DEAD END

Also by Jason Myers

exit here.

the mission

DEAD END

JASON MYERS

Simon Pulse
New York | London | Toronto | Sydney

This book is a work of fiction. Any references to historical events, real people, or real locales are used fictitiously. Other names, characters, places, and incidents are the product of the author's imagination, and any resemblance to actual events or locales or persons, living or dead, is entirely coincidental.

SIMON PULSE

An imprint of Simon & Schuster Children's Publishing Division

1230 Avenue of the Americas, New York, NY 10020

First Simon Pulse paperback edition June 2011

Copyright © 2011 by Jason Myers

All rights reserved, including the right of reproduction in whole or in part in any form.

SIMON PULSE and colophon are registered trademarks of Simon & Schuster, Inc.

For information about special discounts for bulk purchases, please contact Simon & Schuster Special Sales at 1-866-506-1949 or business@simonandschuster.com.

The Simon & Schuster Speakers Bureau can bring authors to your live event. For more information or to book an event contact the Simon & Schuster Speakers Bureau at 1-866-248-3049 or visit our website at www.simonspeakers.com.

Designed by Karina Granda

The text of this book was set in Tyfa ITC.

Manufactured in the United States of America

10 9 8 7 6 5 4 3 2 1

Library of Congress Control Number 2010939783

ISBN 978-1-4424-1430-3

ISBN 978-1-4424-1431-0 (eBook)

For A.R.

I'd like to thank my editor, Emilia Rhodes.
We did it!

And finally, I'd like to thank my editorial director, Jen Klonsky, for standing behind my work and giving me the opportunity to tell these stories.

DEAD END

"This ain't no place for the weary kind, this ain't no place to lose your mind, this ain't no place to fall behind, pick up your crazy heart and give it one more try."

—Ryan Bingham, "Weary Kind"

Dru

PEOPLE LOSE THEIR WAY SOMETIMES. MOST OF THE time, they don't even know until it's too late and the damage is already done. Me, I never lost my way. Even on the run with Gina, I knew where I was going. I was with her. She was my path. She was my destiny. As long as we were together, the roads were set. It's all that mattered.

When you're with someone who makes you feel so good you ache during every moment you're away from them, it's impossible to truly get lost and stray from your path. She's the only one I ever cared about from the exact moment me and Gina decided to make it happen between us.

Her beauty, her smile, her scent, her skin, the way my heart melted with every word she spoke; every time she touched me, even if it was just a slight nudge from her elbow or a quick touch of my hand, it was the greatest fucking thing ever. And, man, to think that some people may go their whole lives without experiencing that kind of love, romance, and intensity, it makes me truly sad. But at least I got it. I got everything from her, Gina King, the prettiest girl in the world. I was just sixteen and she was just seventeen, but my God, she became the pulse that gave me life. Nothing can ever fucking touch that. And nothing could ever be that damn good.

Gina

WHAT ELSE CAN YOU SAY ABOUT DRU? JUST AN awesome guy. A real man. A loyal man. A warm and gentle man. If that doesn't speak to your gut, then you have no soul. Dru has soul. Dru has guts. Dru has my heart in the palm of his hands.

My three favorite things about him:

1. How awesomely handsome he is.

2. How everything he's ever said to me is so beautiful and perfect and nice and has touched me to the core of my being.

3. How he fucks me, the way he handles me and makes me come almost the moment he's inside me.

And also, another thing: The way he makes me feel like I'm a beautiful angel and that our love is the most important thing in the history of the world. The world's greatest and most romantic story. That our love can save each other. That our love can overcome any disaster.

There are so many more things I love about him too. But those are my top three; I mean four. I look at him and my pussy gets wet. I look at him sometimes and my heart skips beats. I could go on and on with my list—I could make ten lists if there was enough time—but you get the point. That boy is beautiful. That boy is special. And that boy has given me everything he has. How much more could anyone ever fucking want?

1

THEY STOOD ACROSS FROM EACH OTHER, THEIR EYES locked. The cold winter wind howled, the deep gray sky hovered above them like some cold pillow marked with indentations from arms and fingers and faces and heads folding it over and poking at it.

She was dressed in a heavy purple coat with a white scarf tied snugly around her gentle neck and a white stocking cap pulled over her long and curly brown hair. Her gorgeous blue eyes blinked once and her tight-pressed lips eased into a small smile. Her cheeks raised an inch as she inhaled the chilled air, inhaled the moisture and the emptiness of the deep land that surrounded them.

He moved closer to her. He was wearing his green coat that had fur on the collar. His hair was short and brown and it blew halfheartedly in the wind that rushed past and through them. He was already smiling. He was always smiling when he saw her or was about to see her. Shit, it was beyond that. He was always smiling at just the thought of her. His green eyes were big and intense. His face was filled with life. It hadn't always been like that for him. It never had, actually. Only after him and Gina talked for the first time did his face turn from the emotionless, dry expression he'd had in every picture, every conversation, every second of every day, into the glowing, grinning, stunning expression he had every time her image floated through his brain. Every time he saw her or was about to see her or jerked off to the movie reel of their sex that projected constantly through his head while he laid in his quiet and dying house, trying to fall asleep at night.

And still looking into her gorgeous eyes, he said, "I wanna leave here with you. Leave Marshall and leave Nebraska forever and go explore the world with you, Gina."

"I'd go anywhere with you, Dru," she said back to him.

"We could run away right now."

"Where would we go?"

"Anywhere else, baby."

He leaned closer to her. He could feel the warmth of her breath. He could smell the Doritos that she'd eaten during sixth-period study hall.

"What about Cuba?" he continued. "I saw pictures of it in a library book. They have white sand there. We could sleep on the beaches at night and swim in the clear water."

"I love that idea."

"Then maybe Paris after that," he said.

"Why Paris?"

He shrugged. His smile shifted to the right for a moment before he spoke. "I guess it's 'cause that's where two kids in love are supposed to run away to. That's how it always is in the movies . . . those old movies I watch late at night when I can't sleep. I mean, right?"

"I don't know."

A few strands of hair blew across her face and she brushed them aside.

"You're so pretty, Gina."

Her cheeks turned pink at the top. "Thank you."

"Prettiest girl in the world."

"Baby, you're so sweet to me. Come here."

They dissolved the few inches of space between them, and their lips met. They kissed slowly and gently and their tongues slid into each other's mouths and moved in small circles until they pulled away.

"What about college?" she asked him.

"What about it? I'd rather be in Italy hitchhiking with you . . . you, baby, in some perfect red dress and your hair hanging down your back."

"I love you, Dru Weiben."

"I love you so much, Gina King."

"And I promise to wait next year for you and go anywhere with you."

"You really mean that, don't you?"

"You know I do. I mean it more than anything. This here, me and you, this is all the life that matters . . . as long as I have you by my side."

They kissed again. As they kissed, there was the sound

of an old pickup truck motoring down a gravel road somewhere far off across the fields.

Four crows landed on the bare branches of a nearby tree. One of them crowed loudly. They both looked briefly at the four birds, and then they turned back to each other and resumed kissing for some time before getting into Dru's truck and driving away.

She lay naked with her legs spread. Her skin was more dark in the winter than any of the other girls because of the Indian blood she got from her mom. Her mom, whom she hadn't seen or talked to in years, in forever, in what seemed like some other lifetime ago.

He was naked and on top of her. He was inside her. They were in his creaky bed fucking. They were in his old house way outside of Marshall. Way off any of the main roads. Dirt roads and gravel and broken fences and dead meadows and dead fields as far as they could see from the drafty window next to his bed.

They weren't loud but they were intense. There was sweating and staring and pounding and pulling, and when they were done, they lay on the blankets and he slid his fingers up and down the side of her body.

The song "First Day of My Life" by Bright Eyes played on repeat from a CD player on the floor next to the bed. They both loved that song. It was the first song they ever danced to, on a cold and rainy night when they drank hot chocolate and split a peanut butter cookie.

It was Dru's idea to keep the song on repeat. He knew it's what she wanted. He knew how that song made her so happy and how it was like their song, written only for them . . .

"This is the first day of my life, swear I was born right in the doorway, I went out in the rain suddenly everything changed, they're spreading blankets on the beach . . ."

Gina rested her head on her arms, her big, round eyes focused on him as he began to speak.

"I don't even wanna wrestle tonight," he said. "I just wanna fuck you and hold you and kiss you till it gets late and you have to go home."

"I don't ever wanna leave this bed," she said back. "Never, ever, ever."

He put his lips against her ear. "Except for white beaches and clear water."

"And red dresses in Italy."

"Let's go, then," he whispered.

"Okay," she whispered back.

2

DRU WAS THE TOP-RANKED WRESTLER AT HIS WEIGHT in the country. Every school was drooling over their chances of him wrestling for their university. It was his life but never his passion. He worked at it because it separated him from the reputations of his dead father and his incarcerated older brother, Jaime.

Before he began to see Gina, he knew wrestling was his only out. But after Gina, there were different dreams and creative escapes and anxious fantasies and a chance to just be happy with someone else. Someone who loves you to the core and would be willing to do anything for you.

The Marshall High gymnasium was packed.

Wrestling and football. The only shows in town. The noise was deafening and it was so warm inside, people were breaking sweats as they sat smashed against one another in the bleachers. There were people spilling through the doorways. The fluorescent lighting of the gym was intense and blurry and the crowd gave off an energy as powerful as that of a Van Halen concert.

Everything was electric.

Dru stood to the side of the mat in his red, black, and

white warm-up suit. His black Asics were laced up and double knotted. His headgear was strapped on tight.

He played the match move by move in his head.

He'd beaten his opponent, Tommy Reynolds, a senior from Carter, three times in the two previous years, one by decision, the other two by pin in the first round. He had no doubt that the fourth match would end like the previous three, except quicker. Dru knew all of the kid's moves, his tendencies, his thinking. All by memory. It's what separated him from everyone else, that and his natural talent.

The match before Dru's ended with Marshall's wrestler in that weight class defeating Carter's six to one.

It was time for Dru's match.

The 135-pound weight class.

The mat cleared, the band played the Marshall High fight song, and Dru looked into the stands at Gina. She was sitting where she always sat, in the top corner at the other end of the gym.

She smiled at him that amazing smile of hers and he winked back at her. The announcer called him and Tommy to the mat. Before Dru ran to the middle of it, his teammate Jacob Brown slapped him in the arm and said, "Fuck that faggot up."

Dru smirked. "He can't beat me, man." He looked to the mat. "Nobody can beat me."

He shook Tommy's hand, and the ref blew his whistle.

Tommy lunged at Dru and Dru turned Tommy around

and locked his arms behind his head. Then he took out Tommy's feet. They both fell to the mat, Tommy on his face and Dru on Tommy's back. It was easier than even Dru thought it was going to be. He flipped Tommy on his back in a second, then drove his elbow hard into Tommy's chest. Tommy's shoulders hit the mat and Dru stuck him there.

"You never had a chance," Dru snapped.

"I know," Tommy said.

The crowd got to its feet. The ref got down on the mat, counted, then smacked his hand down and blew his whistle. It was over. Just twenty-seven seconds was all it lasted.

Dru let go of Tommy and stood up. He looked right to Gina, the first place he always looked after he destroyed an opponent.

She was on her feet with everyone else, smiling, lips glistening, clapping her hands, screaming. Dru ripped his headgear off and waited while the band played the fight song again. The two boys shook hands one last time, and then the ref took Dru's left arm and hoisted it into the air. The crowd cheered louder, and Dru winked at Gina again. She blew him a kiss and it was better than winning. That beautiful gesture made him ache to be in her arms right at that moment. He felt better from that, better from her eyes staring at him, following him, better from a smile from her to him, than he'd felt from winning the match.

She'd done something so special to him in the two months they'd been together. Made him feel a hope he never knew existed. Made him feel like he was really wanted somewhere, wanted by someone. She'd made him feel like he was great because of who he was and not how he wrestled. Wrestling was what made people think he wasn't exactly like his older brother and father. Gina was what made him think that there were more important things than proving to people he wasn't like his older brother or his father.

He'd always been different. He'd seen the damage done and the pain they'd caused and he'd promised his mother that he would be different from them. No way he was gonna fuck up his life or anyone else's. And he'd kept his word to her. He stayed out of trouble, did okay in school, took care of the house and the land. He even took care of his dying mother, took care of what he had to to get them by. And for all of that, for keeping his promise, Gina King was what he got.

He deserved her like she deserved him. Two young lovers who believed in forever. If you can believe in forever, you can believe in anything.

He walked off the mat, wiped himself dry with a towel, put on his warm-up suit, and drank from a cold bottle of water. And when he turned around and looked back up at his girl, she was already looking right back down at him.

MARSHALL WON THE MEET. IN THE LOCKER ROOM
the team's head coach addressed them with his usual
speech about working even harder and not resting on
their continued success. After the coach was through, Dru
showered and dressed quickly. He put on a pair of Lee jeans,
a gray hooded sweatshirt, white Asics, and the same green
coat with the fur collar. He high-fived some teammates and
left the room.

Gina stood against the gym wall a few feet from the
locker room door. She was wearing her purple coat, tight
black jeans, brown Ugg boots, and black fingerless gloves,
and had a brown purse hanging off her right shoulder.

Her face brightened and her eyes grew big and wild as
she practically leaped off the wall. She ran into his arms and
kissed his lips.

"Yeah, baby," she said. "You killed that guy."

"Twenty-seven seconds."

She whispered in his ear. "I'm so glad you don't fuck me
for only twenty-seven seconds."

She pulled back, grinning.

The gym was empty minus the few parents still waiting
for their kids. Dru's coaches and a handful of assistant

coaches from all the big-time wrestling schools were standing around talking near the other end of the gym.

An exit door was propped open with a chair, letting the cold winter wind cool down the warm and heavy air.

Gina nudged Dru in the arm. "Be a gentleman and drive me home."

"It would be my pleasure, darling." He winked. She hooked an arm through his. Then they headed for the gymnasium doors.

"If you play your cards right, you may even get a little present."

"Oh yeah? So what do I gotta do, Gina King?"

Pause.

They were both grinning like children eating ice cream cones.

"Let me play the music," she said.

"I always let you play the music."

She made a face.

"Sometimes I do."

"There's a song I want you to hear."

"And I get the present if I listen to the song?"

"Maybe."

As the two neared the doors, an assistant from Iowa quickly broke away from the circle of coaches and approached them.

Dru's smile went away and he snapped, "Oh great. I just talked to this asshole on the phone last night for an hour. I'm sick of them."

"So don't talk to them."

"I ain't. Gotta date with you to hear a song."

"Yes, you sure do."

As the coach got within a handshake of Dru, Dru flipped his head at him with a hint of old country-boy arrogance and told him, "I ain't got the time right now, Coach."

The coach stopped and put out his hand. "You don't have time for me?"

"Nah, not right now." Dru swung his eyes to Gina, who squeezed her arm even tighter around his. "Gotta get this pretty lady home."

"Well, I'll call you in a couple days."

Dru slipped his hand around Gina's and pushed the door open. "Sure thing, Coach. I'll be waiting by the phone." He led his girl through the doors, laughing as he did it, and they ran down the hallway of the school and out to the parking lot.

It was a relief not to have to stay for an hour after exhausting meets and talk to those coaches anymore. Now that he had his angel, another door was opening, and those possibilities were the ones where beautiful imaginations went wild and old motel rooms in Cuba became a real option.

The idea, the hope, the belief that everything will be perfect and wonderful and fine.

Without the illusion, there's only a constant state of paralysis.

DRU'S TRUCK WAS COLD AND SMELLED LIKED MOTOR oil and dirt. Their breath made clouds. Gina opened her purse and pulled out a CD.

"So what's this song you got me all worked up for?" he asked.

"Have some patience," she said, smiling, kissing the corner of his mouth. "You'll hear it in a second."

She ejected the *Crazy Heart* sound track and slid her CD in.

"This is the sound track to that movie I was telling you I watched on IFC last Saturday night. *All the Real Girls*. It's so good too, baby. We have to watch it together."

"I'm into that."

Dru started his truck and drove it out of the parking lot while Gina hit play and turned the volume up. She scooted up next to him and squeezed his arm.

"The song's by this Will Oldham guy. 'All These Vicious Dogs.'"

"Nice title."

"Amazing song."

She turned up the volume more. "Just listen to these lyrics, baby."

"*And I have been yours, in fall and in praying, and I love to look at you from the side at night with music playing…*"

They looked at each other after those last words.

"That's what I do when you fall asleep after we're done fucking," Dru said.

"I know that. Thought you would like it."

"I love it."

"I love those Sunday afternoons at your house when we lay naked in your bed and listen to those bluegrass records with you watching over me."

"How do you know I'm doing that if you're sleeping?"

"'Cause I can tell. My body feels like heaven when your eyes are on me. Heaven."

"Yeah."

"Plus, sometimes I'm awake and you can't see my face, but if you could, you'd see the biggest smile of the happiest girl ever."

The track finished and he shook his head and said, "I love you."

"You know I love you."

"What's next?" he asked.

She flipped songs to track four, Sparklehorse, their song "Sea of Teeth," and then she said, "This and your present are next."

She scooted over to the middle of his truck, licked the inside of his ear, and whispered, "I love watching you kick ass on that mat." Then she undid his pants, pulled out his hard dick, leaned down, and put it in her mouth.

She didn't come up until he came.

She swallowed.

Then she played "All These Vicious Dogs" again as she ran her fingers slowly and softly down the side of his face.

DRU PULLED HIS LOUD, RUSTED TRUCK UP NEXT TO
the driveway at Gina's house. Her house looked like every
other house on the block. It was white and two stories, with
a front porch and a one-car garage with a netless basketball
hoop attached to the top of it. It was a nice house in a nicer
neighborhood. Nothing like Dru's shack in the country.
Gina lived where the business class lived. Barbecues and
playgrounds with new equipment and young couples who
took walks on warm nights pushing strollers.

Pyramid played on Gina's CD. The lights were off inside
the house.

Gina kissed Dru's cheek and said, "Ya know ya better
not piss those guys off too much."

"What guys?" he asked.

"Those coaches that come to see you wrestle. They
might not wanna give you a scholarship if you blow them
off the way you did."

Dru smirked. "Shit," he said. "I'm an undefeated, two-
time state champion wrestler, Gina. And I'm only a junior.
I'll be able to go anywhere I wanna go after next year. If I
wanna even do that."

Gina squeezed his arm and kissed him again. "And I'll

go wherever you go, baby. I promise, whatever you choose, and I'll be with you all the way."

"You mean that?"

"Of course. I'd love to travel around with you. It would be amazing. And if you do go to college, whatever one you choose is gonna be a good school that I can get into. I can study math at any of those places and then get into some awesome postgrad program. Maybe we can travel after college too. We have the world at our fingertips, so whatever seems best for us, then that's what we do. Together. That's what I want most."

"So you're really gonna wait for me even though you'll be done with school this year. . . . Really?

"Yeah, baby. I told you. I'll take classes at the community college and work as much as I can and make some money while you finish your last year."

Dru nodded and turned to her. "Tell me that you really mean it again?"

She giggled. "I really mean it again, Dru."

"Your dad is gonna hate that."

"I don't care what he thinks when it comes to us."

"He don't like me. That's for sure."

"He doesn't hate you. He thinks you're just part of some phase I'm going through. He doesn't get it, but so what, baby?" She put a hand on his thigh and rubbed it. "I like you and that's all that matters. That's all he will even care about in the end anyway."

She leaned in closer and put her lips to his. She stuck her tongue in his mouth. He didn't care that those lips had just touched his dick or that her tongue had just tasted his come. It was nothing. He'd been with her for two months. He'd eaten her pussy out, made her come in his mouth, and then kissed her while he fucked her, and she never complained once about having to taste herself.

He pulled back and grabbed her gently by the chin, centering her face right in front of his.

"Good night, baby."

"Good night, Dru."

THEY SHOWED UP IN DROVES, PACKING THE convention center in downtown Lincoln, Nebraska. Five hundred people to be exact, seated at nice tables with white tablecloths and candle centerpieces.

They were all in tuxes or nice dresses to honor one of the most powerful but secretive men in the state, Curtis Alderson, for founding Alderson House, a statewide program that provided housing, meals, and work for men who'd just been paroled or released from jail for good.

The idea behind Alderson House was that these men could be rehabilitated into society by working up résumés and not breaking rules and contributing—some for the first times in their lives. The program had been a smashing success for more than fifteen years, with twenty Alderson Houses located throughout the state of Nebraska. Leading state lawmakers, community business leaders, and heads of other charitable organizations decided it was time to honor Curtis Alderson for his achievement.

They booked a night and sent out the gold-stickered invitations. Then there they were, all gathered in a room watching testimonial videos from participants of Alderson House. They listened to passionate speeches by those who'd been affected by the house. Curtis sat gratefully with his elegant and beautiful wife, Tina, and their only child, Beau, at the front of the room, around a table full of five-star food.

The man they were gathered to see was wearing a brown suit with a thin black tie, cowboy boots, and a ten-gallon cowboy hat. He was fifty-four and his face was aged, his body beat up from years of brutal land work and building his brand, building his franchise. He had a large scar that ran down the entire left side of his face from a bull accident and an abrasion from an oil burn just below his right eye. His personality was larger than life and it showed in the way people flocked to him. He was a businessman. He got things taken care of. He had a purpose, a mission, and nothing ever came between him and his desired end result.

But he was also a secretive man who viewed most reporters, except on a night like that one, as the enemy. A function of a sick society where privacy was almost nonexistent and nothing was fact-checked and everything was one-sided. He had an inner circle that consisted of three other men, whom he'd known since his first landgrab, whom he'd all "saved" like so many other men who were loyal to him, and who had devoted their lives to his enterprise. With this devotion, they'd all in turn been rewarded not just with salary, security, and positions of great respect but with a sense of dignity and pride as well. A sense that their good lives were a result of Curtis's vision and his trust. Because of that, Curtis Alderson and his enterprise were to be defended, protected at all costs and by any means necessary. Everyone associated with him and his franchises adhered to that philosophy with ruthless vigor and terrifying loyalty.

Tina Alderson sipped a glass of pinot grigio. She held the glass loosely, freely, but her sips were strong and fluid. She wore a navy blue dress made out of satin that exposed the white, freckled skin of her left shoulder. She had diamond earrings that hung four inches off each ear and a diamond necklace that Curtis had bought her on their fifth wedding anniversary, two weeks after they'd received the shocking news that she was pregnant.

The news was not startling in a negative way. It was startling because they'd been trying for three years to get pregnant and had finally accepted the fact that she could not bear him a child. It was so fucking vicious for Curtis. Because a man like that, a man with an ego larger than the gods, a man who was building his own empire from scratch, a man like that wants nothing more than a child, preferably a boy, to inherit that empire.

And it was absolutely devastating for Tina. A woman like herself, who marries a man with that kind of ambition and power, who marries a man who gives her only the best things, a man who plucked her from the perceived horrors of the middle class, the working stiffs, and the normal, is constantly aware that it is her duty to one day give birth to that man's child. When Tina thought she couldn't fulfill that obligation to the one who had given her everything she'd ever dreamed about, her life became a nightmare.

The fucking guilt became alive.

It began to breathe heavy.

It's the kind of guilt that growls at you like wolves and coyotes. It grows legs and arms and a poisonous head. Tina was asking herself constantly if that man regretted the day he asked her to marry him, if he regretted his life commitment to her. If he wanted to get rid of her and find some other pretty face that could and would bear him the heir or heiress to his great empire. So when she was almost a week late, way back all those years ago, she couldn't believe it when the pregnancy test was positive.

By that afternoon she was sitting in the den with Curtis, telling him the wonderful news. It was right then that they decided they would have only one child, because they didn't want to go through the horrors of failure anymore. Failure was not an option.

For Tina, it was absolute emancipation from the suicidal guilt that overwhelmed every breathing moment of her day and, at times, her dreams. And for Curtis, it was the absolute guarantee of the continuation of his legacy. His own flesh expanding his empire.

Nine months later their son, Beau, was born.

Beau swallowed the remains of a crab cake and followed it with a drink from the bottle of beer in front of him.

He was handsome, with perfectly trimmed black hair that was parted neatly to the left, a very defined facial structure, and big brown eyes. He was as cool as they came. A small smirk of privilege constantly spilled from the corners of his mouth. His body language put out a defined confidence. Most of the time he leaned back in his chair with eyes that spoke of judgment. He scanned the room, picked people apart, and looked for his prey. Sometimes he had his elbow on the table with the back of his hand against his chin. When he moved or gestured, it was with precision and demand. But when he talked, his vocal tone left an impression of arrogance. An arrogance that came from a blessed life, one that came from the insurance of inheriting a massive sum of land and money and power. One that came from a lifetime of being told that he was better than anyone else just by having the last name he did.

Beau graduated with a 3.2 GPA and fucked all the hottest girls, freshman through senior year, and when he finished high school, he went to the University of Nebraska in Lincoln. He flunked out his first semester, and sat out the next one before finally transferring to the University of Nebraska–Omaha, where he was in the middle of his sophomore year. He still had a couple of close friends in Marshall, where he still ruled.

Beau never heard the word "no" anywhere in Marshall and he always got what he wanted, especially when he went after it. He was an Alderson. "Recourse" and "retaliation" were absolutely useless words when it came to him.

After all the overdone praise had been dispensed and the testimonials concluded, there was only one speech left to give. Curtis Alderson's speech.

Curtis stood up as the room filled with loud applause. He was an imposing presence all the way around. He was six feet two inches tall and he seemed like an old giant. His shoulders were broad and his belly stuck out six inches. He lumbered when he walked from the extreme abuse he'd put his body through to get himself to a moment just like this.

A moment for people to kiss his ass and maybe get a favor from him. A moment where he could hear how godlike he was. A moment to cut a few more big-time backroom deals.

He stepped to the podium and everyone rose to their feet, still clapping. He nodded at them and winked at his son and wife and waited until the ovation became less and the folks took their seats. He removed that cowboy hat, setting it next to the microphone, grinning wide, and said, "Howdy, y'all."

Dru

MY FAVORITE THING ABOUT GINA IS THAT SHE'S GIVEN me a chance to really love someone else in a way that you can't love your family. I love my mom, like any kid should, despised my dad for what he did to my family, and was angry at my brother for being the criminal bastard he was and leaving me to take care of everything. Jaime always stuck up for me growing up. But he left me to pick up the pieces after he got arrested.

Then this angel came into my life. This delicate being who saw through the reputations I'd been given based on nothing I had done.

She's it. She's better than anyone. Better than everything.

She was a gift.

She was my chance.

Sure, people loved me because of my talent on the mat, but beyond that, it was all fake. I was still Dale Weiben's son and Jaime Weiben's brother and my clothes were ratty, my house was broken, and eventually the apple wasn't gonna fall far from the tree.

Gina didn't buy it.

Once she got to know me, she knew I was capable of

giving her the affection and the pleasure and the happiness that every kid wants.

Angels don't come around that often.

I got lucky.

This lovely creature appeared in my life. She's stuck by my side. She's loved me back the way I've loved her every moment of every single fucking day.

That's her timeless gift.

Giving me the chance to be in love. Giving me the chance to have butterflies in my stomach. Giving me these sleepless nights.

And those Sunday mornings.

Those have been so nice.

"Easy like a Sunday morning."

That's my favorite thing about Gina.

And those cute freckles on her nose don't hurt either. Or that amazing body. Or that warm voice. Or those soft arms she wraps around me that make my body shake with goodness as the tension of every other fucked-up thing in my life falls from my shoulders.

The warmth of her whispering sweet things in my ear. The words "I love you and will never leave you."

The words "This is forever, baby."

Gina

ADVERSITY DOES TWO THINGS: DESTROYS YOU OR makes you stronger. Adversity destroyed my real mom. It destroyed my first family. For a while it destroyed my hope in that one word that can mean so much when it's truly meant: "forever."

You ever seen a sixteen-year-old kid take care of his dying mom? Pay the bills? Keep up a house and a piece of land while dealing with bullshit history exams, algebra classes, wrestling practices, and broken-down vehicles?

You ever known someone whose dad was in and out of jail and drove himself drunk off a bridge? A person who took on a job picking up litter along the highways for twelve hours a day every weekend for four months to pay back the loan his mom had to take out to pay for the funeral? You ever known anyone like that?

I have.

Dru did all of that stuff and so much more.

He is how I became strong. He is how I went from meek and sensitive to understanding but tough. A lot of people say they're tough because they get into fights, drink themselves into poison, and do it again a week later. That's not tough. That's destructive. That's not real adversity; that's the stupid shit you bring on yourself.

No, Dru is the toughest person and it's rubbed off on me. He's always saying, "Take care of your shit. Take care of yourself. That's what strong people do. No matter what, if you have the ability to make shit happen, then make it happen."

God, he's bright beyond his years. I never once heard him make an excuse about the fucked-up life he inherited. Never once heard him complain about doing what had to get done, no matter how difficult it was.

He's loyal beyond loyalty.

Adversity? Ha! Adversity can't even look him in the eyes.

Smiles to my man forever.

Forever. I finally figured out there could be a real chance at forever with him.

7

THE PARKING LOT OF THE CONVENIENCE STORE WAS
weirdly lit a dull yellow from the street lamps surrounding
it and an annoying white from the fluorescent bulbs
humming from the storefront.

There were three vehicles parked in the lot. One was the
store clerk's car. Right next to it was an unmarked white car
with tinted windows and rusted rims. And in the back was a
Marshall County Sheriff's car.

Inside the unmarked car sat three darkly shadowed
people. Sheriff's Deputy Marty Ollenbeck sat in uniform
in the driver's seat. He was in his early thirties but had the
youthful appearance of a high school boy just barely hitting
puberty. In the backseat was the other sheriff's deputy,
Brian Fehr. He was also in his early thirties, but he had a
rough-and-tumble face with a Wyatt Earp mustache, sharp
features, and eyes that bulged when the vein in his forehead
rose to the surface. Next to Brian was a broken-looking girl.
A sick-looking one. But not sick from any kind of virus; sick
from meth withdrawals. Sick from her body finally feeling
itself again and not liking what it had become, not liking
the way it looked and smelled and not liking the way it felt.
She was in her midtwenties and had dirty blond hair that

looked wet with sweat. There were deep, dark circles under her eyes and a big cold sore, purple-colored, dragging from the left crease of her lips. Her face meat was sucked back against the bone. Her hands shook from being weak and tired and scared. She'd once been pretty. She'd once been popular and shy and happy. She'd once liked to laugh a lot and enjoyed being outside, in the sun, talking to friends.

She'd once had dreams too.

Deputy Fehr grabbed the girl's shaking hands and squeezed them tight, snapping her arms straight.

"Now listen very carefully," he said.

"I am," the girl said, her voice raspy and full of scars from the tobacco and meth abuse.

"Listen better this time."

She put her head down. "Okay."

"Look at me."

She did.

Marty watched them in the rearview mirror. He was too nice to talk to the girl like that. He was there because his boss, Sheriff Cortland, asked him to be. He was there to make sure Brian stayed under control and didn't do anything to jeopardize the sting. Marty wasn't timid. He just wasn't a dick.

"When you are inside the store," Brian said, "you've got to bring at least five packages of Sudafed to the counter and purchase them."

"But what if the clerk doesn't let me?"

"Just push the story on him. Keep pushing that your kids are really sick and that you're desperate. If you're desperate enough, he'll let you. Desperate people almost always find a way," Brian snapped. "'Cause if this doesn't work, none of the charges against you are getting dropped and you're looking at two years."

She looked down and Marty turned his eyes away.

"Are we on the same page?"

"Same page, sir."

"Good," Brian said, dropping her hands. "Now go in there."

The girl got out of the car and walked slowly into the store.

Brain radioed Sheriff Cortland, who was in the sheriff's car behind the store. "She's going in."

"Good," Sheriff Cortland said, and leaned back in his seat. Lyle Cortland had been sheriff of those parts for more than twenty years. He was a serious man who'd seen a lot during his time. He was six feet tall with a head of black hair and weathered, hardened skin.

The store clerk's eyes followed the girl as she walked to the pharmaceutical aisle.

She fingered an assortment of cold medicines until she came to the Sudafed.

Three years ago there had been a law passed that required anyone buying Sudafed, a main ingredient in methamphetamine, to show a form of identification when buying it. The law also limited the purchase of it to once every two weeks. The law hadn't worked in deterring methamphetamine production, so usage hadn't dropped, but the fines and the punishment for breaking this law were quite severe, especially for store owners and their employees who were caught selling more than the allowed limit.

The girl picked up a box of Sudafed and examined it. She sniffled and wiped her nose with the back of her hand and then looked at the clerk. He was still staring at her and she faked a smile, then glanced back down at the box before grabbing four more.

She took a deep breath.

Here was her moment.

She walked up to the counter and dropped all five boxes on it.

The clerk studied them for a moment, then looked back at her and said, "One is all you can buy, miss. Only one. If you want another one, you're gonna have to wait two weeks and come back."

"But my kids are sick," the girl said. "I need more than one."

The clerk shook his head and shook the package even harder. "Only one! Got it? Anything over one is illegal and they will close our store."

She worked herself up and made her eyes fill with tears. She begged, "Please, mister. Please. I need all of these. My kids are sick, I'm sick. Do you understand? I have to take care of my family."

"Miss, miss, miss. You have to calm down and listen to me. If I sell you all these and they catch me, I could go to jail. This many is a felony. The law is clear. You can only get one right now."

"That's not gonna work," she snorted, the tears running down her face. "I have five kids. I am sick. I need all of these now!"

She wiped her face and put it in her hands.

"I'm sorry, miss," the clerk said. "I would if I could. I would. But I don't want to get in trouble. My father owns this place. This is our whole life. They could close it down if we get caught selling this. They've been targeting Indian- and Pakistani-run stores for months. People are being deported for breaking the law. I can't risk it."

"But I won't tell. I promise. I won't. Just do it one time and I'll never come back in here again. Okay?"

She pulled out her wallet and showed him a picture of her and her kids.

"We're all sick and I need the Sudafed."

The clerk's shoulders eased and he looked back at the counter.

"Just this one time, mister."

She wiped her face once more.

"Please," she begged. "And I'll never bug you again."

He nodded. "Against my better judgment, but I'll do it."

"Thank you."

"Just this one time."

"Of course."

She paid and felt horrible as she walked back to the unmarked car and got in.

"How did it go?" Brian asked.

She handed him the bag with the packages in it. He opened it and laughed. He pulled all five out and held them up to Marty.

"Looks like the camel jockey bought the story." He looked at the girl and put his hand on her shoulder. "You did good."

"Thanks."

"Your kids got a good momma."

She didn't say anything.

Brian radioed Lyle. "He took the bait, Lyle. I got five packs of that shit in the car right now."

Lyle nodded. "All right. I'm moving in. Marty, you come with me. Brian, you watch the girl."

"Why?" Brian snapped. "I want this action. Marty always gets the nod."

"Don't question my orders, Deputy. That's the way we're handling this. Okay?"

There was nothing.

"Are we clear, Deputy?"

"Yeah. Ten-four."

"Good. Let's move, Marty."

8

BALLOONS DROPPED FROM THE CEILING AND champagne bottles were popped simultaneously. The ceremony had just concluded and the ballroom reception had just begun. All the tables were cleared out by men with white jackets and black pants. A dance floor appeared. There were four open bars, one in each corner of the room, and a local band quickly took the stage and began playing a cover of a popular country music song.

Curtis stood in a circle of powerful men, a congressman, the two state senators from Nebraska, and the speaker of the state House. They discussed the context of a meeting that would be centered around ten thousand unused acres of land just outside of Marshall. Land that was all owned by Curtis Alderson.

A waitress brought a tray of bourbon to the men, and one of the senators made a joke about how he could use someone that pretty in his office. The whole circle laughed.

Curtis finally emerged from a mural of handshakes and smiles and pats on the back and walked over to the bar where Beau and Tina were talking.

"My son . . . I'm so glad you came tonight." He put his

arm around Beau's shoulders and shook him tight. "It's great to see you."

"Wouldn't have missed this, Dad."

Curtis patted his back. "One day you'll be honored as well."

"I know, Dad."

Beau turned to the bartender and held up a finger. The bartender popped the cap off another bottle and handed it to him.

"How many have you had?" Curtis asked.

"Just a few."

"Do you need a room here for the night?"

"No, Dad."

"So you're driving back to school tonight?"

"Dear," Tina interjected with a smile. "He's driving home. He's staying at the house for the rest of the week."

"Well," Curtis bellowed, his smile almost doubling in size. "And to what do we owe this pleasure?"

"To nothing, old man. I haven't been back since Christmas and I think it will be nice for me. I could use a little pre-spring break from Omaha."

Curtis put his eyes on Tina and raised his hat a couple of inches. "You see what's going on here, don't ya, Tina?"

"What, honey?"

Curtis looked at Beau and smacked his arm and said, "It's because we're gonna be in Lincoln. That's why the boy wants to go home tonight." He glanced back at Tina.

"That's not it, Dad," he said. "I haven't thrown a party there in years. I just wanna go home and relax. All my school stuff has been taken care of. It's just nice to be able to come home."

"That's what you always say, son."

"No it isn't, and you know that. I can party anywhere I want to."

Curtis pushed his hat back down. "Well, okay then. Just relax. I'm only giving ya some guff."

"That's what you always say."

"Sure is. And I think it's good that you'll be around. I'll be able to show you some of the grand ole things I'm working on with this land deal. It's a goddamn winner, just like us."

Beau sipped his beer.

"It'll be great for you to observe some of this stuff as I'm doing it, son."

"I'm sure it will, Dad."

Lyle sat at his desk and read over his report from the store bust. His desk was sparse. There was a glass with pens in it. A wire basket full of other files. A Nebraska Cornhuskers coffee mug. A picture of him and an ex-girlfriend.

He set the report down and rubbed his face. It was time for a drink. He pulled open the bottom drawer of his desk, took a bottle of whiskey from it, and poured some into the coffee mug.

He took a swig, finished it in the next, removed his hat,

and sat back. His head felt fuzzy as he stared at the wall next to him, at a picture of him fishing in Canada last summer near his cabin. It was where he planned to retire in less than six years. The only place he'd been able to relax.

He picked up the file again just to double-check it for any errors.

There was a knock at his door.

Marty was standing in the doorway with his own report in his hand.

"Can I have a minute with you, Lyle?"

"Sure."

Marty sat in one of the two chairs on the other side of Lyle's desk.

Lyle pulled the bottle of whiskey back out and asked Marty if he wanted a drink.

"Not tonight, Lyle."

"I understand." Lyle put the bottle away and closed the drawer. "You look troubled."

Marty's face twitched. He slid a hand across his forehead and said, "I guess it's this bust we did tonight."

"What about it?"

"Well, not just this one. But all of them lately, Lyle. It's like we only bust Indian- and Middle Eastern–owned stores."

Lyle leaned forward and set his arms on the desk. "We only bust the stores we get tipped off to 'cause they're doing illegal things."

"But who tips us off?"

Lyle paused, then leaned back. "You know the answer to that."

"Tips always come from one of Curtis Alderson's guys. Always, Lyle."

"And so what's your point?"

Marty shook his head and slid his hand down the front of his face.

"Well, Deputy?"

"I don't know, Lyle. It just seems like Curtis has us doing special favors. I bet his stores ain't squeaky clean."

"You got proof of that?"

"No, sir."

"You looking to get proof?"

"No, Lyle. Nothing like that. It's just, the store we took down tonight . . . see, that's the last convenience store not owned by Curtis for damn near fifty miles."

"Well, there ain't many convenience stores or towns within those fifty miles." Lyle grinned.

"That's not my point."

Lyle sighed and poured himself another drink. He downed it and poured another one. "We're doing our jobs, Marty. That's all."

"And you're okay with that answer, Lyle? 'Cause you don't look okay with it. You haven't seemed okay for a while now."

Lyle sat silent, staring at his Cornhuskers mug.

"Are you okay with it?" Marty pressed.

"I never said that."

Marty shook his head. "But we're just doing our jobs?"

Lyle washed his throat with another drink. He set the mug down and said, "The store we took down tonight had been selling over the legal limit of cold medicine. That's a felony in this state. So we shut it down. We did our jobs, Deputy."

Pause.

Lyle went to take another drink but realized the mug was empty. He set it down and said, "Now that's all, Marty. You did good. Go home and I'll see you tomorrow."

Marty left the office and Lyle stared blankly at his report. Another favor. Another dump of cash into his personal account. Another instance he could've said no but didn't.

9

A BLACK MUSTANG SPED DOWN THE HIGHWAY. BEAU
rapped word for word to the new Eminem bumping hard
from the speakers. He was excited to get back to Marshall
and have the house to himself for a couple of days.

His phone rang, startling him for a moment, throwing
him off the verse he was rapping so excitedly to.

"Corey Muthafucking Rogers," he said after answering it.

"Where you at, Beau?"

"A couple hours outside of Lincoln. Be in Marshall in
about an hour."

"You bring anything back with you?"

"You know I did, dude. You got any girls in the pipeline
for me?"

"Nah."

"What the fuck, dude? No babes at all?"

"I got nothing, kid."

"Jesus, man. You really do leave everything to me."

"Whatever, man. Just call me when you're back?"

"For sure."

He hung up and threw the phone on the passenger seat.
He turned the music back up and started rapping again. He
loved his life, the way it felt. Not having to give a fuck. Not

having to answer to no one but the one person who wanted to hand everything over to him.

He reached into the front pocket of his pants and slid out a bag of cocaine. It was his favorite. The high was like nothing else. On cocaine, he really had the ambition to take over the fucking world.

While he steered with his left hand, he dumped a small pile of the coke on top of that hand, then he set the bag down next to his phone and put his right hand on the wheel.

He held his left hand under his nose, slammed the pile against it, and sniffed back hard. He grunted and snorted and his face twitched and his throat went numb for a moment and then he sniffed back hard one more time and turned the Eminem up even louder.

All that money at his fingertips.

All that power.

The power was what seduced him.

The idea that nothing or no one could touch him no matter what he did. With no rules in your normal day-to-day life, there are absolutely no limits, there is no normal.

10

DRU SAT ACROSS FROM HIS WRESTLING COACH, KEN
Ludens. Ken was short and stocky with broad shoulders, a
shaved head, and a goatee. He had an enormous ego. It was
always his way or no way.

He was The Coach.

He was also ambitious beyond his current position.
His eyes were set on the next level, a head coaching job at a
smaller college, or as a top assistant at a bigger school with
rich tradition. A position he figured would be guaranteed
with the deliverance of his star wrestler to one of those
programs.

Ken's desk was covered with pictures of past state
championships. The trophy case was full of the accolades
of his past teams. And the wall behind him was plastered
with even more photos of him with Olympic wrestlers and
coaching legends and of his own championship wrestling
days.

Dru cracked his knuckles. They sat in silence for another
thirty seconds before his coach started in.

"You thinking all right in that head of yours?"

"How do you mean?"

"Last meet you blew off that coach from Iowa in front of

me. You just acted like he was no one. They're gonna be at the meet tonight again to watch you take on Schmidt."

"I figured."

"Thing is, you would've never done that last year or the year before."

"Come on, Coach. I was with my girl. I didn't wanna talk to that guy, anyway. I talked to him on the phone for an hour the night before that one. It's always same thing."

"That girl gonna give you a free ride to a major university?"

Dru didn't say anything. He scratched the side of his face.

"Is she, Dru?"

"No. But so what? I'm winning all my matches still. I've never even lost one for you, Coach."

"I know that."

"So what's the problem?"

"Seems to me that your focus just ain't the same as it's been the last two years."

"I won my last match in less than thirty seconds."

"To a pile-of-shit wrestler who has no business being ranked."

"I still won."

"That girl of yours doing something to your head?"

Dru smiled and nodded and let out a small laugh. "Nothing but good things, Coach."

Ken's jaw clenched and his lips pressed tight. He leaned forward and said, "Huge goddamn match tonight for you against Schmidt. Three-time state champion. Grew up into your weight class this year, and now you gotta beat him."

"I know I do. But he's ranked number two and I'm number one."

"Kid's fucking tough, Dru. Tough as nails."

"He's going to Northern Iowa, Coach. That's all."

"Solid program they got."

"Not like Iowa or Nebraska or Arizona. All those better schools want me."

"He's good, Dru."

"And I'm better."

Ken leaned back and nodded. He ran a hand over his mouth. "I think you are too. But your practicing is worse than it ever was. Your preparation seems sloppier too. And besides the last meet and maybe a couple of gimmes at the beginning of the year, you haven't been anywhere close to as dominant in your matches this year as the past two. At some point you're gonna have to win on something other than talent alone."

Dru rolled his eyes. Shook his head. "So what are you trying to say, Coach? You don't think I'm gonna win tonight? 'Cause I am. I'm gonna kill that asshole."

"All I'm saying is that you need to get your head back to the mat and only the mat. Focus on finishing as strong as you possibly can this year. This is your fucking chance, Dru. This is your only chance to be something special. To get the hell out of this place. Ain't that what running around with that girl is really all about? Getting away and not looking back?"

Dru swallowed a ball of spit and snot. "Sir."

"Well, that girl ain't gonna get it done for you. That girl is filling that head of yours with silly distractions and mumbo jumbo. Wrestling is the only way outta this place for you, Dru. And tonight, this match with that punk, this match is gonna go a long way in defining your legacy. Keep that in mind."

"Yes, sir."

"Are we clear on that?"

Pause.

"Yeah. We are."

11

DRU'S HOUSE WAS WHITE BUT THE PAINT HAD BEEN chipping for years. There were two broken pickup trucks in the front yard. A white shed with the windows broken out of it and a missing door sat twenty feet from the house. A big tree with branches that reached to the sky filled the backdrop. Stray cats wandered the yard, skinny, tired, sick-looking creatures. Shingles had been falling off the roof. Even the front porch had crumbling steps and an orange sofa on it. The porch columns were beat-up and ugly.

Dru had been trying his hardest to keep up the house but it was a lot. Sometimes when things begin to fall apart, they can't be put back together by just one person.

A sixteen-year-old boy.

Imagine having to do everything in the world to survive, with almost no help at all.

And he'd never made a single excuse in his entire life about doing any of it.

The sky was gray and the night was approaching fast when Dru shut his truck off and walked into the house. He went through a side door and up two stairs, into the kitchen. There were clean dishes in a dish rack on the counter next to the sink. An uneven table with bread crumbs on it.

Pictures and a couple of get-well cards hung from magnets on the olive-green fridge.

Dru walked into the living room and turned on a lamp in the corner next to the TV. There was a small stack of finished TV dinners on the end table next to the brown reclining chair. He set his backpack on the chair and took off up the stairs, past the pictures of him and his family together that hung on the once white, now smoke-stained wall.

When he got to the top of the stairs, he heard her coughing. The cough had been getting worse and worse. It was full of mucus and blood. His mom lay on her bed in a gray robe with pink roses embroidered on it. The blanket and sheet had been kicked off, and her head was lying sideways on the pillow, right next to a wet puddle of green and red.

He stood at the foot of the bed and watched her cough. She was only ninety pounds of blotted skin and weak bones. She weighed 145 before the cancer broke into her stomach. He leaned down to pick up the blanket and sheet and set them back on the bed without covering her. She was hooked to an IV and he could see tears falling from her eyes.

He walked to the side of the bed and picked up a towel from the cart next to the IV. He dampened the towel in a bowl of water and gently wiped his mom's face and the remnants of her cough from the pillow. He set the towel down and pulled off the note that the hospice lady had taped to the wall. The hospice lady came every other day, while Dru was in school, to make sure his mom was as comfortable as she could be as she neared the final, fragile stages of her short life. She filled prescriptions. Changed the IV. Brought in clean towels. Monitored her heart rate. Changed her clothes. Bathed her. Soothed her by being a warm and kind and constant presence during her slow and painful slide into darkness. She sang to his mom and wiped her tears away, and on his mom's good days they even talked about gardens and the forests around Marshall and how handsome Dru and Jaime had grown up to be. Her boys, they were. Her beautiful, amazing boys.

Dru put the note next to the bowl of water and opened two of the five prescription bottles, dumping a pill from each into his hand. He poured a glass of water from the pitcher on the tray, then he put one of his hands underneath his mom's weak neck, turned it gently, and lifted it to the glass.

"Open your mouth, Mom," he said.

She did. He put both pills on her tongue, then put the glass to her lips and poured the water into her mouth. He watched her throat to make sure she swallowed. He poured another drink of water into her mouth before taking his hand out and setting the glass down.

She coughed and he wiped her face with the towel. She laid her head back on the pillow and grabbed Dru's hand.

"Where's Jaime?" she asked, the words barely audible, slow and raspy.

The medication had diluted parts of her memories. They made her confused. She knew Jaime was in jail, but sometimes she didn't know because she was too sick to have a long conversation.

"He's at work, Mom."

Lying was the easiest when she was like that.

"How come he never visits anymore? He's out of trouble."

"He's busy. I've told you that before."

"Too busy to see his own mom?"

"I'll talk to him tomorrow and tell him you want to see him."

"That's my boy."

Her eyes closed and he held her hands against his until she finally drifted to sleep. Fell away from the pain. Fell back into a world that he hoped was full of oceans and beaches and white meadows and warm smiles.

He slid his hands out of hers and leaned down and kissed his mom's forehead and whispered, "I love you."

12

BEAU AND COREY WALKED INTO THE ALDERSON
Market, one of the many stores Curtis owned throughout
Marshall and the surrounding counties. This one was
directly across the street from the Marshall Farmers Mutual
Bank, which Curtis had almost single-handedly saved a
decade earlier.

Corey wore a Marshall High letter jacket, a gray sweater
with a pink collared shirt under it, faded jeans from the Gap,
and white Reebok high-tops and had two gold earrings. His
brown hair was short but spiked in the front. It was like he'd
stepped out of a bad eighties movie. He was a stereotype of
a stereotype that somehow had made its sick way back into
being cool again.

If it was ever really cool.

Beau wore a black V-neck tee, a gray hoodie with a white
zipper, black jeans, and blue Adidas. The total opposite
of Corey's douchebag look. They'd been best friends since
grade school, though. Corey loved the idea of being best
friends with Curtis Alderson's son. The power and the
respect the name commanded. And Beau loved being best
friends with someone he could manipulate and control.
Who would do anything he told him to do.

It was just past five and they were already fucked-up.

Beau called Corey a faggot as they walked back to the beer coolers and Corey bumped into a stand, knocking over a couple of newspapers. He just kept walking.

Beau grabbed a case of Bud Light and the two walked up to the counter. Behind it was a cute girl with blond hair and red lipstick. Beau set the beer on the counter and eyed her up from her waist, past her tits, to her face. He winked.

She blushed brighter than her lipstick and smiled back at Beau.

"You new here?" Beau asked.

"Me?"

Corey laughed and Beau said, "Yes you." He squinted and looked at her nametag. "Amy."

"Well, I'm new working here but I've lived in Marshall my whole life."

"Do you know who I am?" Beau asked.

"Yes."

"Then go ahead and charge this beer to my dad's account."

"Okay."

She scanned the beer and made a note on a clipboard.

"Amy is a pretty name. I like it a lot."

"Thank you," she said, putting the clipboard down.

"Amy . . . mmmmm. How bad you wanna hang out with me and my friend, Amy?"

"If you're serious . . . pretty bad."

"Good," said Beau.

"Would you really want to hang out with me?"

"Let me ask you something?"

"Okay."

Beau leaned over the counter. "Have you ever sucked a dick and swallowed the come before?"

She laughed nervously and tapped her pen against the counter.

"Have you?" he pressed.

"Maybe I have." She grinned.

Beau stood back straight and smiled. "I'd fucking love to hang out with you, so I'll tell you what. Why don't you call my dad's house after your shift and make it happen for yourself."

"Okay."

Beau winked at her again and took the beer. He turned around and saw this older blonde, probably in her forties, whom he'd seen waitressing at the Marshall Inn Diner for years, standing behind them. He looked her up and down and smiled at her, too.

She just rolled her eyes.

"Old bitch," Beau mumbled to Corey, and laughed as the two of them walked out.

The lady stepped up to the counter and Amy turned around and grabbed two buy-one-get-one free Marlboro Mediums from the cigarette racks.

Amy set them down and went, "Do you know who that was, Nancy?"

"I sure do, dear."

"Beau Alderson."

"I know. They were wasted. He's always wasted. I could smell the drunk on them," Nancy said.

"He's such a hunk, huh?"

"Beau Alderson?"

"Yeah. And he wants to hang out with me."

Nancy pulled a five-dollar bill from her purse and set it on the counter. "Kid is nothing but trouble, Amy. Nothing but trouble."

Amy rang up the cigarettes and said, "Super-fun trouble, I bet."

13

GINA SAT AT HER KITCHEN TABLE HELPING HER HALF-
sister Katelyn with her math homework. Katelyn had snow-colored hair tied back with pink ribbons and enormous blue eyes. She was a wearing a pink wool sweater and brown corduroy pants.

Gina loved Katelyn so much. She was Gina's best friend, even though she was only seven years old. Gina took her to the mall and bought her clothes. They made mix CDs together and danced to them in Gina's room. Gina taught her how to put on lipstick. They would go to the park near their house and talk on the swing sets about cute boys and school until sunset. Sometimes they rode their bikes to the creek and jumped into the water from the tire swing. Gina was Katelyn's exclusive hairdresser. They wrote in the same diary (Gina also had her own, which she kept in her closet under an old Care Bears pillow). Gina loved her little sister as much as Dru.

As Gina went through a long-division problem with Katelyn, her stepmother, Samantha, came into the kitchen. Samantha was thirty-two and had short blond hair and blue eyes. She was very pretty. Samantha married Gina's father eight years earlier. Gina never felt awkward about it, even though she and Samantha didn't have a strong relationship. It didn't matter, because her dad and Samantha had Katelyn.

In her arms Samantha held a medium-size box full of her handmade cards. She set it on the table and asked Gina if she would go and drop the package off for Tina Alderson at the Alderson house.

"Why do I have to do it tonight?" Gina complained. "I heard Dad say on the phone last night that they were out of town."

"They'll be back first thing in the morning, Gina, and I can't run over there that early. Tina needs it right away for one of her scrapbooking get-togethers. Beau will be there. Tina said he'll be expecting you to drop them off before seven."

Gina's back twitched as a shower of shivers ran through her. "I hate Beau Alderson, Sammy."

Samantha put her hands on her waist and shook her head. "That's so ridiculous, Gina. He's an Alderson. How can you hate an Alderson?"

"He's a creep. That's why. He was so mean to girls in school. He was always asking me out and trying to get with me at parties. I just saw him over Christmas break at a party and he was all over me even though I told him I was with Dru."

"Nonsense."

"It's true. He thinks he can do whatever he wants just because he's an Alderson."

"Well, maybe he's changed, Gina."

"Since Christmas?"

"Maybe he has."

"Aldersons don't change, Sammy. I've heard Dad say that again and again since Curtis asked him to run for mayor last year."

Samantha sighed and rubbed her nose. "Don't make up lies and excuses just because it's me who's asking you to do this."

"They're not excuses. Beau Alderson scares me, Sammy. And ya know what else?"

"What?"

"Dru has a huge match tonight."

"Well, if you leave right now, you'll have time to do me this favor. Then you can have the car to drive to the meet."

"But why can't you just do it?"

"Because I asked you to, Gina. Okay? That's why. And you have nothing to worry about. Beau Alderson is a good young man. He comes from a wealthy, respected, powerful family. Maybe if you played your cards right, with your dad running for mayor this fall, maybe you could go out with Beau instead of that boy from that criminal family."

Gina's face turned red and her blood began to boil. "Dru is not shady. I love him. He treats me like a queen. He is everything that's good, and Beau Alderson is a slimebag. Dru is a way better person than him. It's not even close, Sammy. It's a blowout."

"Oh really, Gina? Just look at Dru's family. His older brother is in jail for robbing one of Curtis's stores. His dad did three or four stints, and then got drunk and drove himself right off the Miller Road Bridge when Dru was, what, still in elementary school? Is that really what you want to be associated with? Those types of people. I mean, it's just a matter of time before your little boyfriend starts acting the same way."

"He would never hurt anyone. How dare you say that, Sammy?"

Samantha sighed in frustration.

"I really, really like Dru," Katelyn chimed in. "He's supernice and supercool, and also, he's supercute."

Gina laughed out loud and covered her mouth.

Samantha tapped the box with her fingers. "Well, that's just great, Katie," she said. She looked at Gina and held out her car keys. "Please do this. It was your dad's idea. Please, Gina?"

Gina grabbed the keys from her hand and picked up the box. "Well, that's all you had to say, Sammy. That it was his idea."

"Thank you."

Gina winked at Katelyn. "Make sure you finish those problems before bed."

"I will," Katelyn said.

"I know. I love you."

"Love you, too, Gina. Have fun and tell Dru I said hi."

"I promise I will."

14.

DRU SAT ON THE FLOOR IN FRONT OF HIS GYM LOCKER and stared straight ahead. He took one deep breath after another as he closed his eyes. He leaned back and put his head against the locker behind him. The last thing he heard was the marching band as he squeezed a picture into his brain and locked everything else out.

It was a moving picture, frame by frame, of the match he was about to have, how he was going to exploit his opponent's weaknesses. Even as his teammates walked by him, patting him on the shoulders, he was in that moment of the match. There against Schmidt. Winning the match before it even started. He was there. His mental toughness was that of a professional who'd played his most important game, his most important match, thousands of times.

15.

THE DEN THAT BEAU AND COREY WERE SITTING
in had a fireplace, which Beau lit, two leather sofas, and
spotless brown carpet. The walls were dark orange with
paintings of farms and wild horses and flowers hanging on
them. A flat-screen television was up on the far wall and
there was a state-of-the-art stereo system with subwoofers
in all four corners of the ceiling. There was a glass coffee
table in the middle of the room and a leather reclining chair
in the corner.

The Dirt Nasty song "Nasty As I Wanna Be" bumped
from the stereo.

Corey was wearing the pink shirt with the collar popped.
He had sunglasses on even though it was night and the den's
lighting was turned low.

He and Beau were drinking from a fifth of Jim Beam and
the Bud Light they'd purchased earlier. Corey sat on one of
the sofas and Beau was in the reclining chair. There was a
large mirror on the coffee table with three grams of coke left
on it. Baggies of Xanax sat next to the mirror.

They'd both been doing drugs and drinking since
middle school. It was a habit. Beau was a gram-or-two-a-day
user of coke. That would make most people with a full-time

job go broke, but he could afford it through the stipend he got each week from his dad. He was also a hard pill user. It started with stealing his mother's prescriptions of Valium, then progressed to Percocet and from Percocet to Xanax. Those were very useful to him. He needed them to help him pass out before the comedown from the coke became too bad, too dark, and too ugly.

Beau was messing around with a Polaroid camera he'd brought into the den after the last time he went to the bathroom.

Corey did a huge line. He looked over at Beau. "Where the fuck did you even get that?"

"I found it last night, dude. Upstairs in one of the closets. It used to be my mom's."

"It even work?"

"Yeah. It's pretty cool. Like retro and shit."

"I never even knew you were into cameras and pictures."

"I've always liked Polaroids."

"Since when?"

"Since always, faggot. What's with the questions?"

Corey shrugged and took a pull of the Beam. "Just wondering."

"Pictures keep the real shit alive forever. The memories. The way they really happened."

Corey did another line, licked his lips, and wiped his nose with the back of his hand. "Pictures are the fucking best, man."

Beau laughed. He leaned over and gave Corey a fist bump.

"We gotta get some tail over here, man. Fucking bang some babes before your mom and dad get back," Corey said.

He rubbed his finger on the mirror, then rubbed the residue across his top gums.

Beau shook his head, smirking.

"What?" Corey asked.

"You keep smashing that blast the way you are and it won't matter if there's bitches over here. You'll be too high to squeeze that baby cock into any slab of vag."

"Fuck that, man. Let's just call up some babes."

Beau set the camera on the table. He grabbed the whiskey and took a pull from it. He swallowed it without choking it down and making a face like Corey always did.

"Just shut the fuck up, man, and give it rest. I wanna wait for that King girl to drop off some package for my mom. After that, I'll call some girls."

"Gina King?" Corey asked.

"Yeah."

"She's a fucking babe, dude. We could ask her if she wants to stay and party."

"Maybe I will," Beau said, holding the bottle to his lips. "Maybe we'll make her party."

He took another drink.

"What's that mean, man?" Corey asked.

"What?"

"Make her party?"

Beau shrugged. "Ya know, just see if she wants to stick around."

Corey looked at the floor.

Beau grinned even wider, staring at his friend, then took another drink and asked for the mirror, laughing as he did it.

THE TEAM HUDDLED IN THE CENTER OF THE LOCKER room. They yelled and one of Dru's teammates led a chant, the one they always said before they left the locker room on meet night:

Focus. Fight. Kick ass. Have fun.

They chanted it three times, then ran out to the eruption of their hometown fans in the stands.

As focused and unmoved as Dru stayed in his head before his matches, he always got a huge adrenaline rush, a massive thrill, running out to the gym.

The two teams went through their prematch warm-ups while the marching band played "Eye of the Tiger." Dru looked up to the spot in the bleachers where Gina always sat with a smile and a wave and a kiss to blow, but he didn't see her. He stopped and stared at the empty spot. His guts sank. A stunned look consumed his face. One of his teammates smacked the side of his arm as he walked by Dru.

"You okay, bro?" his teammate asked.

He blinked. "What?"

"You okay?"

He looked around the gym quickly and said, "I'm fine, man."

"You ready to kick some ass?"

"I'm always ready to do that."

GINA DROVE UP THE LONG AND WINDING DRIVEWAY that led to the Alderson house. The drive wove through large trees that looked like scenery from a German expressionist film. Tall steel posts came up from the ground, lit at the tops with orange light.

The sky was dark.

The Alderson house—or mansion, one could call it—was enormous. Two stories tall, three quarters of a football field long, a whole one wide.

Only one light shone dimly through the front windows. She stopped the car and watched the house. A heavy dose of uneasiness settled into her. She wished like hell that Dru was with her. Around him, she didn't fear anything. Without him, her weakness sprang up like weeds through cracks in the summertime.

She became short of breath and hesitant.

She thought about how slimy a guy Beau was.

She wasn't concerned that he'd try anything, but she was sure he'd make her uncomfortable.

The anxiety rode up her spine and got so bad she

put the car in reverse to turn around. She would just tell Samantha no one was home. She wanted to get to Dru. She wanted to get out of the darkness and cold and into the lights and warmth of the gymnasium.

As she was turning the car around, the front of the house lit up.

Her shoulders bunched. She'd almost made it out. She took a deep breath as she shut the car off and grabbed the box. The wind blew her hair in and out of her face. She shivered and her breath made tiny clouds in the air. She walked to the front door, where Beau was standing with a grin.

18

DRU SAT ON THE BENCH WHILE HIS TEAMMATE wrestled. He wasn't watching the match, though. He was staring at Gina's vacant seat. His body shook. He felt sick and hapless.

He thought about where she could be, but no reasonable conclusion came to him. It tore deeply into his core because she'd never been late for warm-ups. She had promised him she never would. That promise meant a lot to him. No one had ever been there just to root for him. He felt a distance from the mat. His head went fuzzy for a moment and he wanted to leave the gym. He wanted to find her and ask her why she wasn't there.

How could she not be here?

What the fuck?

Who could she be with?

With that last thought, the fuzziness dissolved and his demeanor changed. He grew nasty, his eyes turned dark, and he pulled them away from her empty space, down on his hands.

They were red and sweating.

Standing at the top of the stairs, Beau looked Gina right in her eyes and said, "Hey there."

Shivers down her back again.

Noticing her shudder gave him a sense of power.

All she could think of was the last time she saw him, his whiskey breath and wild eyes and how he kept putting his arms around her shoulders. How he tried to pull her into a bathroom, how he told her she was lucky because he'd picked her and not any of the other girls.

Finally, that night, when he went outside to smoke, she bailed from the party and drove to Dru's. She never said anything to him about it. The reason Dru hadn't been with her was that his mom had asked him to stay with her and they watched *Funny Girl* and *Breakfast at Tiffany's* until the medication put her out. Then he and Gina laid on the couch in his living room and watched *The Woman in the Window* on PBS, one of those old black-and-white movies he loved to watch so much.

"Come on in, Gina."

"Why don't you just take the box?" she asked.

"'Cause my back hurts."

She rolled her eyes.

"It really hurts, Gina. Just bring it in and I'll show you where to put it and you can leave."

Pause.

"Fine," she agreed.

As she walked by him, into the warm mansion, he caught the scent of her perfume. It was the same scent she'd worn to that party at Christmas.

His thoughts went to her rejection. No girl had ever denied him before.

A spark of extreme bitterness slammed into him.

His mouth twitched.

He'd almost forgotten about that night. It wasn't just anger he felt but the lack of respect. Nobody told him no. He'd always gotten what he went after.

"Follow me," he said after closing the door. "It goes in the kitchen."

She trailed him into a dining room, then down a long hallway. While they walked, he looked over his shoulder and said, "Ya know what?"

"What?"

"You look better than you did at Christmas."

Her heart skipped a beat. Her hands trembled for a moment. She took another deep breath and forced a smile.

"Thanks, I guess. Did I see you at Christmas?"

He clenched his jaw. "Yeah," he snapped. "It was at some party, I think."

She clutched the box tight. "Oh, I don't even remember. Funny."

"Yeah, funny." Pause. "You look even more grown-up than you did then."

"I don't feel older."

"No one ever does in high school."

He smiled at her as they entered the kitchen. It was huge, with a stone floor, granite countertops, and a long, wide wooden table that shined underneath the bright ceiling lights.

Beau pointed at the table. "It goes there."

"Okay." She walked to the table and set the box down. When she started back for the hallway, Beau grabbed her arm.

"Hey," she said. "What are you doing?"

He smirked and let go. "Do you drink whiskey?" he asked.

"I'm driving," she answered.

"One shot won't get you arrested," he said back.

"Well, I'm good. Thank you, though."

He grabbed her arm again.

"What are you doing, Beau?" she snapped, shaking her arm out.

"Can I show you something?" he asked. "It's in the den. It will only take a second."

She hesitated. She didn't want to go but figured it would appease him. He'd show her whatever he had to show her and she'd say, "Rad" or "Cool" or "Neat" and that would be the end of it. She'd be back in the car. She'd be at the meet. Even though she knew she had missed warm-ups, at least she'd make his match and explain everything. Dru was too in love with her to stay mad.

She followed Beau into the den and immediately regretted her choice when she saw Corey doing coke off a mirror.

Beau held up the Polaroid camera. "You see how old this is? Aren't you super into photography?"

"I took some photos for the school paper."

"Your mom's really into shooting photos, though. She used to have that studio in town."

"She's my stepmom, Beau. But yes, she used to have a photo studio on Main Street."

"Do you want the camera?"

"No, you keep it. Take some pictures of your own."

Beau nodded and set the camera back down. He picked up the whiskey and took a drink from the bottle before offering it to Gina. "Come on," he said. "Don't be such a lady. Take a drink."

"I have school tomorrow."

"So what? Come on, Gina. Just one."

She looked at Corey. His mouth was open and his tongue slid around his lips.

"Just take one," he said. "It won't kill you."

She sighed. She decided to give in again. After that, she was gone.

"Okay," she said. "But just one, and then I have to leave."

"Good," Beau said.

He gave her the bottle. She took a very small sip and made a face while she choked it down. She handed the bottle back to Beau.

"How about some blast?" he asked.

"No, no, no, no," she said. "I'm leaving."

"Just a tiny line," he pushed.

"No, guys. I have to go now."

"Don't be like that," Beau snapped. "Don't deny me again."

"What the fuck, man? I have to go. I have better stuff to do than be here with you two."

Immediately after she said that, she regretted it. Beau's face turned sour and dark. He looked pissed.

Her face went red and she started shaking.

Beau got right up to her. "You don't deny me."

Corey stood up. "Beau, settle down."

"You're fucking crazy," Gina said, and turned for the doorway.

But right as she took her first step, Beau grabbed her hair, pulled her head back, and snapped, "You ain't going anywhere till I say so."

She screamed as Beau twisted one of her arms. He smacked her in the face, leaving a red handprint on it. Then he shoved her to the floor and slammed a foot on her back.

"What the fuck are you doing?" Corey asked, stepping toward the two of them.

Beau turned and grabbed him by the shoulders. "You said you wanted to party, man," Bean snorted.

"Not like this, dude. Let her go."

"Shut the fuck up! Don't be a pussy!"

He shoved Corey back and Corey just stood there. He did nothing. He always did everything Beau told him to do.

Everything.

"You're fucking doing this too," he snapped at Corey. He looked back down at Gina and licked his lips. "Now let's fucking party, girl!"

Dru stood across from the toughest opponent he had ever wrestled and maybe ever would. Brian Schmidt was a three-time state champion who hadn't lost a meet since his freshman season. He was one of the most hyped wrestlers in the state, but even with all of his accolades, accomplishments, and flat-out domination, he wasn't considered as talented as Dru. He wasn't projected to have the same kind of success at the collegiate level.

The ref got between them. Dru looked back to the stands.

Hope swam through his blood.

Dru saw a body in Gina's vacant spot and his heart jumped back into place until he realized it was another girl, not his girl. His shoulders dropped and he looked at down at his feet.

The fuzz returned as the anger became despair.

The ref told the two to shake hands. Brian stuck his out and Dru swatted it with the back of his. The whistle blew and the match began.

Brian went for Dru's legs. Dru didn't react and his knees buckled as he fell to the mat. Brian was in control. The domination was just beginning.

Beau ripped off his shirt. Gina was lying with her face to the carpet. Her nose was smashed flat. Drool spilled from her lips. It was the worst feeling ever. Her heart was smashing into her ribs. She was sobbing. Screaming wouldn't even help. She closed her eyes and braced for the intrusion.

"Quit crying, whore," Beau snapped. He turned her on her back, kicking her hard in the ribs. He knelt down beside her and tore open the buttons on her jeans and slid them down to her ankles. Her body was in a steady tremble. Even with her eyes closed, she covered her face with her hands.

Corey shook his head and looked down at his feet. He wanted to stop it but didn't know how. Beau was stronger. Beau had more power. Like the sheep he'd always been, he bit his lip and kept staring at the floor. In his brain he hummed a song by Beck. It distracted him just enough to not hear Gina's sobbing.

Beau slid Gina's underwear to the side and shoved two fingers into her pussy. It was dry so he slid his fingers in and out a few times over to get her crotch moist.

She couldn't fight back. She'd always thought that if something like this happened, she'd fight and scratch and claw and stop the predator. Every girl thinks like that. Of course they do. But Gina wasn't fighting back. She was helpless and she knew it. There was nothing in her power to make it stop. It was like being buried alive. His fingers sliding in and out of her pussy like the dirt being thrown on her. It was devastating. Every part of her life was being changed without her consent.

Beau stood back up and walked over to Corey. Smacking Corey's arm, he said, "Lighten up, this won't be your first time."

"What are you talking about?"

"Come on, man. I saw you finger banging that passed-out girl in Lonnie's parents' bedroom at his house party last summer."

Corey's jaw dropped. "You did?"

"Yeah, faggot. I did. I was going to piss in the upstairs bathroom and I saw the light on in there and poked my fucking head inside. I saw it. I watched you assault that drunk, sleeping girl, so don't act like you're better than this, 'cause you fucking ain't, man."

The wind left Corey's lungs. Then Beau opened his wallet and took out the condoms he always carried.

"Gotta use these," he told Corey, then kicked Gina's leg. "No physical evidence this way. Her word against ours, and my word always wins."

Corey didn't say anything.

He was white as a ghost.

"I'm smarter than the rest of them assholes," Beau said. "Now hold this bitch's arms down while I make her moan."

"I don't want to," Corey said.

Beau's eyes went wild again.

Corey winced like a pussy.

"What's that you said?" he asked Corey.

"You heard me."

Beau punched Corey in the chest. "Fuck you. You do what I tell you, man. You always do what I tell you."

Corey rubbed the spot on his chest where Beau had hit him.

"Hold her arms down, dude," Beau said. He balled his hand into a fist again and Corey jumped back. "Do it or I kick your ass, then let the word out on your secret party at Lonnie's last summer."

Corey looked into his friend's eyes. He knew Beau was serious.

"So do what I want," Beau said. "And everything will be dandy."

"Okay, man. Okay." He looked down at Gina. Her face was still covered. "Dude," he said. "She's not gonna fight back."

Beau grabbed Corey by the shoulder and pushed him at Gina. "Just do what I fucking say, man."

Corey stood over Gina's head. He knelt down, planting both knees into the carpet above Gina's shoulders. He put his hands on her arms.

Beau unzipped his pants. His dick was already hard. Even though he'd been drinking for most of the day and had done some coke (not nearly as much as Corey had), the control and the power had given him a rush to the crotch.

He put on the condom, pulled his pants to his knees, and guided his dick into Gina's pussy.

The buzzer sounded and the first round ended with Dru down three to nothing. It was the first time he'd ever ended a round behind. Worse yet, he'd been dominated. He hadn't even made a counter move. He was there in body, but his mind was gone.

Furious with Dru's lack of effort, his coach grabbed him by the shoulders. "What's wrong with you out there?"

"Nothing, Coach."

"You're embarrassing me, yourself, and this whole fucking school."

"I'm sorry, Coach."

"Get fucking focused! Kick his ass! You realize if you lose this match, no one will think you're the greatest again. No one!"

"I know."

"So go the fuck back out there and destroy that asshole. Be a fucking hero."

Dru nodded.

He turned from his coach and returned to the center of the mat and got down on his hands and knees. Brian put a hand on Dru's left arm and the other one on Dru's right thigh, and then he leaned down to Dru's ear and said, "Fucking you up was easier than fucking your whore girlfriend."

The ref blew the whistle and Brian pulled Dru's arm out from under him and locked him in a cradle.

Dru closed his eyes.

The only thing in his head was the word "whore."

Beau thrust into Gina hard one last time. His shoulders bunched and squeezed together. He made sure to hold on to the top of the condom so that it didn't slip down when he was pulling out of her.

He finished coming and let out a deep sigh. "Goddamn," he said as he pulled himself out of her. "Wow is all I can say." He stood up and walked to the fireplace, where he took the condom off and threw it into the flames.

He felt no remorse, no humiliation. He felt more manly. He'd bagged the bitch who had turned him down. Never mind that it was through force. To him, he knew she'd enjoyed it. He knew she'd go home later and think about how good it had felt and sleep well.

That's how it played out in his imagination.

He was smiling as he opened a new beer and pounded the whole thing in three drinks.

Gina's crotch was pink and throbbing.

Beau zipped his pants and walked back to Gina.

Corey's head was turned away from Gina. His eyes were closed. He knew what was coming next. It was his turn.

Handing him a condom, Beau said, "Hop on that shit. It's ripe and ready for ya."

Corey didn't move. He couldn't look at his friend.

Beau's cheeks got red and he grabbed Corey by the neck. "I said, hop on that shit, man."

"I don't think I should," Corey stuttered.

"Excuse me?"

"Come on, Beau. You had your fun. That should be enough for you."

Gina's hands still covered face. Her eyes were still closed underneath them. She refused to look. To see. Her ears were full of fuzz. She couldn't hear anything but the feedback from her brain. She wasn't there anymore. She couldn't feel her own pulse.

Beau squeezed Corey's neck even harder. "You listen here, man. You're gonna do this, 'cause if you don't, I'm gonna fucking kill you. You understand? I will fucking tell people what you did to that girl and I will bury you if you don't fucking do this. Okay?"

Corey winced. "Fine. I'll do it."

Once Beau let go of his neck, Corey unzipped his pants. He spit on his hand and jerked himself off. It made him nauseous. He was trying to think about anything other than where he was. He thought about the nasty porn he watched on his computer, sex he'd had with other girls, fucking some hot young actress, anything except for Gina. For a moment, he thought he was going to puke. He stopped briefly. He was sweating badly. When he began to jerk off again, he finally got hard enough to put the condom on. Beau took a drink of whiskey and then he knelt down by Gina's head to hold her down.

She could smell his breath. It smelled the same way it had when Beau had tried to get on her at Christmas. She was sick to her stomach. She held her breath and left the house. But just in her head. On her back, clothes stripped off, she had no other choice than to listen to the fuzz and go to another place in her brain.

She couldn't even hear the words that were being said.

"Just relax and don't fight back," Beau said. "You know you're having the time of your fucking life."

Corey got on his hands and knees. His eyes welled up with water as he dropped another glob of spit in his hand and rubbed the condom. He put a hand on Gina's side and shoved himself into her pussy with the help of the other.

Even though he didn't want it to, it felt good for a moment. She felt good. The pleasure was undeniable.

Suddenly, Beau jumped to his feet. He grabbed the Polaroid and took a photo of Corey raping Gina.

When the camera flashed, Corey jumped off Gina.

"What the fuck, man?"

"I wanted to remember this moment."

"What?"

"Your second rape, man."

"You fuck!"

"You gonna finish?" Beau pressed.

Corey looked down at his dick. It was limp. The condom

was slipping off. He shook his head. "I can't," he said.

"Faggot," Beau said back, and began to laugh again.

Dru didn't fight back. Brian got better leverage and turned him until both Dru's shoulders were touching the mat. The ref put his face to the mat. Brian locked Dru tighter and the ref slammed his hand down once, then blew his whistle.

Brian let go and pumped his fist in the air as Dru just laid there. The crowd was stunned and the gym fell still.

Dru finally sat up while Brian was declared the official winner. He looked up to the bleachers and shook his head. He'd forgotten that he'd even been wrestling.

Corey took his condom off and tossed it into the fireplace. He was shaking as he zipped his pants back up. He walked to the coffee table. As he passed Beau, he went, "You're an asshole, man."

"Shut up."

Corey cut another line and snorted it.

Gina whimpered on. Her hands still covered her face and her eyes still stayed shut and her ears still rang with the fury of a helicopter engine.

Beau put the camera back to his face. This time, he stood directly over Gina and took another picture. Her pussy was red like a tomato.

Beau set the camera back down. He leaned down and pulled Gina's pants back up.

He ripped her hands off her face and yanked her to her feet and told her to get lost.

It's all she wanted, anyway. She was dizzy and she hurt. Getting lost seemed like a dream. Getting lost was the only thing she wanted.

"Keep your mouth fucking shut and nothing bad will happen to you," Beau said.

Gina didn't say anything and looked to the side, away from Beau.

"Nod if you understand what I just said."

She didn't respond.

Beau grabbed her hair and moved her head back and forth. "You're nodding."

"Okay," Gina whispered.

Beau let go. "'Cause no one would ever believe you, anyway. We used condoms, and you didn't even say no, so just keep that whore mouth of yours shut. But if you do decide to talk, just know that your dad will be fucking ruined. You understand that? Your dad will be finished around these parts and your family will fucking hate you for that. Okay? So just don't say a thing and get the fuck out of my sight."

Gina nodded again and left the den. Beau watched her drive away.

In the car, Gina gripped the wheel tight. She didn't want

to go home. She was shaking. Her breathing was heavy. Her chest felt tight. She couldn't face her family. Home was where Dru was. She knew the meet was over. She knew he was shattered because she hadn't been there. He'd be angry. But he was where she had to go.

There was no other place than him.

Dru changed right back into his clothes without a shower. He spoke to no one.

When he was done, he grabbed his duffel bag and slung it over his shoulder. Coach walked into the room as Dru started for the door.

"Where the hell do you think you're going, Weiben?"

"Home."

"Not till I'm done addressing the team."

"Address them without me. I don't give a fuck about what you have to say. I lost. We fucking lost. What you say won't change any of that."

"Excuse me, son?"

"You heard me, Coach."

Dru left the school, hopped into his truck, and drove home.

Gina

NUMB.
Fractured.
Sore.
Confused.
Angry.
Guilty.
Fucking go ahead and pick one. Pick all of them. It's all going through me, pushing through my blood, crushing my heart, making my head throb and my hands shake.

19

DRU SAW GINA'S STEPMOM'S CAR PARKED IN FRONT of his house as he whipped into the driveway. All the lights in the house were off. His head spun. Confusion overwhelmed him. He noticed his hands—they were trembling. He'd never seen his hands shake before.

Dru got out of the truck and looked around for a moment before calling out Gina's name.

Nothing.

An eerie silence consumed the property. He shivered in the cold breeze before running into the house and yelling her name again.

Still no answer.

He moved swiftly into the living room, flipping on the lights.

He stopped and listened.

A whimper from upstairs.

He stormed to the top of the stairs and turned the hallway light on. The sound was coming from his room.

Racing inside, he found Gina curled up on his bed, hugging one of his pillows. Her body was silhouetted from the moonlight that barely crept through the window.

"Gina," he called out, putting his hands against her shoulders.

She shook at his touch.

"Hey," he said. "Gina."

Still nothing. She wouldn't speak. She wanted to but she couldn't tell him. She was too sickened, too ashamed.

There was something else, too.

She didn't want to hurt her Dru.

She just whimpered while Dru kept pushing her. He shook her gently. Begged her to talk but her body was stiff and her lips were glued to the pillow.

"Gina!" Dru continued, as his aggravation grew. "Fuck! Tell me what's wrong."

She gripped the pillow tighter.

Dru stood up.

He put his hands on his face.

He'd never gotten angry with her before, but her silence was killing him. His mind raced. He thought back to the meet. Her not being there. What Brian Schmidt said.

What he called her.

That horrible word.

Whore.

It was pinned in his brain.

"Gina!" he yelled again.

More whimpering.

So he snapped. He went, "Did you do something terrible,

Gina? Did you do something behind my back tonight?"

Still nothing.

"You weren't there tonight. What were you doing?"

Nothing.

Dru's mind was going crazy at all the possibilities cropping up in his imagination. It was speeding at a thousand miles an hour. His heart pumped tough against his chest.

Gina knew what he was thinking, yet she wasn't ready to talk. She was so fucking ashamed. So fucking embarrassed. So goddamn aware that nothing was going to be the same. Dru was going to be crushed and devastated just like she was.

And in the very back of her head, she was also thinking that Dru might not believe her. That he'd break up with her. She'd die without him. She didn't like those thoughts, but they were there. They existed. Lurking destruction in every corner of her head.

Then Dru went for it.

"Were you with another guy?" he pressed. "Is that it? Huh? Did you sleep with some other guy tonight?"

Even though he knew she would never do something like that to him, her silence made him question everything. This was all so new and weird. Emotional vulnerability had set in like a stone.

"Just come out and tell me, Gina. What other guy did you fuck tonight?"

She had to stop it. She couldn't let this go on. She

couldn't take this from the love of her life. She had to say something.

She ripped the pillow from her face. "Will you just stop it?" she screamed.

"I won't stop it! Screw that. Who were you with?"

"Nobody!"

"Don't lie, Gina. You weren't at my meet and I find you here crying. What guy's dick was inside of you tonight?"

"Fuck you!" she screamed out. "I didn't sleep with anyone. Beau Alderson and Corey Rogers raped me! All right! Are you happy to hear that? They raped me one right after the other so that's why I wasn't there."

The breath left his body. It was like he'd just been punched in the stomach.

"Are you satisfied now?" she asked. "Are you happy to know whose dicks were inside me tonight?"

He staggered back and his vision blurred. He wanted to yell at her. He wanted to blame her.

He knew it was wrong.

But that's the first instinct.

Blame the victim.

Hate them until it hurts.

"Dru," Gina cried out.

The sound of her voice made him blink. His hands stopped shaking and his eyes refocused.

She was sitting up with her arms around her legs.

Even in the dark room, even with the sad voice, even

with tears on her cheeks that shined in the sparse light, she was the most beautiful and precious thing he'd ever seen.

He rubbed his face and knelt down in front of the bed. "What are you even saying exactly?"

She wiped her eyes. "I was raped, Dru. They raped me at the Alderson house."

"But why were you there? Why weren't you at my meet?"

"Because . . ." Her face dropped in her hands.

"Because why? Did you want to hang out with them?"

"Don't fucking blame me, Dru."

Dru screamed and pounded his chest. "Did you even fight back?"

"Why are you doing this?"

"You shouldn't have been over there, Gina."

"It's not my fucking fault!"

He jumped to his feet. "Fuck!" he screamed. "I'm going over there. I'm gonna kill those fucks!"

"Dru, just wait. Come here!" Gina pleaded.

"I'm going over there, Gina."

"To do what?" she screamed, jumping off the bed. "What are you gonna do?"

"I'm gonna kill them."

"No you're not. Don't be fucking stupid. No one will ever take our side over an Alderson's."

He hung his head. "But they hurt you so bad, baby."

"I know! I can feel the fucking pain still! But you can't blow this up."

"Why are you talking like that? I'm gonna deal with it."

"No, no, no," she cried. "You can't. My dad will lose his whole career. We'll be run out of town."

"So what are you saying, Gina?"

"To just let it go and help me through it. I need you. I can't get through this fucking shit by myself and I can't tell anyone else either."

The fury returned.

Violence swarmed over him.

"Fuck your dad," he said. "You can stay here and do nothing, but I'm gonna go over there and deal with it."

"Don't. Just stay here."

"Can't do that, Gina," he said, backing away. "Just can't."

He turned around and ran outside and got into his truck.

He paused for a moment.

Everything had changed.

He slammed his fists against the steering wheel until they got sore. Then he started his truck and slammed out of the driveway.

Gina listened as he roared off.

The tears had quit coming and the numbness had subsided. She began to really feel the soreness in her hips and her crotch. Her head was throbbing. She went backward in time. The blurriness faded and she began to remember the things they'd done to her.

She remembered how she didn't fight back.

It made her sick.

The reel played out as the physical memories flooded in. The smacking sounds. Bodies thrusting together. The breathing noises. How her pussy was wet even though she didn't feel good.

They were going to have to pay. Dru was right. She jumped to her feet and ran outside and headed back for the Alderson house.

20.

COREY AND BEAU STAYED IN THE DEN EVEN AFTER
Gina was gone. Beau went on like nothing had happened.
He talked about the hot bitches he screwed in Omaha. He
talked about how rich he was. He told Corey that it wasn't
really all that bad what they'd done.

"Her pussy was wet, man," he said. "And she never
said no."

"I should go," Corey said, standing up and turning
toward the door.

"You done partying like that?"

"Yeah," he said. "I'm tired. I'm kinda over the buzz."

"Okay," Beau said with a smirk. "Suit yourself. I was
about to call some snatch over."

Corey shook his head. "You're nuts."

"You are too."

"Not like that," he said.

"You've done it before."

"It was different."

"Fuck you, man," Beau said. "It's never different."

"How come you never told me you saw that?"

Beau shrugged. "Ya know, I don't really know. I didn't
care, actually. It didn't bother me. I thought it was funny,

really, how you were finger banging a bitch who wasn't even conscious."

Pause.

"I mean, what a stupid whore," he continued. "My thing is like this: If you're gonna get fucked up like that, black out and not give a fuck, then be ready for whatever comes your way and don't complain when it happens."

"Gina was sober, man."

"Gina didn't say no."

Corey took a big breath and nodded. "Right."

As he was leaving the house, Beau stopped him and handed him one of the photos. It was the one he took standing over Gina.

"I don't want that," Corey said.

"Just fucking take it, man. Ya know, as a reminder of what you couldn't finish."

"What about the other one?"

"The one with you in it." Beau grinned. "I keep that in case you do something stupid."

Corey stared at Beau.

"Just take the fucking picture. It'll be fun for you one day."

"How's that?"

"When I'm gone and you're sitting around your house all stoned and bored. Pull that baby out and finish the job."

"Whatever."

"Take the fucking picture," Beau pressed.

"Okay, man. I'm taking it."

Corey snapped it out of Beau's hands and left.

"What an asshole," Beau muttered to himself, then walked back to the den without locking the front door. He looked at the photo and set it back on the coffee table. He grinned and shook his head. Then he cut a huge line of coke and snorted it up.

21

DRU SLAMMED HIS TRUCK TO A STOP AT THE TOP of the Aldersons' driveway. He didn't have a plan. He wasn't even thinking. Rage was the only thing making him move. He ran to the door and pounded on it.

No answer.

He pounded again and then twisted the knob. He was surprised when the door opened. He walked in and saw the light coming from the den straight ahead.

Music was bumping loud.

Dru started toward the den, but he'd taken only three steps when Beau appeared at the top of the stairs.

He didn't even flinch at the sight of Dru.

"What the fuck are you doing here, trash?" he snorted.

"Fuck you," Dru snapped.

"What?"

Dru closed his fist. He ran at Beau and swung as hard as he could into the side of Beau's face. The blow was loud. It sounded like a piece of wood hitting cement.

Beau staggered back a couple of feet but wasn't fazed by the blow. He was loaded on coke. He hardly felt a thing.

Dru jumped at him.

He wrapped his arms around the back of Beau's neck

and started hitting him repeatedly wherever he could land a shot. Beau took it for a few seconds before he slipped out of Dru's grip.

The key moment.

Beau punched Dru in the ribs. Dru swung back and missed and Beau gave him a shot to the neck. Dru winced. He lunged back at Beau. Their arms locked around each other. It was a scrum. The pile of two moved back and forth until Dru pushed with all the force he could muster. Beau lost his balance, stepping on the top step while still hanging on to Dru. They both lost their footing as they tumbled down the stairs into the den.

Their arms untangled as they rolled on the floor. Dru stood up. He spun around and dove for Beau, but Beau had already grabbed the glass ashtray from the coffee table. He slammed it into Dru's head. It made a cracking sound and Dru's ears started ringing. He fell to the floor and Beau jumped on him. He dropped a knee against Dru's chest, and a forearm against his throat, and then he ripped out a pocket knife and popped the blade.

He was sweating from the fight, sweating from the coke.

He held the blade against the left side of Dru's face. "I'm gonna slice you up and kill you, motherfucker!"

"Go ahead, man. But you won't get away with it."

Gina rolled her car to a stop behind Dru's truck. She froze for a second at the idea of walking back into the house of horror where her body's fragile innocence had been ripped away forever. But then she thought about Beau's smug face, that cocky grin and that dick he'd forced inside of her, and the hesitation and fear dropped. She sprinted from the car. As she was passing Dru's truck, she grabbed the tire iron she knew he kept in the back of it. She gripped the iron tight and ran for the door.

Beau still had the knife to Dru's face, laughing. "This is self-defense, pussy. You found out I fucked your whore of a girlfriend, got pissed off, broke into my house, and tried to assault me. I thought my life was in jeopardy so I took action before you could kill me."

"You're pure fucking evil, man,"

"So were your dad and your older brother, asshole."

"Fuck you!"

Beau slid the knife down to Dru's neck without putting a cut in him. "You're about to die, man. You know how many bodies my dad has buried around these lands? No one will ever care you're even missing."

Gina flew into the den.

She was horrified at the sight of the knife.

She screamed out like a warrior and Beau had barely turned his head when she swung the iron as hard as she'd done anything in her whole life.

CRACK

SNAP

POP

The sound of a nut being crushed under a shoe.

Beau's head split open. The knife dropped from his hands. His head slunk to the side. He blinked once, and then blood began to gush down his face.

He tried to stand up but collapsed to his knees.

Dru scooted back away from him on his hands and heels.

"Shit," he said.

Beau tried to stand again but he just couldn't. He fell to the floor. He twitched on the carpet like a fish on land while blood kept gushing. He made these gurgling noises that sounded like a wild beast being choked by rope. The blood went everywhere. It formed into puddles. It soaked his clothes. And then he quit twitching. The noises stopped.

Dru pushed himself to his feet and wiped his face with his shirt.

He turned his eyes on Gina.

He barely recognized her face in that moment.

She was staring at Beau's body with eyes bigger than Jupiter. Her upper lip was curled. Her face was wet with sweat.

She looked crazy.

It spooked him at first.

Everything was upside down and wrong.

Dru took a deep breath and looked at the body, still gooey with red, and then back at Gina.

He watched her lips. They creased into a smile and her chest started moving and a noise, this eerie noise that sounded like howling demons, began to move from her stomach and up through her lungs and chest, blowing past her throat. She dropped the tire iron and shook from the laughter.

"Gina!" Dru yelled. "He's fucking dead!"

Gina quit laughing. "Shut up, Dru," she snapped, her words colder than ice. "He got what he deserved."

"We're so fucked, Gina!"

"Just shut up!" she screamed.

Dru scanned the room. His eyes grazed the coffee table and he saw the picture. He stepped over Beau's legs to pick it up.

"Holy shit," he said. "Gina. This is it."

"What is?"

"This right here. This is all we need. We can clear it up with this."

He held the picture out and she ripped it from his hands. Her eyes grew enormous again as she looked at it. The evil came back to her face.

"You sick fuck!" she screamed, kicking his body. "You sick, disgusting fuck. You took pictures! Fuck you!" She kicked him over and over and over.

And then in the next instant, without any hesitation, she spun around, took a step, and flung the picture into the fireplace.

"No!" Dru yelled.

The picture melted in the flames, dissolving into smelly black smoke.

Dru dropped his face into his hands.

"Have to burn it!" she yelled. "Have to kill it all."

Dru lifted his head. "But that was the only thing we had against them, Gina."

"No, no, no . . . you're not listening. Destroy everything," she snorted. "Kill everything about this night."

"Gina!" he yelled. "That was all we had to show that we're innocent. The only fucking thing and now it's gone."

Gina started kicking Beau's body again. Dru grabbed her arms tight and told her to stop.

"Look at me, Gina."

She stopped kicking and did. As she looked deep into his eyes, a calm came over her, and she finally saw what he was saying. Her face went white. Her body went limp.

"Hey," he said, shaking her.

She stared blankly at him.

"Hey there," he said again.

She looked at the body, then back to Dru.

"What are we gonna do now?" she asked.

"We have to leave."

"I know that. It's not like we can stay here."

"No, Gina," he said. "We're gonna have to leave town. We have to leave Marshall, baby. Get away from here."

"But how . . . I mean . . . leave forever?"

"Yes. At least, I have to. You said it yourself earlier, how no one will believe us at all. They'll think you had sex with Beau and that I got jealous and came over and killed him.

They won't see anything else. They'll see my brother and my dad. I'll never get a fair shake here. This is Curtis Alderson's town. He has all the gold."

Pause.

They looked into each other's eyes again.

"And whoever has the gold makes the rules," they said at the same time.

"Well, you're not going by yourself," she said.

"Gina. Maybe you should stay."

"Fuck that, Dru. I'm a part of this. No way you're leaving alone. No way!"

"So then we have to go now."

Gina nodded. "Okay," she said. "We'll leave town tonight."

The panic had set in. It was their only chance. To run away and hide forever.

Gina

I'VE NEVER HAD A VIOLENT BONE IN MY BODY.
Never had one violent episode or breakdown in my whole
fucking life. I've never hurt anyone, not even the guys I've
broken up with. Always been a gentle letdown kinda girl.
That was me. It's probably still me. But I used to believe
that no one should ever respond to violence with violence.
I used to believe in a lot of stupid things.

1. The tooth fairy

2. The Easter bunny

3. Elves

4. Unicorns (well, that's not stupid, but
   I don't think they're real anymore)

5. Gwen Stefani

Even though I hit that sick fucker with the tire iron to
help Dru, I honestly can't say that I wouldn't have tried to hurt
him anyway. Fuck that "turning the other cheek" bullshit.

I didn't mean for him to die. But I don't care that he's dead. If that makes any sense.

Hurting me like that.

I wish a ton of pain onto Corey Rogers, too. That might be the most tragic thing about what happened . . . that we won't be able to find Corey and confront him.

Whatever.

He'll get what's coming to him in some way. He'll have to live every day with the memory of what he and that animal did to me.

Dru

IT'S FUCKED HOW LIFE CAN CHANGE ON A DIME without you even having much say in it. I'm still on the right path but the route has changed.

I was just sticking up for her. I can't believe I let that fucker get out of my grasp and take me down. Now here we are. Two lovers on the run. As long as we stay by each other's side, I know we'll be okay. As long as she stays in my sight, no one can hurt her again. I can protect her and get us to a safe place.

Now, I don't exactly know where that is, but I do know someone and maybe they can direct us to the right place.

Keep us on pace forever.

Because nothing less will do. If me and Gina can't have forever, then we might as well be dead too.

22

DRU CLEANED BEAU'S BLOOD OFF WITH WARM water and a towel. His head was sore from the ashtray that was slammed into it. When he was finished cleaning himself, he took an army bag from his closet.

Dru took two blankets off his bed and stuffed them inside while Gina went to his dresser and opened the drawer. She pulled out two handfuls of underwear and socks. Dru went back to his closet and grabbed three hooded sweatshirts, a scarf, and two stocking caps.

Dru packed it in and zipped the bag.

Gina grabbed his hand. "Hey," she said.

He looked up. "Hey."

"I love you," she said.

He shook his head. "I'm sorry for yelling at you earlier."

"It's okay, baby."

"It's not."

"Yes it is. I know you were just in shock. You were confused. It's okay."

Pause.

She let go of his hand. "So what are we gonna do?" she asked him.

"I have one idea," he answered.

He walked over to the dresser and pulled a scrap of paper out of a cup full of rubber bands, loose change, and paper clips. The paper had the address of Carl Sheer on it. Carl had been Jaime Weiben's partner in crime. They were best friends and had done a lot of stealing and running drugs over the years but weren't together the night Jaime got busted. He'd told Jaime that it wasn't a good idea to hit that store, but Jaime was high and insisted his plan was perfect. It wasn't. He slipped up and got put away.

After it was all said and done, Carl came by the house one afternoon and told Dru that if he ever needed anything, any kind of help, to come and see him.

That was two years ago.

He didn't even know if Carl still lived there, but he was the only person Dru could think of who would know what to do.

He read the address a couple of times. It was for a trailer park about a mile outside of Marshall.

"We're gonna go see this guy," he told Gina, holding up the piece of paper.

She took it from him and looked at it.

"If anyone can help us it's him. Jaime trusted him."

"Okay," she said. "I trust you, baby."

She set the paper on the bed and Dru handed her the bag and told her to meet him at the truck.

"You saying good-bye to her?"

"Yeah," Dru said.

"Wish I could say good-bye to Katelyn."

"Yeah."

She nodded and went downstairs. Dru waited till he heard the side door shut.

He walked into his mom's room.

She was sleeping and he knew he wouldn't be able to wake her up. The medication was way too strong for that. He didn't want to, anyway. What would he even be able to tell her? She couldn't help him anymore.

His face bunched up and tears came to the surface. He put a hand on her forehead. She was always so warm from the medication.

He took his hand off her forehead to dig out his wallet and pulled out a family photo taken at the hospital the day Dru was born. He set it next to her head and he leaned down to kiss his mom's forehead one last time.

He whispered, "I love you, Mom," into her ear.

Gina was waiting for him by the truck. She had tears in her eyes. He was still wiping his dry.

"How was it?" she asked.

He shrugged. "I don't know."

Pause.

"Sorry," she said.

"What the fuck?" he snorted. "What are you sorry about?"

"This mess we're in."

He threw his arms around her. "Don't ever apologize to me again. Those motherfuckers hurt you, baby. He deserved what he got."

"I should've fought back."

"Hey, quit it." He stepped back, his hands on her shoulders. "Stop it right now. It's not your fault. Okay? It's not, Gina."

Pause.

"Just tell me you get that."

Pause.

"Please."

She nodded. "I get it."

"Okay, then." He looked around the yard. "I need the keys to your car. We need to get it out of sight from the road."

"Oh." She pulled them out of her pocket and dangled them from her fingers. "Here."

He traded them for his set and went, "Now follow me in the truck."

He knew the land like the back of his hand. There was a small cove of trees deep in the field on his property that was barely noticeable from the road. He drove the car behind the trees and parked it. No one would see it unless they went out there and stumbled upon it.

He was exhausted.

His head was sore.

It felt heavy on his neck.

The day felt like weeks.

When he got back to the truck, Gina scooted over to the passenger side of the cab and Dru put his seat belt on. He placed a hand on her knee.

"Ready?" he asked.

"Ready," she said back, and he drove the truck back through the yard, past the house, and onto the dirt road.

23

ABOUT A MILE OUTSIDE THE SOUTH ENTRANCE
of Marshall was a trailer park with twenty trailers in it. Dru
drove the truck through its only entrance and followed a
gravel path that wound around a handful of trees.

This was hope.

An escape plan that began in the middle of the night.

Born in a trailer park.

Born from the lips of a criminal.

Dru stopped at the last trailer, which sat more than a
hundred yards away from the one before it.

The sky was full of stars.

Carl's trailer was white with green and brown trim.
There was a red rusted shed about thirty feet behind it. Four
old pickup trucks and a gray car were next to the shed. All
the lights were off inside the trailer.

Dru sighed and looked at Gina. "Just wait here, baby."

"Of course."

He got out of the truck, and right when he closed the
door, a light in the trailer turned on and Carl appeared in
the doorway.

He was very rough, rugged, and handsome. He had
short black hair that was trimmed neatly and a goatee. He

wore jeans and a plain white T-shirt and was barefoot.

"Who's there?" he asked, stepping out on the wood steps.

Dru stopped. "It's me, Carl. Dru Weiben."

"Dru Weiben?" he responded, surprised as hell. "What are you doing here? How the hell are you?" Carl walked down the stairs and shook Dru's hand.

"Not good, Carl. I need your help bad."

Carl squinted and looked past him to the truck. "Who else you got with you?"

"She's my girlfriend."

"So what the hell is going on?"

Dru exhaled and told Carl the whole situation, every single detail.

Carl's jaw dropped. His shoulders bunched. He looked scared for a moment before pulling it back together.

Just as Dru finished, Carl's girlfriend called out from the steps, "Everything okay, Carl?"

Carl turned to her. "Everything's fine, baby. Just go back inside."

She didn't move.

"This is just an old friend, Haley. It's all fine out here."

"Okay," she said back in a worried tone. "Old friends have gotten you in trouble before."

"Just go back inside, baby."

She went back in, but Dru could still see her shadow near the door.

Carl looked up at the sky and nodded slowly in thought.

"So can you help us?" Dru asked.

"Shit, Dru. Curtis Alderson will have the whole state on the lookout for you two. He'll send his own guys."

"I know."

"Fuck."

"You're the only person I know who could maybe help," Dru said.

Carl lowered his head. "I got one idea and it's a long shot. But if there's any place that can hide you forever, it would be this place."

"Anything," Dru said. "We'll go anywhere."

"There's a place up north along the Montana-Canada border. It's called Jameson's Crossing. It's on the eastern side of the state, past the town of Red Valley. It's outlaw land. They got cowboy gangs on horseback. There are arms dealers and Indian tribes and separatist groups. Tons of drugs get passed through there. A lot of stolen gear and technology. Me and your brother used to do crazy business there."

"It sounds like the Wild West."

"It is. Shit is lawless for the most part. The law works for gangs and everyone is out to control a running route."

"And we can go there and do what?"

"I have some contacts at a house deep in the hills there. They can hide you two and get you across the border if you need to go. You'll be safe there if you make it. I'll get in touch

with them, and when you get near there, you call me from
a pay phone and I'll tell you where to go. They'll probably
only wanna hide you for a couple days, though. After that,
it's up to you. You'll have to get lost there, disappear forever,
and start over."

"We know that, Carl."

"All right, then. Just wait here."

Dru noticed Haley disappearing as Carl headed back to
the trailer.

Carl took a tin jar out of a drawer next to the kitchen
sink and pulled out a wad of cash. He ran back outside and
gave it to Dru.

"How much is it?" Dru asked.

"Four hundred. It's all I got on me, man."

"Thank you so much, Carl."

"You're like family, man. Come with me."

They walked over to one of the trucks and Carl handed
Dru the keys to it.

"This one runs the best," he said.

"Sure."

"It'll get you through the night and most of tomorrow.
I wouldn't push it after that. I'll take care of yours. Don't
worry about that. But you'll probably have to boost another
one or two to make it there."

"I figured."

"You remember how to jump-start, right? From me and
your brother showing you when you was younger?"

"Yeah."

"Most of them old-time farmers don't even lock their shit up. Hell, most of them leave their keys in the damn things."

"Yeah?"

"That's right. And stay off the main roads as much as you can. Try and only take gravel and dirt roads and just keep going north. You'll get there. You can take the back roads almost all the way to Jameson's Crossing if you stay on the path north."

"Okay, then."

Dru looked back to the truck and motioned for Gina to come over to them. She grabbed their bag of stuff and did so.

She walked slowly, gingerly. She was so tired. She got to Dru and he took the bag from her hands.

"This is Carl, Gina."

A moment of silence followed their introductions.

"Damn, guys. Tough break," Carl finally said.

"Happens like that sometimes," Gina said.

"Shouldn't," Carl responded. "Not to a couple of good kids like you."

Both Gina and Dru looked at the ground.

"You guys better get moving now," Carl said.

"Thanks again, man," Dru said. "Can I ask you one more favor, though?"

"What's that?"

"Can you check on my mom tomorrow and make sure

she gets her meds? I figure after tomorrow, everything will break open on the news about this, and the state will do something with her, but the hospice lady won't be there tomorrow and she can't miss her meds."

"That's really risky, Dru."

"But she needs them so bad."

"Fine. I'll get Haley to do it so there's not a chance of me being seen there."

"Thank you, Carl."

"Be tough, guys."

"We will," Dru said, shaking Carl's hand.

"Good luck."

24

DRU AND GINA STARTED DRIVING ON THE HIGHWAY while they knew it was still safe. Miles and miles out of Marshall and they were the only ones on the road except for the few semis that blew past them every few minutes or so. They didn't speak for so long. Their bodies were drained and their brains were running on fumes.

Late into the night, Gina leaned her head against the window and spoke about her birth mom.

It was rare she ever did this. Since they'd been together, Dru could recall only two times that Gina spoke of her real mom.

She wondered aloud, "Maybe we can find my mom on the way up. I think she's in South Dakota. I got a letter from her once and the envelope was marked from there. Maybe if we found her we could stay with her. I know she'd hide us and help us start all over. I know she loves me still, even though she left. She didn't leave because of me, Dru. She left because she couldn't handle my dad blaming her for Ben dying."

Gina lifted her head and slumped down in the seat.

She said, "I'm sure she has a tribe she's back with now that knows the lands and has protection. We could start over there and make our own way after that."

Pause.

"In South Dakota," she said. "That's where I got the letter from."

Dru stared straight ahead with both hands on the wheel. "Maybe we'll find her when we're driving through," he said.

"I know she wouldn't turn away from me twice."

Another pause.

"I just know she would love to see me again and listen to our story."

"Our story," Dru whispered.

"What, baby?"

"Nothing."

Gina's head slid toward his shoulder as the truck went over the top of a hill. The taillights disappeared on the other side of it.

25

IN THE MORNING, SAMANTHA MADE BREAKFAST for the family. Katelyn sat at the table using crayons to draw a deer running across the road. By the time Samantha was through with the French toast and scrambled eggs, Gina still hadn't emerged from her room. Samantha stood at the bottom of the steps and yelled for her to wake up and get ready.

"Maybe she's not here, Mommy," Katelyn said, looking up from the picture.

Walking back into the kitchen, Samantha said, "What would make you say something like that? She's never stayed out all night on a school night before."

"Because she had your car."

"I know that, sweetie."

"Well, I didn't hear her drive into the garage last night and I always hear her come in when she has your car."

Samantha whipped off her apron and hurried down the hallway to the garage. Her car was gone. She slammed the door and raced back into the kitchen with red cheeks, shaking her head.

She put her hands on her hips, fuming, "I can't believe she would stay out all night with that loser boy just because

I asked her to do me this one damn favor. I never ask her for anything and the one time I do, she pulls this crap and has my car with her! Damnit!"

Katelyn jumped in her chair. It was rare for Samantha to raise her voice.

"I can't believe the nerve of her to stay out all night!" she yelled, as Craig King, Gina's dad, was walking down the steps wearing a gray suit with a blue tie. He had a thick black mustache and dark hair

Curtis Alderson had big plans for Craig. He saw a future congressman, a senator, or a potential governor in Craig. They were close in the way that most people were close to Curtis Alderson. Craig did what Curtis asked him to do and never asked any questions.

Craig walked into the kitchen and asked Samantha what all the huffing and puffing was about.

"Your daughter isn't here. She's been out all night with my car."

"Do you know that for sure, Sammy?"

"Jesus, Craig. Yes. The car isn't here and she's not in her room! And ya know what I think?"

"What, honey?"

"She did this just because I was the one who asked her to drop that package off for Tina. Because I asked her to do one damn favor, she spit in my face!"

Craig walked to his wife and grabbed her left elbow. "Just calm down, Sammy," he said. "I'm sure it's nothing.

I'm sure there is a reasonable explanation for why she stayed out."

"Are you serious, Craig?"

"We'll talk about it when I get home from work."

"You don't care that she was out all night with that boy?"

"Sammy," Craig said. "Take it easy. I said we'll talk about it tonight."

She pulled her arm out of his grasp. "You always take her side, Craig. Always!"

"That's just ridiculous. There are no sides in this family. Neither of us knows what happened, but we will. I promise you, we will discuss it tonight with her. I'm sure she's at school and everything is fine."

Craig leaned in and kissed her cheek. Not a worry about his daughter even flashed through his head. So she stayed out all night with a boy he didn't much care for. He trusted her enough not to think anything more than what it was, a silly teenage rebellion. Maybe she'd fallen asleep on his couch watching movies. She'd done it before and come home really early in the morning. That's what it had to be.

He pulled out a chair to sit down next to Katelyn and picked up the picture she was working on.

"That's just beautiful, sweetheart."

"Thanks, Daddy."

He gave Katelyn a hug while Samantha put breakfast

on their plates, then set them down hard on the table.

Her face was red.

Craig ignored her.

She turned away and walked out of the kitchen.

26

DRU AND GINA DROVE DOWN THE LONELY ROAD. They'd taken the highway until dawn, before turning to the back roads that ran north. They were slowly but surely nearing South Dakota.

He could drive only around forty miles per hour on the back roads. He had to be careful where he turned to make sure they didn't ever get too far off track. It was miserable but necessary. Patience was the key. But it's hard to have patience when you don't know exactly what's coming after you.

The hour changed to nine. They were listening to the radio, waiting to hear the news updates. As the report began, his grip on the wheel got real tight. His back went straight. His throat became dry and his heart beat fast.

Gina squeezed her lips together and tapped her fingers nervously against her legs.

They traded a quick glance as Dru pulled the truck over to the side of the road and they listened with heightened ears.

It was so excruciating.

There was all this stuff about the wars. A lawmaker who was arrested for corruption. The stock market was down.

The economy lost more jobs. Some famous football player was in trouble because of a nightclub shooting.

And then it was over.

There had been nothing about Beau Alderson. Nothing about the two of them missing.

Dru turned the volume down and let his heart fall back from his ribs. He looked over at Gina. Her eyes were huge and her forehead was moist with sweat.

"Nothing about that sick fuck at all," she snapped. "I think we might just make it to Jameson's Crossing, baby."

He rubbed his face. "Eventually the cops are gonna go ask Carl about us."

"How do you know that?"

"'Cause he's got such a past with my brother, Gina. They're gonna look at all of that. Everything."

"So what if they do?"

"They're gonna wonder where one of his trucks went."

Panic returned to Gina's face. "Baby?"

"We're gonna have to ditch this truck soon."

"How will we get to Jameson's Crossing if we do that?"

He rubbed his face again, groaned, and put the truck in gear. "Find another truck," he said.

Then he hit the gas and turned the wheel as they continued north on the gravel.

27

SAMANTHA STOOD IN THE KITCHEN AND CLEANED THE dishes from breakfast, still furious about her stepdaughter, her car, and what she perceived as her husband's lack of urgency and understanding. Her relationship with Gina had never been that good or very smooth. They were never at each other's throats and they were never even shouting, for that matter. It was just cold between them. The conversations were mostly short and brief and incredibly insincere. Neither side was right or wrong. It's just tough, is all. It's tough to fall in love with a man who's been married before and is older and has had two children and has one of them die, which was the sole reason his first marriage ended up fractured, then falling apart. It wasn't two people falling out of love or doing things to purposely ambush the relationship, the family, the life. It was an accident and overwhelming guilt and unanswered questions that can never be answered because the question itself is of an action that had no intention.

And it's so hard to be a little girl with a perfect family and a beautiful mom who brushes your hair at night and reads you sweet stories and sings soft songs to your little baby brother from the room next door while she cradles him in her arms and kisses him and watches over him until his eyes shut and he's fast asleep. A little girl whose mom and dad are inseparable, fun, always smiling and laughing and being silly college sweethearts, the perfect kind of love. And then it's gone. In a few brutal moments. And it's no one's fault at all. But it has to be, right? There has to be blame and there has to be reasons and there has to be answers and if nobody can adequately accept the blame and give a sufficient reason and provide an answer, the love, no matter how strong it is, the family, no matter how tight it is, the life, no matter how good it is, will always buckle, then snap, then drown completely under the pressure of itself, the reality of the mistrust, and the weight of its own history, because if there are no answers, the blame and the guilt become stronger than the love and those two things together become a force that no amount of love can ever break down and overcome.

This was Gina King's reality.

This was what Samantha King had married into and brought another life into.

When the phone rang, interrupting Samantha's thoughts, she shut the water off and hurried to answer.

"Hi," the voice on the other end said. "And to whom am I speaking?"

"Samantha King, ma'am. And who is this?"

"This is Julie Reynolds over at Marshall High. I'm the secretary."

"Hi, Julie. What's going on?"

"Well, Gina's not in school today and we haven't received a call or a note from either you or Craig so I was checking to see if she's out sick."

The blood in her veins began to warm again. "She should be in school, Julie."

"No one has seen her all day, Mrs. King."

"That's very strange."

Pause.

The obvious popped into her brain. "Is Dru Weiben in attendance today?"

"No, Mrs. King. He's absent as well. Why do you ask?"

Samantha's grip on the phone tightened. "I just wanted to know."

"Okay."

"Well, thanks for calling, Julie. Craig and I will be certain to get this straightened out as soon as we can."

"Okay. You have a good day, Mrs. King."

Samantha slammed the phone down and put both hands against her red face.

28

CURTIS AND TINA DROVE PAST THE FRONT OF THE
house and around to the garage. They saw the front door
open and thought it was odd, but when they noticed Beau's
car in the garage, the suspicion faded. He probably had
people over and passed out. It had happened before.

They grabbed their bags and went inside.

It was silent.

That eerie kind of silence when you realize that
something's a little off.

Items from the cupboard and fridge were still out on the
counter. All the lights were on even though it was daytime
and natural light flooded the house.

Curtis called his son's name.

There was no answer. He set his hat on the shining oak
table and looked back at Tina.

"Something don't feel right," he said.

Tina walked past Curtis, into the front room. She saw
a chair tipped over and the umbrella holder lying on the
floor.

Her eyes traced the flow of the scene to the den. She
wasn't more than a step through the door when she saw her
son's body on the floor, covered in blood.

Dried blood on his face.

And on his neck.

Brain matter stuck in his hair.

Stuck to the floor.

She screamed out. Her hands flew to her face. The horrific and disgusting image of her only child lying facedown, dead, on the floor was overwhelming.

Curtis's chest filled with pain.

He ran into the den and saw the scene. He also saw something else. He saw the bigger picture.

On the floor, along with his dead son and the brains, was the end of his bloodline. The end of his family name. The guarantee that there would be no heir to the Alderson enterprise.

That realization was just as crushing to him as his son's lifeless body. That's not heartless. It's the truth. What his son represented was something bigger than just a person. It was larger than just a son. Anger took over, but like always, he stayed in control.

Never let your emotions show.

Never let anyone see weakness.

Never show your hand to anyone else.

He grabbed his devastated wife and told her to go to the kitchen and get some water.

Curtis took a deep breath and gazed at the scene of the crime. Shaking his head, he took note of the drugs and the booze. He'd known for a while that Beau was using but always thought he'd straighten himself out. Aldersons work through everything by themselves.

He leaned down and rummaged through the pockets of his son's jeans to see if there was anything suspicious or illegal on him. There wasn't. Touching the body was a neutral feeling. It wasn't the first dead body Curtis had ever touched.

He instantly transformed into his problem-solving self. He pulled his cell phone out of the case hooked to his belt and called the sheriff.

"I need you here right away, Lyle," he said. "This can't wait."

Lyle said something, but Curtis cut him off.

"It's about my boy, Lyle. He's been murdered."

It was only after he put his phone away that he noticed the Polaroid camera. He walked over and picked it up, fingered it. He hadn't seen it in years. He looked at Beau and then back at the camera and then looked at Beau again.

He fingered it for a while longer before walking to the kitchen. There, he grabbed a trash bag. Then he walked back into the den and threw all the booze, the mirror, the drugs, and the camera into the bag. He pulled the yellow straps tight and tied them into a knot. Then he walked out to the garage and stuffed the bag into one of the green plastic garbage cans.

His son was dead but there was still a reputation, a name, an empire, to protect.

29.

GINA AND DRU CAME TO THE END OF A GRAVEL ROAD that led to a highway. Flat earth and fields and fences and trees. There was a sign for a town six miles away with an arrow pointing east.

"I know that town," he said.

"How?" she asked.

"Been through there on a couple trips to wrestling camp at South Dakota State. There's a gas station that sells food and snacks right off the main road," he said.

"Is it worth the risk?" she asked.

"We have to eat, Gina. There still hasn't been anything on the news, so I think we'll be okay."

"I trust you."

"I know you do, baby."

She reached over and held his arm as he turned onto the highway and drove toward the town.

The sky was gray and moody. There were two trucks at the gas pump and a few cars parked in front of the store. While Gina waited in the truck, Dru kept his head low but took notice of the two men filling their trucks. Neither paid Dru any attention.

Even if it meant nothing, it gave him a sense of calm. It eased him.

As he walked into the store, he saw the security camera and turned his back to it and went to the coolers in the back. He grabbed two jugs of Crystal Geyser water by the handle, then went down an aisle and picked up a jar of peanut butter, a jar of grape jelly, and a loaf of bread.

At the counter, he saw a small rack with U.S. maps in it. He grabbed one and set it next to the rest of the stuff.

"Taking a trip somewhere?" the guy at the counter asked.

Dru looked at the camera and then at the guy. "Just heading to Colorado."

"What's in Colorado?"

"I don't know yet, but there's nothing here for me. Not anymore at least."

The guy nodded. "Well, good luck to ya."

After twenty minutes back on the gravel, Dru noticed a field opening and drove about a half mile into it, where trees hid them from the road.

He shut the truck off and opened the bread and both jars. Gina took everything from him.

"I have this," she said. Then she spread the peanut butter and the jelly on both pieces of bread with her finger, exactly like she used to do it as a child.

They ate in silence and passed the water back and forth.

Through the window, they saw only brown and gray and space that looked like it never ended.

30

SAMANTHA CALLED CRAIG ON HIS CELL PHONE. HE was at his office downtown and had just finished up a fundraising meeting for his mayoral run.

"She's not at school," Samantha snapped. "Neither is Dru."

"They're probably playing hookie and went to a movie or something, Sammy."

"Maybe they're in trouble, Craig. That boy is no good. I mean, do you even care?"

"Of course I do. She's my daughter, but I know she's all right. I just do. I know Dru's not the best kid, but Gina is just trying to rebel."

"You should've stepped in when she started seeing him. I told you it was just a matter of time till he turned into garbage."

Craig stood up from his desk. "Would you relax, Sammy? Just take it easy. She's my daughter. I know her better than anyone. If she was in trouble, she'd call me."

"Would she?"

"Yes."

"With what phone? Hers broke two weeks ago."

"She'd find one. Now just stop it. I'll go right now and drive to Dru's house and see if they're there."

"That would be nice, Craig. She has my car."

"I know she does, dear. I'll leave right now and call you when I get there."

"Good. Finally a sense of urgency with you."

Pause.

"Leaving right now, Sammy."

31

PHOTOGRAPHERS TOOK PICTURES OF THE CRIME
scene. Deputy Fehr put on gloves and picked up the tire
iron. He looked it over, paying attention to the dried blood
and brain matter.

He bagged the iron, handed it to the crime scene
specialist on-site, and told him not to do anything with it till
Curtis Alderson had talked to him.

Tina was upstairs crying in her bedroom. She lay on the
bed, her face smothered against a pillow, a glass of wine on
the nightstand.

Curtis and Lyle sat in Curtis's office at the back of the
house. The walls of the office were dark green. His desk
was oak and thick and spotless. Pictures of Curtis with
congressmen and even one with both former presidents
Bush hung on the walls. The office had no windows. Curtis
couldn't stand the idea of anyone being able to see into his
office without his consent.

They sat across from each other in two-thousand-dollar
brown leather chairs.

When Lyle had arrived at the house, he could feel the
anger and madness beaming from Curtis's eyes. He knew
Curtis wanted blood, so he promptly gave the orders to

everyone at the scene, then went straight back to Curtis's office. He needed to gauge Curtis. Get a sense of how far he was going to go.

"Anyone been giving you trouble, Curtis? Anyone I should know about?"

"Folks is always giving me trouble, Lyle. You know this. But I haven't been getting any threats, if that's what you're getting at."

"You've made lots of enemies in your life, Curtis."

"As have you, Sheriff. Anyone close to you been killed 'cause of it?"

"Nope. But this land deal you got working is big news."

"It's goddamn huge, Lyle. But what happened to Beau ain't got nothing to do with that."

"How can you be so sure?"

"We'll call it a gut feeling."

Lyle leaned forward in his chair. "There something you haven't told me about, Curtis? Something you may have found or seen this morning when you got back?"

"I've told you everything."

"Sure about that?"

"What the hell are you implying?"

"Ain't implying nothing, Curtis. Just asking. This is part of my job. To ask the questions . . . even to you."

"I told you everything, Lyle. What you and your guys saw is what Tina and I saw. But more importantly, when you

finally get whoever fucking did this to my boy, you bring
them to me first."

"You know I can't do that, Curtis. Not this time. Not
with a homicide. This ain't some petty thief or embezzler. I
gotta go by the book on this one."

Curtis raised his arm and slammed his hand down on
his desk. "You'll do what I tell you to do, Sheriff. I made you
what you are. I am responsible for everything you've got. I
call the shots around here, not you. Are we clear?"

Lyle shook his head.

"We aren't?"

"Curtis, this can't look like we're doing you favors."

"If it's done improper, then you make it look proper.
That's what you do, Lyle. That's your real job."

The last part stung Lyle. There was some truth to it, but
it felt to him like Curtis was rubbing his face in it. Sure, Lyle
had covered up for Curtis and helped Curtis obtain more
and more power for years. He was one of Curtis's yes-men
and he had taken a lot of Curtis's money to promote his own
ambition. But he had also done a lot of good. He'd cleaned
up Marshall County a great deal. He'd gotten domestic
abuse reduced to an all-time low. Petty crime had dropped
significantly. Drug-related crimes were at an all-time low.
Yes, he'd been on the take from Curtis. But he'd still done
good work for the county above and beyond what Curtis
Alderson had ever asked of him.

And those words from Curtis—*That's your real job*—

were like a smack in the face, but Lyle didn't flinch. He wasn't gonna show his hand that early. So when Curtis said again, "I want to see those killers first," Lyle just nodded.

32

AS CRAIG NEARED DRU'S DRIVEWAY, A BLUE FORD pickup truck was pulling out of it. A young lady was at the wheel. Craig brought his car to an immediate stop and stared at her as she drove past him. Craig watched the truck in the rearview mirror until it disappeared.

He had no idea who that was. He knew Dru's mom was under hospice care, but the girl in the truck looked too young to be her caretaker.

He parked his car and stormed into the house. He yelled for Gina and Dru. He searched the basement and the all the rooms on the first floor before ending upstairs. He saw Dru's mom asleep on the bed. He didn't know much about Dru's family besides the stories of his Wild West–like dad and his older brother's life of crime. He'd never met Dru's mom, only known she was sick.

He stepped away from the door and continued down the hallway till he found Dru's room. The first thing he noticed when he walked in was the scrap of paper on Dru's bed with Carl's address on it. He picked it up and read it.

It was lying out for a reason.

His daughter was gone.

He put the paper in his pocket and called Samantha.

"Sammy, call Lyle."

"Is everything okay?"

"I think they may have run away together."

"Are you sure?"

"Or he kidnapped her, but something's not right and no one's here except a dying woman, so call Lyle and tell him they're missing. I'm gonna call nine-one-one and get an ambulance out here for this kid's mom."

"Okay, Craig."

Craig went back to Dru's mother's room and looked around. He looked at the medication and the pictures and the frail body on the bed.

He was sick to his stomach.

The only thing he could think of was his beautiful daughter.

He cursed himself for not having had a better sense of urgency this morning.

Maybe she was just skipping school.

But something dreadful in his gut told him she wasn't in Marshall anymore.

33

SAMANTHA IMMEDIATELY DIALED THE SHERIFF'S Office and got put through to Lyle. In a frantic tone, she told him that Craig and she had reason to believe Gina was missing.

"Why do you think that?"

"She didn't come home last night. She's not in school today and neither is her boyfriend."

"Who's her boyfriend?"

"Dru Weiben."

Lyle's eyes lit up. He still remembered the day he put Jaime Weiben in jail. "Tell me when the last time you saw her was, Mrs. King."

"Last night at the house. I asked her to drop off a package to Tina Alderson."

Lyle sat up straight. "Really? To their house?"

"Yes. She took my car and was headed there."

Lyle cleared his throat. A huge fucking break. "I'm gonna need to talk with both you and Craig down here at the office as soon as possible."

"Okay. I'll call Craig right now and tell him to come pick me up."

"I'm gonna have Curtis Alderson present too."

"Why?"

"We'll talk about that when you guys are all here."

"Okay, Lyle. Thank you."

"Thank you for calling, Mrs. King. We'll get to the bottom of this."

"I know you will."

Lyle hung up the phone and called Marty about the development.

"You know what it looks like we got, Lyle."

Lyle sighed. "Looks like we might have a coupla teenage fugitives on our hands."

34

THE SUN STILL HADN'T APPEARED, AND THE GRAY SKY loomed heavy.

The two kids drove and ate sandwiches. The tension lay heavy in the truck. It wasn't contentious or weird or edgy.

It was uncomfortable.

Dru didn't know what to say to Gina, how to comfort her, if she even wanted to talk about what happened or hear any of his words. He was speechless for the first time in their relationship. He couldn't imagine the horror of what she had to be feeling. All he could do was say stuff here and there, usually about the journey they were on, but even that didn't help. There was a hopeless feeling that had entered both their thoughts, even if neither of them wanted to acknowledge it.

Just stay on the path north.

Stick tough with each other.

Get there, disappear, start over.

He turned off a dirt road and onto gravel.

He looked over at Gina as she covered a single piece of bread with just peanut butter.

"Hey, baby," he said.

She looked up. "Hey."

"What are you thinking about?"

"Peanut butter."

He smiled. "Anything else?"

She shook her head. "Nah. Just wishing we could be there already."

"Me too."

Pause.

"How do you feel?"

She squeezed her lips tight, nodded, then said, "I feel like we're doing the right thing."

"We are."

"The only thing we can do."

She took a bite of the bread, then held it in front of his face, offering him a bite.

"I'm good right now, love. Thanks."

"Just let me know when you want some."

"I will."

Pause.

"I think at the next town I'm gonna call Carl," he said.

"Don't do that."

"I think we have to. We need to know what's going on back in Marshall. Carl will know more than the radio will tell us."

"I'm sure they're looking for us by now, Dru. Let's just keep going with that in mind."

"I just wanna get a sense of what they may know. That's

the important thing. Do they think we just ran away or do they know about Beau?"

"I'm sure they know about Beau."

"How can you be so sure?"

"His parents were supposed to be home this morning."

"How do you know that?"

"'Cause that's what Sammy told me before I dropped that package off for Beau's mom. That's why I was over there. Did you even know that?"

"You never told me why you were ever over there."

Pause.

He rubbed his face and whispered, "Jesus . . . I never waited for an answer."

She looked at him. "My dad asked Sammy to have me drop off a package there. She said Beau was expecting me and that Tina needed it first thing when she got home. So I took it there and was gonna drive to your meet right after. I knew I'd miss warm-ups but I would've easily made your match."

"Oh shit."

She reached over and put a hand on his arm. "Did you win?"

He shook his head. "No."

"Because I wasn't there?"

He looked over at her. "No. He was just better than me."

She knew he was lying to her but that the lie was intended to protect her in some way. She appreciated it, actually. She leaned over and kissed his cheek.

"Are you still going to stop?" she asked him.

"Yes."

She sighed.

"Hey," he said. "I promise you, Gina, it'll be okay. I won't put us in any danger. We'll be so careful."

"I know we will. I just hate the thought of stopping anywhere we could be seen."

"It'll be fine. Please just trust me on this."

"I do trust you, Dru. I'll always trust you."

"That's what I need to hear, baby."

She took another bite of the bread and put her head against the window, eyes drifting to the sky, body sore from the violence and the duress. She closed her eyes and thought about the boy sitting beside her, who had stuck up for her, and she was happy. After everything that had happened—the way her life had been stabbed, chopped into pieces, and left over a crime scene that was not her fault— just being next to her man gave her a feeling of protection and love that she never thought she'd experience.

It's those moments when timeless and never-ending bonds are formed. The bonds that make outsiders jealous. The bonds that truly mean friendships and relationships are real things and not mirages that come and go over the years, because they can come and go often with so many people. But not with these relationships. Not when two people can do this much for each other and flee from a life because of forces beyond their own control, yet at the exact same time, taking with them an idea, a pipe dream, that they will have a better and more perfect life somewhere else together, starting all over again from the beginning.

That's fucking romance.

That's fucking true love.

Gina

EVERYONE KNEW WHO DRU WAS BECAUSE OF wrestling. But even though he was being recruited by every big college and was winning titles, and even though he was one handsome, beautiful man, he wasn't very popular in school. He was usually by himself, aside from practices and meets. I rarely saw him at kegs or basement parties or any of the hang-out spots. I'd heard he was a good fuck, though. The year before we started going steady, one of the senior girls talked about how she fucked him sometimes after school. She would go over to his house with friends and drink beer and wine coolers and smoke cigarettes. She talked about the way he touched her, like a man. The ferocity and passion in how he fucked her, like an animal. The amount of times he made her come before he was finished, five at the least. She was a pretty popular girl too, so I knew he could've had all that, the friends and the party invites and the cutest, hottest, most popular girls, but he didn't seem interested in that.

I'd known him, not well, though, since I moved to Marshall in fifth grade. I hadn't even spoken more than a few sentences to him in the seven and a half years before

we really talked for the first time. It was when I had my own
car still. A red Chevette that was so old and broken and not
really worth the trouble anymore. But I drove it because
that's what my dad had passed down to me. It was freezing
and everyone had left school except for the night janitors
and a few students waiting for a late bus. I had stayed after
school to work on my part of a group project. When I went
to leave, I noticed my dome light on. There were no other
cars, just a truck, in the parking lot, and it was just so cold.
So, so cold. The wind was like ice and hurt my face. I got in
my car and of course it wouldn't start. The battery was dead.
I tried two more times before screaming at my steering
wheel and slamming my hands against it. I got out, ready to
go back into the school and call my dad from a pay phone,
but before I went in, I kicked the car really fucking hard a
couple of times, and that's when, out of nowhere, I heard
him say, "That's no way to treat the thing that gets you
around."

I turned and saw him standing there with a library
book and notebook in his hand. He had on a brown tweed
jacket with a black hoodie under it and a black stocking
cap and blue jeans. He was so cute. I'd always thought
he was cute—most of the girls did. It was just that no one
really talked to him much because he was never hanging
out. It's not like people think it is. The way it can be
portrayed in movies and TV shows. Just because you're a
star athlete and hot and the center of attention on nights

when you're doing the thing you're great at doesn't mean everyone loves you. It wasn't like that at all in Marshall and especially not with Dru.

See, in Marshall, family meant more than accolades. Dru came from a family of criminals with horrible reputations around town. Kids weren't allowed to spend the night at his house. He wasn't allowed to spend nights at their houses. They weren't allowed to play with him after school. So it didn't matter when people found out he was different from his dad and brother. It didn't matter that he was the best wrestler in the state. He was a bad seed. A wolf in sheep's clothing. He never got close to anyone other than me. And that's for real.

All because of the day my car died.

He set his books on top of my car. "How about I help you so you don't have to kick that thing anymore? I have jumper cables in my truck over there."

"Thank you so much," I said.

He smiled. "My pleasure."

His smile warmed my heart. It sounds cheesy, but it did. It was beautiful.

He walked to his truck and drove it over. I glanced at the book he'd been carrying. It was called *Long Time Gone*, by William Lee Brent. I looked at the back. It was the memoir of a former Black Panther who'd hijacked a plane to Cuba and had lived there ever since.

Dru got out of his truck, holding the jumper cables.

He opened my car door and popped the hood.

"Why are you reading this?" I wondered out loud.

"It's for a book report."

"About a Black Panther?"

"The assignment was to pick a real-life figure whose life we knew nothing about. What's more interesting than a former Black Panther who hijacks a plane to Cuba and lives in exile there, teaching at universities and speaking about the revolution?"

"Doesn't seem like there would be anything more interesting than that."

He hooked the cables to my battery and said, "It's really damn good, too." He walked to his truck and did the same thing. "Cuba is beautiful. It's so pretty. The pictures in the book don't look anything like the ones I see on TV. It's like paradise."

He glanced over his shoulder and smiled again.

Melting heart.

He continued, "I wanna go there one day, I think. I bet I'd really like it."

"That's cool."

He got back into his truck and started it. "Okay," he said. "Try yours now."

I did and it started right up. "Yes." I sighed.

He hopped out of his truck, closed his hood, and took the cables off my battery.

We stood there staring at each other.

"Thank you so much," I told him. "I'm glad you were here so late."

"I'm always here this late."

"Why?"

"I have nowhere else to be, really. So I work out until my body feels like it's gonna break."

He looked at the ground and kicked a rock.

"I heard you are the best wrestler," I said.

"You know about me?" he asked.

"Duh. The whole town does. You're the big shot. The best ever or something."

He smirked and blushed just a tiny little bit. He was so modest. He's still so modest. "I'm all right. You ever see me wrestle before?"

I shook my head. "I do the football and basketball thing usually. I've never made it to a wrestling meet before."

"I see."

We smiled at each other and then turned away from each other. I grabbed his books off my car and handed them to him.

But as I was getting back into my car, he said, "Hey, here's a thought."

I came to a standstill and my heart jumped a beat. "What's that?"

"My first meet of the year is in two days. It's a tournament right here in Marshall. Why don't you come to that? Then you can start doing the wrestling thing, too."

I could feel my cheeks get warm. "That's a Saturday."

"So what?"

"What time?"

"Starts at nine."

"Maybe," I told him.

"Okay."

He headed for his truck but turned around before he got in, and grinned.

"Why are you smiling?" I asked him.

"'Cause I got this good feeling that 'maybe' means 'definitely.'"

I laughed and closed my car door. He watched me drive off. Two days later, I went to the tournament.

I got there at eighty-thirty just so I could talk to him before it even started. We had a really sweet talk and I knew right then I'd be in love within a week.

Dru

IT RAINED HARD THAT NIGHT. IT HAD BEEN RAINING for days, downpours, and everything was messy. It was the spring, early May, and farmers were upset about losing planting days. Rivers and creeks were rising, and towns in Nebraska and other states had been flooding. I hadn't seen my dad in more than two weeks. He was living out of his truck somewhere between Marshall and the town over, working odd jobs, beating up the girlfriends that he was cheating on my mom with, being the only thing I knew him to be. A total asshole. A professional dick. The meanest prick in the world.

He was a miserable drunk. Whiskey all day and night.

He was constantly in and out of jail for something or other.

He'd been out two months before that night. Living out of that shitty truck that barely ran. He was too drunk to fix it and too stupid and poor to pay anyone else.

The police said he'd been seen at some dump bar between the co-op and the ThriftRight grocery store drinking the bar special for most of the day. Then no one knows where he went or what he did. If anyone did see him, they never came forward. All I remember is it rained

so hard that night. The type of rain you can't see through.
Thick like fur. Headlights become useless. It's something
you shouldn't even be driving in sober.

My dad was pretty stupid, though.

Stupid enough to beat and cheat on and leave a woman
who loved him to the end and never asked him for anything
except money for groceries, shoes, and clothes for me
and Jaime. He never graduated high school. He learned
everything on job sites that paid him just enough to drink
and put gas in his truck, which meant my mom worked
two jobs to pay the mortgage and the heating bill. They
were never divorced. She worked so hard and never got
nothing but bruises and lies and, I'm sure, regrets, regrets,
regrets. Every once in a while, he'd sober up and give her
some money. He'd mow the lawn and barbecue and say nice
things to her until the night would come and the demons
would take over. Phase out the real man inside for a while.
Phase out the sanity and the love instincts, and suddenly
it's not your family around you. It's not your wife or your
boys or your house or your land. It's the reality of all the bad
choices you've made. It's the real-life version of the things
you didn't want to do and did. You can try to destroy only
that which you hate.

He hated his family.

And so that night, Sheriff Cortland knocked on the
door at three in the morning. My mom went downstairs in
her bathrobe and Jaime hid in a closet because Jaime was

already stealing shit from people, selling weed, and running things up north.

I stood at the bottom the stairs, poking my head around the corner.

He took his hat off. He didn't want to come inside. He talked but all I could hear were the words "accident," "bridge," "dead," "drunk," "drunk," "drunk," "drunk." My mom thanked him for stopping by, and after he left, my mom told me to go back to my room. Said she'd talk to me tomorrow.

She sat in the kitchen the rest of the night and smoked cigarettes and cried. Sometimes she would stop. She would clean something. Then she would cry some more and open another pack of cigarettes.

Me, I never went back to bed. I just moved farther up the stairs and away from my dad's death.

Away from my dad for good.

36

SAMANTHA, CRAIG, AND CURTIS SAT IN LYLE'S OFFICE, around his desk, Curtis wondering what Craig and Samantha were doing there, Samantha and Craig wondering exactly the same thing about Curtis.

Nothing had been connected yet.

Word hadn't spread about Beau's death or Dru and Gina's mysterious departure.

Lyle and his deputies were the only ones who had both sets of information.

Curtis had never been kept in the dark this long about anything. It's why Lyle wanted him there with the Kings. To prove a point to Curtis that he was gonna be in charge of the investigation.

Lyle walked into the office with a cup of coffee and sat down.

"What the hell is going on, Lyle?" Curtis snapped.

"We've got a couple of breaks in both cases."

"Both cases?" Curtis wondered aloud.

He looked at Craig and Samantha.

"What's going on here, Lyle?"

"Their daughter is missing, Curtis."

Curtis took his hat off and set it on Lyle's desk. "Jesus,

Craig. I'm so sorry to hear that." He looked back to Lyle. "But what does this have to do with Beau's death?"

Samantha gasped. Craig turned to Curtis. "Beau died?"

"He was murdered, Craig," Lyle said, cutting in.

"Yeah, killed in cold blood," Curtis snapped. "But what do these things have to do with each other?"

"The last time anyone saw Craig's daughter was last night, right before she left to drop off some kind of package for your wife."

"You can't think that Gina would ever—," Craig started, but Lyle cut him off.

"I haven't said anything of the sort," Lyle snapped. "Now, everyone, just hear me out. There's somebody else missing. That's Dru Weiben."

"What's that gotta do with this?" Curtis butted in.

"Dru is Gina's boyfriend."

Curtis looked at Craig. "Your daughter is dating a Weiben?"

Craig nodded.

"Jesus Christ, Craig. You think you could've disclosed that to me when we were discussing your goddamn office run."

"I didn't think it would matter. I wouldn't let her date someone I ever thought would be a threat to her."

Curtis shook his head. He swung his eyes back to Lyle. "So what's going on here, Lyle? You tell us now."

"I will. I just need everyone to sit tight and listen to me."

"Just tell us, Lyle." Curtis was staring coldly at him.

Lyle looked at Craig and Samantha. He was about to espouse a theory he himself didn't truly believe, but he wanted Curtis to think that was the direction he was taking the case.

"First off," he began, "I don't think Gina had anything to do with Beau's murder whatsoever."

All of them listened intently as Lyle spoke.

"From everything my deputies have found out so far, Gina never missed one of Dru's meets since they started dating and the season began. What we think is that Gina went over to your house, Curtis, to drop off the package, and Beau, being that charming kid he was, talked her into hanging out with him instead of going to the meet. So they hang out and Dru doesn't see her in the crowd. He gets all lost. Remember, he comes from a family with a history of men who lose their minds on the flip of a switch. Kid loses the meet. He got creamed, which we think says something about the state of his mind. So he notices that she wasn't there, and either knew ahead of time that she was going to drop the package off to Beau or she told him later, and he lost it. He erupted. He felt betrayed. So he goes to confront Beau with a tire iron and things became heated. They struggle and Dru swings that old tire iron into Beau's head. Once he realizes Beau is dead, he goes to wherever Gina is and he threatens her, kidnaps her, and now they're on the run or hiding out around here still. According to one of my deputies, kids say that Dru had a jealous streak in him when Gina even talked to other guys in school or at parties. So the question is . . . where are they going? Or are they still around here and hiding?"

"Well, shouldn't we put a wire out to other law-enforcement agencies around the state to alert them that my daughter has been abducted by this kid?"

It was exactly the question Lyle was hoping to get from Craig. He opened his mouth to answer when Curtis cut in.

"Not yet," he said.

It was the telltale sign that Lyle had hoped for. He had a hunch that Curtis knew more than he'd told him in his office.

"I don't think that's the best route to go just yet," Curtis said.

"My daughter's out there with some maniac kid, Curtis," Craig snapped. "Why wouldn't we want to put on a full-court press to find them?"

"I understand you're anxious, Craig. And trust me, I want justice to come swift and hard."

"So let's put out the alert, then."

"I think we should make the least noise as possible right now. Let Lyle and his deputies handle everything for the moment since they know the evidence, and I'll put my own feelers out with my people. Most of the time, they can be more effective than the authorities. I have eyes everywhere, Craig."

"Why don't we do both?" Craig suggested.

"Ask Lyle," Curtis responded. "Ask him about these types of situations. You got a desperate kid on the run. Anyone with a badge is gonna freak that boy out, and if he freaks out, he's got your daughter with him. What's he gonna do to her? I know you don't think this is the right call, but have I ever let you down or been wrong before, Craig?"

"No, Curtis, you haven't."

"There are a lot of stupid cops out there waiting to make a name for themselves. They see an opportunity like this and they mess up because their ambition gets in the way of protocol. Go ahead . . . ask Lyle."

"He is right about that, Craig. A lot of eager officers would love to make a career from something like this."

"So you suggest Curtis's way, Lyle?"

"I'm not—"

Curtis cut in. "The bottom line is the safety of your daughter and bringing that boy to justice. We need to get Gina back from that monster. If we put out a wire and they are out of town and on the run, then we got every hillbilly cop in the state or every young, brash, cocky officer just itching to take them down. That's when mistakes happen. When ambition blinds your common sense and judgment."

"Curtis," Lyle popped in, "people are gonna find out anyway."

"Not for another day or two. These kids are not to be hunted like that. Caution works best here."

"But that's my daughter."

"Craig," Curtis snapped, "I get that, and this is why you should trust me and trust my approach."

Pause.

"I've brought you this far with my advice and mentoring. You think I would let you down at a moment like this?"

"I don't think you'd do that."

Curtis looked back to Lyle. "Does that sound like something we can all agree on?"

Lyle's plan had worked perfectly. Keep Curtis in the dark but still let him think he's calling the shots. Everything was in play. Lyle said, "I can live with that."

"Okay, then," Craig said.

"Good," said Curtis. "Well, I guess we should let Lyle get back to work. I need to make some calls and get some of my people on this. Come on, Craig. Let me walk you and Samantha out."

All four of them stood up and Lyle walked them to his office door. Before Craig stepped outside, he turned back to Lyle, "Find her, Lyle."

"We're gonna do our best, sir."

"Thank you."

Curtis, Samantha, and Craig walked out, and Lyle shut the door.

"I need to use the restroom," Samantha said.

"It's just down the hall," Curtis said. "Last door on the left."

"Thank you."

Curtis tipped his hat.

As soon as the bathroom door shut, Craig turned to Curtis and lowered his head. "I'm so sorry about this whole mess, Curtis. I'm sorry my daughter was mixed up in your boy's death. I'm so sorry for your and Tina's loss."

"I know you are."

"Jesus, I can't believe your son's dead."

Curtis lowered his head. "I can't either. Infuriates me and disgusts me. Having my wife find his body all bloodied up in the den."

Craig shook his head. "I don't know what to say, Curtis."

"Say nothing. He's dead. Ain't nothing gonna bring him back."

"My Gina," Craig said. "I bet she's so scared."

"You should've told me she was dating Dru Weiben."

"I know, Curtis. But it never crossed my mind like that. I never had any ambitious intention by keeping that from you. She's my daughter. I wouldn't let her go out with someone I thought might be dangerous or violent. But I was wrong about him. He's just like his family. Sammy was right. I should've listened to her."

Curtis put his left hand on Craig's right shoulder. "You're a good dad and one helluva worker. I know where your heart and priorities are."

"Thank you."

"But I want you to think hard now. Is there anything

you can tell me? Anything that could help us out?"

Craig said no at first before Dru's house came back to him. "Actually, there is. When I was going to the Weiben house to see if Gina was there, I saw a woman in a truck leaving."

"Anything stand out about her?"

"Just that she seemed really young. In her early twenties. I know his mom has a hospice woman that comes to the house and checks in on her, but she didn't seem like a hospice worker. She seemed too young; she seemed out of place."

"What kind of truck was it?"

"A blue Ford pickup. Probably a late nineties model."

"Anything else?"

"Yeah. In Dru's room, I found a piece of paper with an address for some guy named Carl Sheer lying on his bed."

"You know who that is?"

Craig shook his head. "No."

But Curtis did. He knew that was Jaime Weiben's old friend and partner in crime.

"You tell anyone else about it?" he asked Craig.

"No."

"Good."

"Shouldn't we say something to Lyle?"

"I will. I'll tell him before I leave. I want my guys to know too. My connections go much deeper and further than his do."

"Whatever you say, Curtis."

Craig looked at the ground.

"If there's anything else you remember, you come to me first, okay?" Curtis asked.

"Sure, Curtis."

Curtis took his hand off Craig's shoulder. "I know this is tough for you, but we'll get Gina back."

"I know we will."

"And I'll get that son of a bitch who murdered my boy and it won't be pretty."

"What's that mean?"

"That I'll get some time with him before he ever steps behind bars. I'll show that punk what the meaning of the word 'justice' really is around here."

The tone in which Curtis said that made Craig cringe. His back shivered. He looked at Curtis and took a deep breath.

Curtis's eyes were black.

He looked like a monster.

37

THERE WAS AN OLD OUT-OF-BUSINESS SERVICE station, decaying with frayed edges and a broken structure, about 120 miles into South Dakota. There were no lights and no noises. Dru parked the truck next to the garage and went to the pay phone. Gina watched him from the truck while eating another slice of bread and peanut butter. He put a quarter in and called Carl.

"Hey, it's Dru," he said.

"Where are you?" Carl asked.

"Just inside South Dakota."

"How far?"

"A little bit over a hundred miles."

"Shit. I figured you'd be deeper than that."

"Gravel and dirt, man. Plus, I don't know these roads like you and Jaime do."

"I know."

"What's the word back there?"

"There's been nothing about that dead kid."

Dru was jolted by that answer. "Nothing at all?"

"No, man. Maybe no one's been to that house yet."

"That's not it. Gina said his parents were due back this morning. I'm sure they found the body already."

"Well, nothing's come out, man. I've been in town, watching the news and listening to the radio all day. Nothing about that dead kid."

Dru shook his shoulders out, looked back at Gina, and smiled. "That's great news for us. We can take the main roads tonight, then be at Jameson's Crossing in a day."

"Well," Carl started. "Not so fast. There is something you need to know."

"What's that?"

"I had Haley go over and check on your mom like you asked."

"Yeah."

"And Haley said that there was a car pulling in when she was leaving."

"Does she know who it was?"

"Some man. Older. Like late thirties, early forties. Black hair and a mustache."

"What kind of car?"

"A blue Honda."

"Oh, shit," said Dru. "That was Gina's dad, man. Fuck. And he saw her leave? She's sure?"

"She's sure. He had his car almost stopped and he was staring right at her."

"Fuck! This is no good," said Dru. "Now what? Ditch the truck?"

"No," Carl said. "You need to find another truck at an old-looking farm or something and switch the plates out."

"Okay."

"Stay off all the main roads until you get to Jameson's Crossing."

"I got it."

"Promise me."

"Yeah. I promise."

"Move now, then, and don't call here anymore until you get to Jameson's Crossing."

"All right."

Dru hung up and jumped in the truck, explaining everything to Gina.

She put her face in her hands and shook her head. "My dad will go straight to Curtis or Lyle with this."

"I know. We've gotta switch the plates out."

"Then what?"

"Then the same shit. Off the main roads still until we get past Red Valley and to Jameson's Crossing."

"Jesus."

"It's the only way, Gina."

"I know it is," she said softly. "It's just more real now."

"How's that?"

"Now people know we're on the run from something. We look guilty now."

"Carl said there hasn't been anything about the body yet."

"But it's been found. Curtis Alderson is in control. You get that, right? He's controlling the flow of information. It hasn't been announced about his son because he doesn't want it to be."

Dru inhaled. He exhaled.

"We've got a whole new problem on our hands now."

"That's crazy, Gina."

"It's not, Dru. And they're gonna spin it against you. Right now they're painting me as your victim and not Beau's."

"Fuck it, then," Dru said. "It doesn't matter how they spin it, because it doesn't change what we have to do. We have to keep moving, switch the plates, and get to Jameson's Crossing. Same plan, baby."

"Same path," she said back.

And so they drove for miles and miles down the dirt and the gravel. It was all the way dark now, but the clouds still hovered heavy, the moon was barely out, and they went for what seemed like hours, sometimes in between farms. Gina took a sip of water, then slid the jug to Dru, who put it to his lips. Some of it spilled over the sides of his bottom lip. She wiped it away with her coat sleeve and kissed the corner of his mouth.

"Thanks for the sip," he said.

"You're welcome, love," she said back.

At the next farm, near a crumbling barn, was a truck that looked about forty years old. The whole layout looked ancient.

"This is the one," Dru said.

She held a hand above her eyes and peered out the window on his side.

"That looks perfect," she said.

He drove about two hundred yards into a field entry across the road from the farm and stopped.

"Just sit tight, baby," he said.

"Nope. I'm coming with you. I can act as a lookout."

"Really?"

"Yes. We're doing this together, aren't we? Both of us taking the same chances."

"All right."

They both got out and closed their doors very quietly. Dru went to the back of the truck and found a toolbox. He pulled out a screwdriver.

"Let's do this," he said.

"Yep."

They jogged to the end of the field and crossed the road, into the yard of the house. It was only eight and all the house lights were off. Only a large yard light at the beginning of the driveway shone.

When they got to the truck, Dru took the back plate off first. He knelt down and she stood above him, facing the road. He worked fast and had it off in less than a minute. Then he put Carl's back plate on.

Both their chests were thumping hard.

He moved around to the front. Same story. The plate popped right off and Carl's slid right into place.

"Done," he said.

"Good job, baby," she said.

They ran back to his truck. Dru put the replacement plates on and they drove out of the field, driving until they found a dirt road that got them going north again.

"Stay on the dirt and we'll get through the night," he thought aloud.

"Are you scared, baby?" she asked.

"No. Are you?"

"Kind of." She shook her head and wiped her eyes, which had begun to tear up. "It just sucks," she sniffled. "'Cause we didn't do anything. It's not fucking fair. We were just sticking up for ourselves."

Dru grabbed one of her hands and squeezed it and said, "I know, baby. Nothing in my life has ever been fair. Nothing except you."

38.

THEY DROVE DEEP INTO THE NIGHT, THE TWO OF
them. Sometimes she held his hand, sometimes she would
inch over to the middle and lay her head on his shoulder
and leave it resting there, her eyes gazing out into a blur of
uncertainty and night and hurt and headlights that led to
nothing but north.

He loved her touch. It gave him the strongest sense
of calm and safety and assurance he'd ever known. It gave
him goose bumps, even in those bleakest of moments,
when she dropped her head on his shoulder or put her
hand around his and squeezed. It still gave him butterflies
and the tender nervousness usually associated with the
first words, the first kiss, the first time, those beautiful and
innocent moments that the world and the cynics will eat
away at because that's what they do. That's their job. To
pull back those white curtains of innocence and snatch
them away. But even then, in that most brutal reality
and sudden bottoming out of life, her touch, her breath
on his neck, her presence, was the most comforting and
intoxicating and beautiful thing in the world still. They
were the things pushing him to make it to Jameson's
Crossing.

It was beauty. It was God's hand painting the sky. It was the most amazing feeling in the world.

The night wore on and he kept pushing the truck through the roads and past the flat earth of fields. He pushed the truck past the barns and broken silos. At one point, she sighed or yawned (he wasn't sure which) and put her head back on his shoulder and closed her eyes. She wrapped her arms around him and began to talk about the future.

Their future.

They were going to make a dream. A real one, though. One they could hug and go to bed and wake up with and be a part of all day. Unlike the other kinds that leave us with nostalgia and questions as they disappear from our memories until they're gone forever.

This was going to be a different dream.

One that they could have forever. Together. Forever.

She said, "Once we get settled and know we're out of danger, we'll get jobs and save money. I'll cut my hair and you'll grow a beard and when we have enough money saved, we'll get a house on a patch of land miles away from any town or other house. We'll get dogs. Bad dogs . . . unruly ones that make messes and tear through the house and jump all over us and everything else."

She looked up at Dru for a second before flipping her eyes back out the window.

"It's why we won't be able to have nice things," she continued. "And maybe we'll get a rooster and some horses.

Some outdoor cats that the dogs can play with. And then when we're ready, really ready, we'll start our family. We'll have three kids, hopefully two boys and a girl, and we'll live on that land and in that house forever. We'll make our dream there, away from this madness, where no one will ever be able to hurt me or us or anyone we know again."

She looked back up at him.

"That's all I want, baby," she went on. "Bad pets and a house and you. Doesn't that sound amazing?"

Dru pulled her arms into his chest. "It sounds like the best kind of life, Gina. The kind where we're happy because we made what we have ourselves. Not what anyone else wanted."

"It will be amazing," she said.

"It will be our dream," he said back.

39

COREY SAT ACROSS FROM CURTIS'S DESK TREMBLING and sweating. He knew Curtis didn't like him all that much.

It was early in the morning. Corey had received a voice mail from Tina, who had found his cell phone number in Beau's room the night before while going through his things, trying to keep her son alive, at least in her head, for a few more hours.

He'd been sleeping when she called. He'd gotten up to go to the bathroom and when he finished, he checked his phone and listened to the message about Beau's murder.

His body went limp. His gut immediately told him that what he and Beau had done to Gina was most likely the reason he'd been killed.

His future flashed before his eyes.

It wasn't pretty. The panic took hold of him. He had found himself mixed up in rape and homicide. He cursed himself out for an hour for not having had the guts to stand up to Beau that night. He cried because his best friend was dead. A feeling of absolute doom encompassed him. He thought about going to the police with the photo.

No, he thought. *That's stupid. It's too soon. I might be in jail by the end of the day. Fuck!*

That's when his common sense smashed into him like a ton of bricks. His only way out of the mess was Curtis Alderson. Corey had the other photo. He figured Curtis would do anything to protect the reputation of his son and especially of the family name. So he called Curtis and told him he needed to talk to him about Beau's death as soon as possible.

Curtis was agitated. "How do you know about that?"

"Your wife, sir. She called and left me a voice mail."

Curtis sat up in bed and looked at Tina. He was furious she'd called behind his back. He gripped the phone tightly.

"What exactly do you need to talk to me about?"

"The night he was killed, sir."

"Yes."

"Something that happened. I don't wanna say it on the phone. I need to see you in person, right away."

"Jesus Christ."

The cold tone in which he said that into the phone sent chills down Corey's spine.

"All right, then. Come over here immediately, Corey."

"Okay, sir."

So there they sat in the early morning. Curtis in a black button-down shirt, black jeans, and black cowboy boots. Corey in blue jeans, a white button-down polo, and a blue stocking cap.

Curtis stared at him with ice in his eyes. He grinded his teeth and rubbed his hands together. His skin was dry and rough and it sounded almost like sandpaper being moved across a wood surface.

The noise made Corey's shoulders tense.

"Well, what is it, boy?" Curtis finally asked. "You come to tell me something important. So tell me."

Corey rubbed his face and looked to the ground, shaking his head, his fingers finding a resting spot on his bottom lip.

"Well, come on with it," Curtis pressed.

Corey swallowed the lump in his throat. "I was with Beau the night he was killed."

Curtis quit rubbing his hands together. He placed his right hand around his chin and nodded slowly. "Were you there when he died?"

"No. I was with him earlier."

"Go on. Tell me the story."

Corey put his face in his hand and tears welled around his eyes. He looked back up. "Beau was my best friend, sir." He sniffled.

"What are you talking about, son?"

"We were here at the house that night together, and this girl came over to drop off a package." Corey took a big breath. He said, "We'd been partying all day. Drinking and doing coke."

"Go on," Curtis pressed.

"So this girl, Gina, she came over and I don't know what happened to Beau. Something snapped in him. He got really aggressive with her when she tried to leave."

Corey looked back to the ground and shook his head again.

"What happened?" Curtis snapped.

Corey lifted his head. "He threw that girl to the ground and raped her, sir."

Curtis remained calm and focused. All his years of backroom dealing, taking care of issues, and fixing unfortunate problems gave him a steady hand at all times.

Nothing fazed this man.

Not even the news that his son might've raped the now-missing daughter of his handpicked mayoral candidate Craig.

His guts were made of steel. He dressed Corey down with those cold, dark eyes.

Corey trembled even more.

"I don't believe you," Curtis said.

"But it's true," Corey answered.

Curtis's stare grew even more intense. "Don't disrespect the memory of my boy with that kinda crap. He was your best friend, son."

"I know."

"And you're gonna come over here, to my house, and smear his name with that nonsense."

"It's not crap, sir. Here." He pulled out the Polaroid. "Beau took two of these of the girl. He gave me one and kept the other."

Curtis took the photo from Corey and looked at Gina,

pants down, face covered with her hands, the carpet the same shade as in his den. His mind raced backward to the morning before, when he and Tina discovered the body. The Polaroid camera he'd fingered while staring at Beau. He hadn't seen another photo in the room. He'd searched Beau's pockets for any kind of embarrassing items and found nothing. He'd gone around and around and around the room and never saw anything resembling a Polaroid.

His nerves stayed steady. He set the photo down.

"This isn't good, son," he said.

"I think that's why he's dead, sir. Maybe she came back with some people and they killed him."

"Do you know that she's missing?"

"Sir?"

"The girl is missing."

"I didn't know that at all."

"Christ," Curtis snapped, rubbing the left side of his face as all the pieces finally connected in his head.

Rape.

Revenge.

A struggle.

A murder.

It all came together and fit in one big picture. And what was left, after the puzzle had been pieced together, was the land deal.

The millions and millions of dollars.

His name, his reputation, his empire.

All of it in jeopardy.

He knew the truth. That the boy and the girl had come back after the attack. There was a fight that resulted in the death of his son.

But the second picture of the rape.

Where was it?

It would ruin everything if it came out. If anything improper about his boy was made public, the land deal would be done, he'd lose favor and clout in the political world, and it would be the real beginning of the end. The only end he ever really cared about. His legacy and his brand.

The boy and the girl, he quickly convinced himself, *must have the picture.*

"Does anyone else know anything about this?" Curtis asked.

"No, sir."

He nodded. "Good . . . that's good. No one can know about this, Corey. It's very important that you understand this. Absolutely no one else can know a thing about the attack, the photos, any of it."

"But I feel so bad. Beau was my buddy and he's dead because of what happened to that girl."

"We don't know that for sure yet. But if that's true, my son is dead because those two killed him and ran away! So don't you forget that. They murdered my boy in cold blood with a goddamn tire iron. His brain and his blood were spilt all over the floor."

Corey began sobbing. He hid his face in the collar of his polo. Curtis had little patience for weakness in times of crisis.

He told Corey to knock it off.

Corey tried his best to gather himself. He put his face in his hands while Curtis regained the composure and emotional edge he'd momentarily seemed to have lost to get Corey's attention.

"Now look at me, son," Curtis said.

Corey pulled his face out of his hands. His eyes were puffy and red.

Curtis began rubbing his hands together again. "How's your dad's dry-cleaning business going? I've heard it's been rough on your family with all of his medical bills from that car accident."

Corey looked up. "We're struggling pretty bad."

"Probably be nice if the situation got better."

Corey wiped his eyes. "Sir."

"Would you like that, son? For your dad's business to get better?"

"I guess, sir."

"You just guess?"

"Yes, sir. That would be nice."

"Then you're gonna keep your mouth shut and your head down from here on out, and if you do that, then your father's business fortunes will change very quickly."

"Sir."

"You'll stay out of jail and your dad will become a fortunate man."

Pause.

"Nod your goddamn head if you understand me."

Corey nodded.

"Now get the hell out of my house and keep your mouth shut."

Corey jumped to his feet and left the room. Curtis leaned back in his chair. With the reputation of his name crumbling down his eyelids letter by letter, he took out a key that was taped to the cover of a file and he unlocked the middle drawer of his desk. He reached in and pulled a cell phone from it.

He punched in a number by heart and put the phone to his ear.

"I need you here today," he said into it. "Yes. Leave this instant. This is the most important job I've ever had for you."

Curtis put the phone away. He taped the key to the folder and locked up the drawer.

He got to his feet. He fought off a very brief spell of dizziness caused by these words: *He threw her to the ground and raped her.* His son was a monster. His son had destroyed himself. His son had put his land deal in jeopardy. Curtis was furious at Beau. The news would be out today anyway about Beau's murder. He'd already planned to have the local news and radio stations announce it on their noon broadcasts.

He walked over to a large cabinet and pulled out a crystal bottle full of five-hundred-dollar bourbon. He opened it and poured some into a glass, then went back over to the desk.

He picked the picture back up and stared at it.

He shook his head.

If another one really did exist, he had to get it before anyone else did. If those kids had it, he now had to get to them for sure before anyone else did.

The game had changed.

Everything was now at stake.

Gina

IT'S MY BIRTHDAY AND I'M A LITTLE GIRL. I THINK SIX or seven, but I'm very young and my mom wakes me up earlier than usual.

She sits on my bed and runs her fingers through my hair. She has the biggest and prettiest smile on her face and she's so beautiful. Her dark Sioux Indian skin, her snow-white teeth, the perfect shape of her face. She's wearing her white nightgown and her hair is hanging down her back. Her blue eyes are sparkling as she says my name so softly, so warm, and I open my eyes, yawn, and say, "Hi, Mommy."

And she says, "Hi, sweetheart."

I notice that it's darker than usual. "Is everything okay? What time is it?"

"Of course everything's okay, Gina."

I sit up and yawn again. "I'm really sleepy, Mommy."

"It's your birthday, silly," she says. "Happy birthday."

"Oh yeah." A smile eclipses my face. "I forgot."

"It's okay. Come here, sweetie."

She holds her arms open and I jump into them and she squeezes me tight. The warmth of her makes me feel like the safest little girl in the world.

She lets go and says, "Let's go downstairs. There's a surprise for you."

I smile and take her hand as she leads me from my room, through the darkness of the upstairs of the house, down the steps, and into the living room.

The living room is lit with a lamp and my dad is sitting in a chair with my baby brother, Ben, sleeping on his lap. There are four wrapped presents on the floor in front of the TV, with purple bows on them.

My mom leaves and my dad, who doesn't want to wake up Ben, whispers, "Happy birthday, sweetheart."

"Thanks, Daddy."

My mom comes back in holding a small cake with a candle in the middle of it. She and my dad sing—well, they whisper sing—"Happy Birthday" to me.

I close my eyes, make my wish, and blow out the candle. My mom claps and goes, "Okay, sweetheart. Open your presents."

I go for the smallest one because I always think the big ones are gonna be better. I rip open the wrapping paper while my mom takes pictures.

Inside is a pair of red cowgirl boots. I turn and smile and take them out and put them right on my feet and skip around the living room and hug my mom.

The next present I open is a CD player and radio that I saw on television. There are two CDs in it. A Madonna one and a Dean Martin one. Madonna is my most favorite singer in the world, and my grandpa and I used to listen to Dean Martin records when I would go visit him and my grandma in Chicago during the summer.

The present after that is a white cowgirl hat.

It's very cute. There's a blue ribbon wrapped around it.

The last present is my favorite. It's a huge net with a wooden pole so I can catch snakes, grasshoppers, frogs, and small fish in it on my hikes with my mom or dad or when I'm playing in the backyard.

"I love it," I say, and smack the heels of my red boots together. "Thank you, Mommy and Daddy."

"You look beautiful in those boots," my mom says.

"My sweet darling," my dad says.

But when he speaks, my baby brother, Ben, begins to cry. His eyes open and I look away, back to my presents, when a gust of cool air blows past me. It gives me chills. I look back over my shoulder and my mom and Ben are gone. It's just my dad and his face is buried in his hands.

He's crying and it's painful to see.

"Daddy," I say. "Where did Mommy and Ben go?"

"They're gone," he says, without looking up.

"But where did they go, Daddy?"

"Gone, baby. They're just gone."

Her eyes popped open. The sky was light. She jumped off him and gasped. She couldn't believe she'd slept through the night.

"Are you okay?" he asked.

She was a bit shaken. Sweat dripped down her forehead.

"Baby," he said.

She swung her eyes onto him. He looked so tired. Dark bags sunk deep below his bloodshot eyes. Yet even in his exhaustion, he looked worried for her. She always came first to him. No matter what, her comfort, her happiness, her life always were his first concern.

"Hey," she responded.

"You okay?"

"Yeah, love. Just a weird dream."

"What was it about?"

"My birthday when I was younger."

"A real birthday that you had?"

"It was part real and part dream, I think."

"What happened in it?"

She shook her head. "I don't know really. It's already starting to slip away. My mom was there, though, and so was my little brother. It was sad at the end."

She slid up right next to him and ran her fingers through his hair. She put her lips to his ear. "You look so tired, Dru."

"I feel all right, baby."

"You promise?"

"I promise, Gina."

She kissed the bottom of his ear and leaned back. "As long as you promise."

"I do."

She looked out in front of her for the first time since she'd been awake. They were on a gravel road. Everything was brown and gray.

40

IN THE LATE MORNING, THEY CAME TO A SMALL TOWN with a population of four hundred people. The only store was closed and boarded up, but there was a diner on the main shoot through town that was open.

Out of desperation, despite the risk, they decided to stop.

Dru turned the truck around and parked it on the side of the diner, as far out of sight from the main road as he could. They went inside and sat down at a booth.

An older waitress with wrinkles and a perm came over with water and set two menus on the table. Neither of them said anything to her and she walked away.

Gina noticed Dru fidgeting with the silverware in one hand and his other hand shaking against the tabletop. It was horrifying for her to see him so tired and nervous. She lost her breath for a moment, regained it, then got up and went to the bathroom.

She looked at herself in the mirror. She was tired even though she'd slept a few hours. She washed her face with warm water and noticed a map pinned to the wall with a red dot for where they were. Still two hundred and fifty miles outside of Montana. The wind left her sails again. As hard as Dru was trying, he didn't know the roads—he couldn't. It wasn't his fault. But the back roads were failing them. Still, what could they do? The highways were too dangerous. They had plates on a truck that wouldn't match the registration. She wetted her face once more and went back out to sit down, next to Dru this time, and gave him a hug.

Dru

WHEN THEY CAME FOR MY BROTHER, IT WAS DAYTIME, a weekend, and I was mowing the lawn for my mom. Three police cars stormed into the driveway and came to a halt, and six officers jumped out with guns drawn. Five of them ran into the house while one of them pointed a gun at me and ordered me onto the ground with my hands behind my head.

It was humiliating.

I felt horrible for my mom.

I knew it was about to be just the two of us for good.

I knew right then that it was Jaime who'd pulled off the store robbery a few days before.

There was yelling coming from inside the house.

I didn't move.

With a gun drawn on you by the law, you tend not to do anything but what they say.

They brought my brother out in cuffs with his face roughed up. He was bleeding. They threw him in the back of one of the cars.

He wouldn't even look at me.

I raised my head and saw Sheriff Cortland walk out of the house. He stopped at the top step and looked at me and the officer who was still pointing his gun at me and went, "Get that goddamn gun off that boy."

The deputy did as he was ordered and Sheriff Cortland told me to get up.

My mom came out of the house, broken, just so fucking broken. She slumped against the side of the door. Then Cortland told me, "Get up here and console your mother, son."

I ran up to her and hugged her and all the cars and men left and it was just us two standing there for what seemed like the rest of my life.

The rest of her life.

Until the other day when my Gina was hurt.

41

DEPUTIES OLLENBECK AND FEHR WALKED INTO THE
station and found Lyle sleeping on the couch in the lobby.
On the floor surrounding him were the case files and
pictures of Dru and Gina. He'd gone to both their houses
and combed over their rooms, read some of the notes they'd
written to each other, found a shoe box in Gina's room
where she'd placed all these mementos from their dates (he
knew this because she'd labeled them).

Lyle shot up, startled.

He looked worn-out.

"How long you been here, Lyle?" Deputy Fehr asked.

"I never left. Was just catching a quick nap. Anything
new to report?"

Both deputies said no.

Lyle stood up and they all went into his office.

His desk was covered with paperwork as well.

They sat down.

"What's wrong, Lyle?" Deputy Ollenbeck questioned.

"Yeah," Deputy Fehr said, before Lyle could get a
word out. "All the information we've gathered tells me we
got an open-and-shut case. Why are you digging further
like this?"

Lyle pinched the bridge of his nose and sighed. "I'm having doubts about just how open-and-shut this might actually be."

"What kind of evidence you seen that we ain't?" Deputy Fehr asked.

"No evidence. But going through these kids' stuff, reading the things they wrote to each other . . . I don't know. Just something in my gut tells me we're missing some pieces. That there's more to this than meets the eye."

"That Weiben kid was nothing but trash from a criminal family," Deputy Fehr said.

"But just leave the kid's family out of it for a second," Lyle said. "I'm having a hard time believing this kid snapped. I've been asking around about him. I mean, how did he know she was with Beau during his wrestling meet? No one had ever seen Beau and Gina together before."

"What does that matter?" Fehr asked.

"It matters a lot," said Lyle. "Jesus, are you telling me that these two kids, who by everyone's account have been inseparable for months, had a falling out that quickly?"

"Kids we talked to at school said he had a jealous streak," Deputy Fehr responded.

"Sure . . . but that leads him to murder?"

"It's happened before, Lyle," Deputy Ollenbeck said. "They're just teenagers. You know how it was to be a kid. Emotions can change on a dime and do crazy things to you."

Lyle shook his head.

"Lyle," Deputy Fehr said. "All the evidence points to Dru Weiben. He snapped and took the girl because he couldn't let her go."

"Let's just go back to Dru and the girl for a minute," Lyle said. "Look at what everyone has said about them together. Inseparable! And you're telling me that she goes to the Alderson house on the night of Dru Weiben's biggest wrestling match, skips the meet to have sex with Beau, and then somehow Dru figures it all out, kills Beau Alderson, then tracks down the girl and takes her on the run with him? It don't make a ton of sense to me the more I think about it."

"It don't have to, Lyle. Murder ain't always supposed to have a sound reason. Sometimes people, they just snap," said Deputy Fehr. "Kids especially."

"I know they do. But not this kid. Everything about his life was about not repeating his brother Jaime's and his daddy's mistakes. Everything was about making his momma proud. I've been to the house and read things he's written. I've talked to his teachers. No way I'm thinking he goes down that path."

"Blood is blood. It's stronger than anything else."

"I have my doubts in his case, though."

"So what exactly are you saying, Lyle?" Marty asked.

"Something don't smell right to me at all. Just ain't sure what it is yet. Something about that Alderson boy, though. He wasn't totally innocent here. He played a bigger role in his death. I'm positive of it. I just need to put the pieces together."

"You really sure you wanna go digging around Curtis's dead boy like that?" Deputy Fehr asked.

"It's my job," Lyle said. "Besides, Curtis is one of the reasons I wanna dig deeper. He's acting like he's hiding something."

"Why would he do that?" Deputy Fehr asked. "That's crazy. What could he even be hiding?"

"He found the body," Lyle answered. "There could've been evidence that we never saw. Things that could be embarrassing for him that we don't know about."

"That's crazy talk, Lyle."

Lyle sighed. "Look, I'm not saying that Dru Weiben didn't kill Beau Alderson. What I'm saying is that there could be more to it than that. Something caused someone to snap that night and I don't believe it was Gina King sleeping with Beau. It's bigger than that. Meaner than that. And I intend to find out exactly what Curtis is hiding."

Pause.

Lyle looked at Marty. "Okay?"

"Okay, Lyle."

Lyle turned his eyes to Deputy Fehr. "Okay?" he said again.

"It's crazy, Lyle. Hasn't Curtis and his family been through enough?"

"Listen," Lyle said. "I'm not closing the investigation until I'm satisfied with the conclusion."

Pause.

"We clear?" Lyle asked.

Deputy Fehr shrugged. "Dig your own grave, Sheriff. Go right ahead."

42

CURTIS SAT IN HIS TRUCK AT THE TOP OF THE HILL. HE was on one of his pieces of land in the middle of the county, surrounded by nothing but giant earth and quiet. It was the middle of the afternoon. A brisk wind blew through all the emptiness.

He knew he was taking a sizable gamble by waiting for the man he'd called that morning, but he felt it was worth the risk. The man he was waiting for was the only person he could truly count on for a job like the one he was about to propose. The man was the best at this kind of work.

Plus, he had a place to start thanks to Craig King.

The day had been long. Reports of his son being murdered had finally come out. He took condolence calls in his office for most of the day while staring at the Polaroid of Gina. His wife made preparations for a memorial for Beau at the United Methodist church in Marshall for the next day. His mind was worried but his resolve was steadfast. He felt in control of the situation even though he didn't know what exactly the situation was.

It takes a crazy man to think and act like that.

A pair of headlights came into view.

Curtis's window was rolled down, his left elbow resting

on the door, and he swiveled his head around to look over his shoulder. A battered navy blue Chrysler, mid-eighties model, drove to the top of the hill and stopped next to Curtis's truck.

Curtis got out and walked around the front of the car to meet him.

He had long, black hair that stopped at his shoulder blades and blew wildly in the wind. He wore a black leather jacket and black jeans and sunglasses. He was smoking a cigarette.

It had been a while for the two men.

They sized each other up. It wasn't contentious. They both knew their roles in the relationship of convenience.

"Hank," Curtis said, tipping his black cowboy hat at him.

"Sorry to hear about your boy, Curtis," Hank said. His voice was deep and he always spoke slowly, in the same controlled manner.

"He was a fine boy," Curtis said.

Hank took a drag of his cigarette. "This job got something to do with him?"

Curtis didn't say anything; he just looked harder into Hank's face and Hank knew the answer. He nodded and finished his cigarette, then lit another one.

"What's the job, Curtis?"

"Need you to track down two kids."

"These kids do your boy in?"

"I believe they did."

"You don't wanna use the authorities?"

Curtis shook his head. "Not for this one. I need you to beat the authorities, actually. This job is too precious and close to me."

Hank exhaled a large wave of smoke through his nostrils. "These kids," he said. "You want me to bring them back to you?"

Curtis shook his head again. "There's a picture," he began. "A Polaroid that they have. It could be nothing but it could also be embarrassing to my family. I need it back from them."

"So that's it? Just the picture?"

"No."

Hank nodded again. "Dead."

"Dead."

"I understand."

"I knew you would." Curtis pulled out three stacks of bills from the inside of his jacket. "Ten thousand in each one. You'll get the other thirty when the job is done."

Hank took the money. "Anything you can tell me to get started?"

"One thing." Curtis pulled out a piece of paper with Carl Sheer's address on it and handed it to Hank. "Something tells me that this guy knows where those kids are headed."

Hank folded the piece of paper and put it in his pocket.

"Here's a picture of each kid."

Hank took those, looked them over briefly, and started for his car.

"And, Hank?" Curtis said.

Hank looked back.

"No loose ends."

"Yes, Curtis."

Hank got into his car and started it. He turned the headlights on and drove away, leaving Curtis all by himself.

43.

AS THEY FOUND A NEW PATH OF GRAVEL GOING north, Gina watched Dru. She looked at the bags under his eyes, which had grown darker and deeper. She watched him yawn with his teeth clenched, attempting to mask the exhaustion that had washed over him. It was her turn to take over.

She said, "I should be driving, baby."

"No, I'm fine. I'm finally getting the hang of these roads now."

"All we need to do is stay north. I can do that."

"I'm fine. It's better that I drive."

She touched his arm and massaged it gently. A soothing calm came over him.

"You need to sleep, baby," she said. "You need to rest at some point if we're gonna make it there."

He yawned again.

"Please?" she said. "I'll be just fine driving."

He knew she was right and he trusted her. He pulled the truck over and they switched sides.

"Don't stop anywhere unless you wake me up first."

"Okay, baby. I won't. Now just relax for a while. You've been so amazing this whole time."

He squinted at her. "I love you," he told her.

"I love you more," she said back.

"Not possible," he responded.

"Very possible," she responded back.

They both laughed lightly. It was a nice sound. Laughter instead of silence and uncertain voices.

Dru laid his head on the window, his eyes on her. She was so pretty to him no matter what.

That face.

Those dreamy eyes.

That warmth and kindness.

His own eyes closed all the way. His head slid down the window a few inches as he fell into his own dreams for the first time in almost two days.

Dru

I'M IN COLLEGE GETTING READY TO WRESTLE FOR the national championship. My hands are sweaty and there's thousands and thousands of people watching. There are tons of cameras, flashes everywhere, and I'm feeling the pressure and the nerves until I look up in the stands and find her there. She's in the fourth row, standing on her feet, smiling, pushing me through with those eyes and that gorgeous stare. Next to her is my mom. She's totally healthy again. Her hair is shiny and professionally styled. Her skin has color. Her lips are full and pink. She's whistling and yelling. Both her and Gina wave at me. I read my mom's lips. She's yelling for me to do good out here. And like that, the pressure fades, the nerves sink, and I walk to the middle of the mat. And, boy, I do really fucking good.

Gina

WHEN YOU KNOW YOU'RE GOING TO LOSE, SOMETIMES you just quit fighting back. I just couldn't fight them. I lost all feeling and went to another place. I went to Dru. I went to the meet that I was supposed to be at that night. I went to the parking lot where he revived my dead car. I went to his face and all his kindness and his love for me and I didn't feel the violence. All I felt were his arms wrapped tightly around my body. Him whispering into my ear. Him telling me how much he loved me and what I meant to him and what that had done for his life.

How he said I saved him.

And now here he is, exhausted, trying so hard to make it happen, trying to save us.

That's fucking beautiful.

What happened to me hurts like hell. My crotch is still sore. I can still feel the part of my face that was slapped. I can still feel my body slamming to the floor and I can still see Beau's face when he answered the door. That fucking pig.

I have hate in my heart for the first time ever. When I think about it, my body swells and my blood boils. I wonder how there can be monsters like that out there. I wonder how someone gets to be a monster. A person without a conscience or a soul. A person who thrives on the fear of the others around him. It confuses the fuck out of me and pains me, but I know now that anyone can get hurt at any moment.

It's a pretty shitty way to learn a lesson.

I wonder about those monsters and I start shaking. I wonder about those monsters and I see red, and then I look over across the truck and I see the opposite of a monster. I see a tender and gentle boy pushing us through this ordeal like a motherfucking champion. And when I look at him, the hate slowly erodes, my blood comes to a simmer, and love and romance and forever encompass everything inside me.

But the damage is still there. The terror and the darkness and the hate still linger in the background, waiting to make their grand appearances. Our old lives are gone but we're on our way to a new one.

To a dream.

To a place where we can start from the beginning and build it the way we want to build it, and that's what keeps me going. Knowing we're gonna get to Jameson's Crossing and start all over. We'll have those bad dogs and that house and that love that we've had since he saved me that night in the parking lot. He's going to save me once again.

I know this.

And I'm going to help save him too.

44

LYLE RUMMAGED THROUGH BOXES IN THE EVIDENCE
room at the station. He was going over all the physical items
collected from the scene at the Alderson house. Nothing
seemed off or out of place until he moved a box from the
top of a rack that wasn't even part of the Alderson case.
It slipped from his hands, crashing to the ground. All its
contents spilled.

"Shit," he said, climbing down from the foot stool he
was using.

The case had become his obsession. Something about
those kids had awakened a raw emotion in him. Whether
it was the cute notes or the stories some of their classmates
told about them, he couldn't get their faces out of his head.
The school pictures he saw at their houses haunted him.
He had become obsessed with the mystery. It wasn't only a
matter of what Curtis was hiding anymore; it was about Dru
and Gina, too.

But right when his feet touched the ground, his eyes
landed on something that made his stomach turn. Lying on
the floor, with evidence not even from the same case, was
the tire iron still bagged up in plastic.

He became enraged. He wondered how his team could

be that sloppy, who the hell had mixed up and put it there.

He picked up all the other evidence, put it in the box, then grabbed the tire iron and headed outside to his car.

It was time he took control of this case back.

He sped twenty miles to the lab that ran all the evidence tests.

In all of his rummaging through the kids' personal belongings and theorizing about Curtis's meddling, he never thought to question why he hadn't received the lab report from the fingerprint test.

He was furious with himself about that.

His old mind had lost a step or two.

He stormed in and found the lab tech who was in charge of running the tests for the Alderson case.

The tech jumped back at the sight of Lyle coming at him with a bulldog snarl glued to his face.

Lyle slammed the tire iron on the desk and snapped, "Why hasn't this been tested?"

The lab tech look shocked at the question. "Orders came not to dust it for prints," he answered.

"Where did those orders come from?" Lyle demanded to know.

"Deputy Fehr," the tech said. "He said he talked to you about it."

Lyle was beside himself. "Is this some kind of conspiracy," he wondered loudly.

"Come again, Sheriff?"

"Nothing," Lyle snapped. He waved a finger at the tech. "Curtis Alderson is not the law around these parts," he said. "He is not running this investigation, nor is Deputy Fehr. I am. I'm the sheriff and I make the calls."

"Yes, sir."

Lyle left and drove back to Marshall. Nothing was adding up at all anymore. There had been some cases in the past when Curtis was very much a part of the investigation, but he'd never subverted Lyle's authority like that. Having one of Lyle's own deputies give an order about a piece of evidence without Lyle's knowledge.

It confirmed all of his suspicions about Curtis trying to conceal evidence.

He was beside himself. His first thought was to confront his deputy, then confront Curtis, but if he started ruffling things too much, he'd never get to the bottom of anything.

He made the choice to inform only Deputy Ollenbeck of the real details of his investigation. Deputy Fehr was to be given only little scraps and crumbs of the case from there on out.

45

HANK WOUND HIS CAR THROUGH THE TRAILER PARK until he came to Carl's. He was cautiously relieved to see all the space on the other side of it, facing away from the other trailers.

It was a near perfect setup for what he needed to do. The other trailers were easily far enough away that once he was inside, no one would hear a thing.

He parked his car and stepped out of it, noticing people moving inside the trailer.

He crept around to the front of it, where Carl was standing outside.

"Can I help you?" Carl asked.

"Carl Sheer?" Hank asked back.

"Who wants to know?" Carl asked.

Hank reached inside his jacket and pulled out a gun with a silencer attached to it. "I want to know."

"What the fuck?" Carl snapped.

"Get back inside," Hank ordered.

Carl turned around and walked for the door. Hank followed him. Carl knew the deal but he wasn't scared. That's one thing he'd never been.

Scared.

Once they were in, Hank grabbed Haley by the hair. She was holding their two-year-old son. He pulled her to the couch and made them all sit there while he stood tall above them, holding them at gunpoint.

"Who the fuck are you?" Carl asked.

Haley was crying and so was their son, shaken up by the intrusion of a man dressed in black, ordering them around with a killing machine.

"I'll ask the fucking questions right now," Hank replied. "And I wanna know where those two kids are running to."

"I don't know what you're talking about," Carl answered.

"Yes you do. Where are they going?"

"I told you I don't know what you're talking about," Carl said. "I don't know what you want to know."

"Fine, then," Hank said, stepping toward Carl. He grabbed his shirt and began to pound his face with the butt of the gun. He hit him over and over so hard, blood began pouring, fucking gushing, out of Carl's face.

Then he stopped.

Blood dripped from the gun. It covered Carl, the couch, and the floor.

"Now tell me, where are those kids going?" Hank said one more time.

"Fuck you, motherfucker," Carl snapped.

So Hank began to whip Carl again to the point that bones showed through on the left side of his face.

It was a real-life horror-movie moment.

Carl puked.

Before he could retort, Haley yelled out, "Just tell him, Carl! Tell him where they're going!"

"Tell me," Hank said, bashing him again so hard that a tooth stuck momentarily to the gun before dropping into the puddle on his lap.

"Okay, okay," Carl snorted. "I'll tell you. Fuck."

Hank stepped back. "Good."

Carl started laughing while blood kept coming and two more of his teeth fell out. He knew they were all fucked. This was a hit. Carl had been a career criminal. He knew the moment Hank asked him his name. No matter what he said, they were all dead.

"Where are they going?" Hank asked

"They went home." Carl laughed. "To sleep." He laughed again. "They went home to sleep."

Hank began to wail on Carl even harder until Haley screamed, "I know where they're going! I'll tell you. Just leave us alone!"

"Don't say anything, Haley!" Carl screamed back.

"But he's gonna kill you."

"He's gonna kill us anyway."

"I just wanna know where they're going," Hank said. "After you tell me, I'll leave you alone."

"Don't tell him anything, Haley."

But she didn't understand what was going to happen.

Only Carl knew they were dead. There was no point in giving up information on Gina and Dru.

"They're heading for this place," she said.

"What place?"

"It's on the Montana-Canada border."

"Shut up!" Carl yelled.

She looked at Carl.

"What place?" Hank asked.

"Don't say it," Carl said.

"He's going to kill you," she cried.

"What place?" Hank hit Carl again.

"It's called Jameson's Crossing," Haley yelled.

Carl cried out immediately after she said that.

"So just leave now," Haley yelled. "You have what you came for."

Hank smirked.

"Leave!" she screamed again.

"Sure thing."

Hank turned like he was going to leave. Haley reached over with one arm to grab Carl, her other arm holding their crying child tight against her body.

"See. It's okay," she said to Carl. "He's leaving now."

"No he's not," Carl said.

Haley looked up at Hank, who had already spun back around and had repointed the gun at Carl.

"You said you were leaving!" Haley screamed.

Hank shrugged. "I lied."

He shot Carl in the head.

His body went limp and he fell off the couch, directly into his own puddles of blood.

Haley cried out, "No!"

Hank shot her in the head before she could get another sound out.

She fell sideways, her head landing in a pool of Carl's blood on the couch.

Their child fell back. He was crying, his head lying between his mother's thigh and the back of the sofa.

Hank took two steps forward so he was standing directly over the boy.

No loose ends, he thought.

And without hesitation, he pulled the trigger and the boy's head exploded into pieces.

They were all dead.

He washed his gun off quickly in the sink. He ran a wet towel down his jacket to make sure all blood splatters were removed. He wiped his shoes clean. When he was finished, he grabbed two gloves out of his pocket and dragged all three bodies into the back bedroom and shut the door.

It was time to move.

On his way out of the trailer, he shut off all the lights. Then he hurried to his car, got in, and drove away.

At the entrance of the park, he turned north.

46

DRU WOKE UP AND THE TRUCK WAS STOPPED IN A field. It was nighttime. He could hear Gina crying. He shook his shoulders out and gathered himself and looked around. She was outside of the truck, her back against the front end of it, her face in her hands.

He jumped out of the truck.

The stars and the moon were both shining bright.

He hurried around to the front of the vehicle. "Gina," he called out. He grabbed her into his arms. "Why did you stop driving?"

Her crying was painful for him to hear. It destroyed his heart.

"Why are you crying, baby? What happened?"

She finally looked at him. "It's all my fault," she said, sobbing. "This whole thing is my fault."

"What are you even saying?"

"I thought I was strong enough not to break down," she cried. "I thought I could do this without losing it, but once you fell asleep . . . everything came back to me and I couldn't handle it."

"Why didn't you wake me up?"

"I don't know. You needed your sleep, I guess."

"Jesus, baby." He squeezed her tight for a moment, then let go. "Those monsters hurt you. It's not your fault."

"I fucked up so bad, though. That picture could've saved us and I ruined the rest of our lives when I destroyed it."

"No you didn't. We just have to keep going, Gina, and we'll be all right. We just need to keep going north."

"What if there's nothing there? What if it's just some illusion, Dru? Some kinda wild dream?"

"It don't matter, Gina. There's still us and that's all that matters, anyway. Us making it somewhere together. We'll get to wherever we feel is right for us and make a new start and nothing bad will happen again. I won't let it. I won't let anything bad happen to you ever again."

She cried more, and no words were spoken for what seemed like an aching eternity before she finally went, "You promise me?"

"I promise you."

"Okay."

She looked up at him again and he wiped the tears off her face.

"How long have we been stopped for?"

"A couple of hours, I guess. Maybe more."

"What?"

"Maybe more," she said again.

"What time is it?"

"Maybe midnight."

"Fuck."

"I'm sorry."

"No. Stop it, Gina. Just . . ." He put his hands on top of his head. He was still tired. "How far off the road are we?" he asked.

"Pretty far. A mile maybe, maybe two."

"All right," he said. "Fuck it, we'll just stay here for tonight. It's obvious that we're both exhausted and nervous. Let's just get some good sleep."

"But shouldn't we keep going north?" she asked.

"First thing tomorrow, baby. Tonight we rest here and take care of each other."

47

"YOU GOT SOME AMBITION, DON'T YOU?" CURTIS wondered aloud. "I know you do, Deputy Fehr. I can see it in your eyes. You got killer in them. You want to be the Sheriff one day."

"That's my goal, Curtis," he said back.

The two were standing on the edge of one of Alderson's properties a few miles outside of Marshall.

It was late.

Curtis rubbed his chin. "Lyle's getting old and weak. He's become something of a liability to me lately."

He paused and shook his head.

"Weakness is a damn terrible thing," he continued. "Wouldn't you agree?"

"I do agree, Curtis. That's why I've been helping you as much as I can. I think Lyle's lost his loyalty and his heart."

"I know," Curtis said. "There's no place for weak people in this tough world."

"Agreed, sir."

Curtis turned to face the deputy for the first time. "Why hasn't Lyle closed the investigation on this case yet?"

"Because he thinks your boy was mixed up in the attack."

"How so, Deputy?"

"That somehow he was an instigator in the struggle. He don't believe that Weiben kid could've snapped the way he did with your boy being just some innocent victim."

Curtis felt his blood get warm. He grinded his teeth together. The words were like knives cutting into his back. "Is that right?" he asked.

"Sure is."

Curtis looked back at his parked truck. "What's your take on my boy's death?"

"Same as yours. Your boy hung out with his girlfriend. Weiben lost his match and he just snapped."

A huge grin eclipsed Curtis's face and he turned back to the deputy. "You know what, Deputy Fehr?"

"What's that, Sir?"

"I have a feeling that you're gonna make a fine sheriff one day very soon."

HANK DROVE WITH BOTH HANDS ON THE WHEEL. HE
sped down the highway at eighty miles an hour, smoking
a cigarette and staring straight ahead. He was determined.
He'd never fucked up a job for Curtis before. He got paid
well. Curtis kept him in the background. He never worked
more than five or six times a year. Curtis had saved his life
twice. Hank was forever and ever indebted to him.

Hank rolled down the window to throw his cigarette
out. Then he lit another one.

He was going to find those kids.

He knew the land all the way through Montana. He
knew all of the back roads and the safe routes and he knew
Jameson's Crossing especially well from his days of running
drugs and goods as part of a motorcycle gang before he got
put in jail and wound up in the Alderson House program.

Those kids were as good as found.

That's how confident he was.

Sixty thousand dollars pays for a lot of down time and
relaxing. It pays for a lot of whores and beers and card
games and horses.

Those kids were as good as dead.

THEY LAY IN THE CAB OF THE TRUCK, HUDDLED under a blanket, shivering, their breath visible. Their hearts pounded in their chests and their chests pounded into each other. Both of them lay there with their eyes open, unable to sleep from both the cold and their incredible journey and the uncertainty that lay ahead of them.

There were easier things than confronting the unknown.

It was easier to lay there and stare at the ceiling of a pickup truck. It was easier to pretend that the happy end of the journey was a guarantee.

Dru

ON OUR FIRST DATE, WE WENT OUT FOR PIZZA AT this local joint. I was nervous, not gonna lie, sweating and anxious. I'd never dated anyone in my life. I had just been with some random girls here and there.

Gina said she'd be waiting by the window for my truck. I pulled up and she walked out of the house in a brown jacket, a black scarf, and jeans. Her hair was pulled back and up, held in place by bobby pins and a hair clip.

She was smiling really big. I got even more fucking nervous. Enough so that I forgot to unlock the door to her side.

She tried to open it twice before I realized what I'd done. I slapped my forehead and leaned over and unlocked it. My palms were sweaty. I was blushing. She climbed in.

"I'm sorry about that."

"It's totally fine."

She smelled so good, like vanilla and sandalwood. She was intoxicating. And adorable. I had yellow tulips for her that I had handpicked at a flower store in Brantley, which is like a half hour away. It was the best flower store in the county. I remember my mom talking about it with a friend once.

Gina sniffed them.

"They're so pretty," she said.

"Pretty flowers for a pretty girl," I said back.

"Thank you."

"You're very welcome."

I took a deep breath.

So far so good, I thought.

"I've never gotten flowers from a boy before. Only from my aunt after a dance recital when I was in middle school."

"What kind of dance?" I asked.

"I took ballet classes," she said.

"Did you like it?"

"I liked it okay."

I pulled away from her house. My hands were dry again and my confidence was high.

I was playing the Neutral Milk Hotel album *In the Aeroplane Over the Sea.* I knew she liked them because I'd seen the CD case on the seat in her car the night I helped her out in the parking lot.

"Nice choice in music." She grinned.

"I like these guys a lot."

"Me too."

She grinned wide and I knew before we even got to the pizza place that she was gonna be someone so special to me.

We ate Hawaiian pizza and had a pitcher of Pepsi and we played five games of Pac-Man.

I won high score four times, her once.

It was so fun. So relaxing. She said I was the most handsome boy in school.

I blushed and fed her a bite of cheesy bread.

"You're pretty easy on the eyes yourself."

I paid the bill and we left.

It was such a great night. It was like my body had been injected with a dose of excitement and hope.

Before we got to her house, she told me to stop a half block away from it, so I did.

"Why are we stopping here?" I asked her.

"Because I want you to kiss me."

"Yeah?" I smiled.

"Yes, please."

"I can do that."

She put on lip gloss and then we both leaned over and met in the middle. We kissed for what seemed like days. Her lips were so soft and tasted fruity. Her tongue and my tongue danced, and when we pulled away, she said, "So this is it."

"What's that?"

"Me and you. I want you to be my boyfriend. Is that okay?"

I was fucking on fire when she said that.

"Yeah, it's okay."

"Good."

We kissed again, for even longer, and she even rubbed my crotch.

When we pulled away, she shook her head.

"What?" I asked.

"I got a great feeling about you."

"Yeah, I was thinking the same thing about you."

"Good." She scooped up her flowers and smelled them again. "Gorgeous," she told me. "Thanks."

Then she got out of the truck, closed the door, took a few steps, and turned back around. It's always great when they turn back around just as you are about to part ways.

She blew me a kiss and then ran to her house.

Me, I was in fucking love right then with that beautiful girl.

Gina

IT WASN'T MY MOM'S FAULT. IT WAS A HORRIBLE mistake. My dad told her that there would be an important phone call that she needed to answer because he was going to be meeting with clients all day. She'd carried the phone around all morning, but when Ben woke up from his nap, she set the phone down on his dresser and gave him a bath. She warmed the water and set him in the bath and then she heard the phone ring. She was just going to be gone for a moment. She figured that was the call and left Ben in the tub and went to answer the phone in the other room.

Who knows how long she was really in the hallway or how long she really talked before she went back into the bathroom. When she did, Ben was facedown in the water. She threw the phone down in mid conversation and grabbed Ben from the tub. He wasn't breathing. He was blue. She grabbed the phone and called 911 and gave him CPR, but it wasn't working and by the time the paramedics and my dad got to the house, Ben was gone and things were never the same.

My father needed answers and the answers my mom gave weren't good enough. Slowly, the guilt and the blame were too much. She couldn't live like that. The erosion began and my parents crumbled and fell apart and she left one day, in the afternoon, and I never saw her again. But it wasn't her fault. She was responsible but it wasn't her fault and it was too late then. She left and said her good-byes in a letter. Besides the one letter I never heard anything from her again.

50.

CURTIS SAT IN HIS TRUCK IN THE PARKING LOT OF ONE of his convenience stores waiting for Lyle. He knew it was the same store Lyle bought his first cup of coffee from every morning.

The sun still wasn't shining but it was significantly warmer than the day before.

The first thing Lyle saw as he walked outside was Curtis's truck parked on the side of the store. Curtis rolled down the window and said, "I need a word with you, Lyle."

"I've got work to do, Curtis."

Curtis shook his head. "Just get in the truck. This won't take long."

Lyle nodded. He walked around to the other side of the truck and got in.

And there they were. The titan of Marshall County business and enterprise with the titan of Marshall County law. Two titans that had helped make each other. Two titans that were falling quickly apart.

Curtis looked straight ahead and started right in. "We've come up all these years together, Lyle. Working as a team, me and you, building what we wanted for ourselves and helping each other out with almost anything. I think that's been the most successful aspect of our relationship up till now. The loyalty we've given each other, the great trust we've had between us. How we made it work and never even needed to ask the tough questions."

Lyle took a drink from his coffee. "Why are we talking about the past, Curtis?"

"Because the past is what links us to the present."

"So what's your point?"

"I want those killers brought to justice, Lyle. But I also want the investigation closed. Dru Weiben killed my boy out of jealousy and kidnapped a good man's beautiful daughter. Why haven't you accepted this and moved on? There's nothing else to see."

"I'm only doing my job, Curtis."

"Your job is to do what I say. Not to dig into places where your nose don't belong. Why are you being so goddamn stubborn about this?"

"I'll ask you the same question, Curtis."

"Because I have a hell of a lot to lose right now. Any hint that my boy's death was something other than what it was could seriously jeopardize this land deal and I will not allow that to happen. I fucking made you, Lyle. We were a team. So I'm asking you right now . . . no, I'm telling you right now, to end this nonsense and stop digging in the mud."

"Are you threatening me, Curtis?"

"I'm asking you to quit disrespecting my dead son."

"I can't stop the investigation. Not until I get to the truth."

Pause.

Lyle could see the anger rising in Curtis's face. The same anger he'd seen so many times. It was ruthless and brutal and had ended the careers and lives of so many men.

Lyle looked out his window and took another drink of coffee. "I'm sorry, Curtis, but I won't."

"You ungrateful piece of shit. Get the hell out of my truck before I take a swing at that old mug of yours."

Lyle opened the door and began to step out.

And Curtis said, "If you won't stop it, Lyle, then I will."

"I don't doubt that you'll try, Curtis. Don't doubt that for a second."

51

GINA WAS THROWING UP IN THE FIELD WHERE THE two slept the night before. She was on her knees, vomit spilling over her lips. It was green and black with some red mixed in. A frozen canvas of liquid hate and hurt. Dru stood behind her and watched her back muscles spasm, then loosen, only to spasm and tighten all over again.

And she whimpered. There was no real crying. Just the whimper that comes when your body has had enough. The whimper that comes from days of shooting the hate out of yourself and pushing the water through your eyes.

When she thought she was done, she turned to Dru, who knelt down beside her and wiped her face off with his shirt.

"I think I need to eat again."

"Okay."

"Next town."

"Next town, baby."

He kissed her forehead and helped her to her feet.

52.

ONCE AGAIN THE TOWN THEY CAME TO WAS VERY small. The only service station and store were closed.

"What should we do?" she asked.

They passed a diner.

"Stop there," he said.

"You think we'll still be okay?"

"I don't think we have a choice," he said. "You look sick, baby. You look so hungry."

They were less than sixty miles away from Montana.

All the spots in front of the diner were taken, so Dru parked the next block up in the parking lot of a co-op.

While they walked to the diner, Dru said, "We should take advantage of our status as fugitives."

"We should start robbing banks," Gina said back.

"Bonnie and Clyde for the twenty-first century."

"A new breed."

"Might as well get rich while we're running, right?"

The smile disappeared from Gina's face. Just another fleeting illusion. Another unrealistic dream. Another dose of the new reality they were living.

They walked inside and sat down at the counter. Dru wasn't really worried about anyone recognizing them. None of those old diners in those old towns in those old forgotten parts of those states had any televisions in them.

There would be no breaking news happening like it did in the movies, with people at the restaurant or bar or public place noticing the fugitive was among them.

"I'm gonna go to the bathroom," Gina said.

"All right, baby."

The bathroom was old and was for both men and women. Gina locked the door and she sat on the toilet and peed. When she was done, she took a paper towel, wetted it with cold water, and wiped her vagina because the coolness eased the soreness. Then she grabbed a few more towels and put them in her pocket.

While she was in the bathroom, Dru ordered both of them scrambled eggs and bacon. A sudden uneasiness of the truck being a whole block away struck him. He didn't like that it was out of his sight. Beads of sweat formed on his brow. He wanted to get a visual before he ate so he could just relax for a few moments. He went outside and walked to the edge of the road and looked down to where it was parked.

His guts floored.

A highway patrol car was parked by his truck and a patrolman was peering in the window of it.

Dru walked back into the diner like nothing was wrong, even though he could feel the color leaving his skin. He walked back to the bathroom and knocked on the door.

"I'll be out in a minute," Gina said.

"Gina, it's Dru. We have to go."

"What?"

"Open up, Gina. We have to go now."

Gina's heart raced. She unlocked the door and Dru pushed himself in.

Her face was white and full of returned panic. "What's going on?" she asked.

"There's a highway patrolman looking at the truck."

"What the fuck are we gonna do?"

Dru looked above the toilet. There was a small window that was just the right size for both of them to slide through. It was already open a crack. He jumped on the back of the toilet and peered out.

Open country as far as his eyes could see. He pushed the window open all the way and jumped down.

"We make a run for it."

"What about our stuff?"

"Who cares, Gina? We have to go now. You first."

Gina got on the back of the toilet and grabbed the window ledge to pull herself up while Dru supported her with his hands.

Once she made it through, she hung on the ledge and let her legs swing for a moment before she let go and hit the ground.

Dru did the same thing.

He picked himself off the ground and the two of them

climbed over a fence behind the diner and entered a field. They ran as fast as they could.

Everything—their future and the dream and the house and the bad dogs and the forever—had been struck by a fucking lightning bolt and a fire had started.

There was smoke everywhere.

53

LYLE LEANED AGAINST A WOODEN POST AND STARED out into an open field that stretched for miles and miles and miles. Almost fifteen thousand acres of it. Unused and prime and full of potential.

He held a coffee mug in his right hand. He took a drink from it and just stared until the silence and concentration were broken by Marty's deputy car pulling up next to his.

Lyle glanced over his shoulder as Marty approached him holding a Styrofoam cup full of coffee. Marty tipped his hat at Lyle. It went back to total silence except for the harsh wind that had picked up and was blowing past them.

Finally, after taking a sip from his coffee, Marty said, "Why did you want me to meet you here, Lyle?"

"To get a look at all of this, Deputy. Just take a good gaze at all this land and absorb it."

Marty turned his eyes away from his boss and onto the giant stretch of brown and black. He inhaled the fading winter's air and the age-old soil and the moisture of all the elements that sat in the wind.

"Can I trust you, Marty?"

"Have I ever given you a reason not to?"

Lyle shook his head. "Nope."

"Of course you can trust me, Lyle."

Lyle took a drink of coffee. "Can't trust Brian anymore."

"Why is that?"

Lyle sighed. "He's been undermining my authority throughout this whole investigation."

"How so?"

"His attitude about this case. Evidence that was in his possession and never tested. Curtis Alderson giving him direct orders behind my back."

"So fire him if you can't trust him."

"I won't get away with it."

"You're the boss."

"He's got a perfect record so far. Legally, it probably wouldn't stand. Plus, Curtis would bring the heat on me."

"So what do you plan to do, Lyle?"

"Gonna have to catch him in the act and make it stick."

"Jesus."

Lyle slid his eyes toward the ground. "I know that Curtis Alderson is hiding the truth about his boy's murder," Lyle snapped.

Marty exhaled and looked back at Lyle. "Now, why would he want to do that, Lyle?"

"Because of what's in front of us right here."

Marty was confused. "It's just unused land, Lyle."

Lyle shook his head. "You're not getting it, then, Deputy."

"No . . . I guess I'm not."

Lyle gestured outward to the land with his mug. "These fifteen thousand acres are about to be developed by the federal and state governments to the tune of about fifteen million dollars."

"I still don't get it, Lyle. What's that got to do with that boy's murder?"

Lyle turned to his deputy. "Who do you think owns every square inch of this land?"

"Who?"

"Curtis Alderson."

"Sir."

Lyle sighed again and went, "If there's even a hint that his boy's murder might not be innocent, that his boy was up to something sinister, something that might've even brought on his own death, then you can bet your ass that this whole land deal with Curtis would be killed off in a second. His name, his legacy, would be drug through the mud and he'd lose his power. That land deal . . ." He paused and shook his head again. "It would be dead."

"Jesus, Lyle. You know what you're implying?"

"I do."

"And what if you're wrong?"

"He is hiding something, Marty. I mean, just think about it. . . . He was the one who found the body and called it in. His hands have been mixed up in this investigation at every corner like he knows something we don't. He gave Brian orders not to have the weapon dusted for prints. He's the one who didn't want an APB put out on those two kids immediately."

"What do you mean, immediately, Lyle? Did he change his mind about that?"

"No. But I put one out last night."

"Without his consent?"

"Yes, Deputy. Without his consent. Curtis Alderson is not the law in this county. We are. It's my call in the end."

"You really think he'd rather protect a land deal than get to the truth about his own boy's death."

"That's what he is *doing* already," Lyle said. "Since the beginning, and I intend to find out what the real truth is."

"Even if it costs you everything, Lyle?"

Lyle paused and stared back out at the land in front of him. "Especially if it costs me everything, Deputy."

54

THEY RAN AS HARD AS THEY COULD THROUGH THE field. The doomed kids in love and in an impossible situation. They ran even though their bodies were weak and sick and sore. They ran even though they knew the chances were slim and their hopes of that dream were prancing away with every step of their mad dash toward something unknown.

Toward the illusion.

Gina

When I grow up, these are things I want to be:

1. Married to Dru

2. Married to Dru

3. Married to Dru

4. A better person

5. Stronger

6. A mother and a teacher and an artist

7. I want to paint and take pictures and make homemade movies and make beautiful clothes for Dru and myself and my kids

8. Happy all the time

9. With Dru forever

10. Safe. Always.

These are the things that keep my legs moving through this stupid and hard and painful field full of big dirt clumps and ancient stones.

Dru

I DID EVERYTHING DIFFERENTLY THAN THE OTHER men in my family. I tried hard and threw myself into things that could make me a better person. I was nice and respectful and I put on a full shield to block out the demons that my brother and dad had been consumed by. The demons that ate through them and made them into people who weren't really people. The demons that killed their whole lives. I had to live in and with the ruins of their actions. Even though I was a star wrestler, a champion, who had never done a thing to hurt anyone, a kid who spent all my free time taking care of my dying mother and getting better at the thing I was best at, I was still typecasted as the same person as my brother and my dad were. I was them because I looked like them. I was them because I lived in the same house as them. I was them because my last name was Weiben, and around Marshall that name was poison. I loved them both. But you can love someone and at the same time hate everything about them and what they do. Ask anyone who's ever been divorced.

Truth is, it never really bothered me like it would most people because I knew I was different. I was good at something and my name had nothing to do with it. It was me. I was already my own man but it didn't really matter and never would've as long as I lived there. And when those fuckers raped my girl, it didn't matter how many hours I'd dedicated to the mat and taking care of my mom and loving Gina and not doing anything wrong to anyone else. What mattered was my last name. My reputation built on the mistakes and the pain that those who came before had caused. This is the reason I'm running in a field for my life with the only person who was ever able to truly look past that stuff and see me for me. This is why I'm running for my life in sheer exhaustion. This is why I'm running for a new dream.

Even though I had nothing to do with those other people.

55

AS THEY RAN, PUSHING THROUGH TOUGH AS FUCK on their empty tanks, which hadn't been filled with food for more than a day, they were quickly approaching a barbwire fence. Gina began to slow down but not Dru. He decided he was going to hop it and help her over to the other side of it, but about six inches away from the fence, he stepped on a rock that was covered in dirt. His ankle slid to the side and he tripped and fell into the wire and got tangled in it.

The sharp edges of the rusted fence ripped into Dru's skin, tearing through his arms and through his legs. He screamed and tried to squirm his way out of the tangled mess. Gina stood horrified, her hands on her face, as he yelled, blood running though the threads of his clothes.

She pulled herself together and knelt down beside him. "Hold still, baby."

"Goddamn, this hurts," he said. "Ahhhhhhhh." He winced as she moved one of his arms.

"It's okay," she said, and quit for a second. "Look at me, baby."

He exhaled and did. He stared into her and saw a piece of heaven.

A piece of his own self.

He became immediately calm.

"You're an angel," he said.

"You're beautiful," she said back, before resuming.

Very carefully, with the same gentleness as when Dru took care of his mother, she started to untangle him, one line of barbwire at a time, until he was finally out.

He began to stand up and she grabbed him. She told him to stop and rest for a moment but he couldn't.

"We've already lost too much time," he snorted, pushing himself up, moaning from his sore ankle. "We have to keep going."

"Are you sure?"

"What else can we do?"

She shook her head.

"We have to, baby."

And so he grabbed her hand and they helped each other over the fence, and they continued through the field without a true end in their sights.

56

HANK CAME TO THE FIRST DINER DRU AND GINA had been at. He wanted coffee and a piece of apple pie. The place was as usual. The cook was smoking in the back. The waitress smelled like Dorals and cheap perfume.

When Hank finished ordering, he asked the waitress if she'd recently seen two teenage kids who looked distressed and out of place.

The waitress thought for a moment with her finger against her lips. "Ya know," she started.

Hank watched her eyes perk.

He had the answer he wanted.

"I did serve a couple of kids yesterday who looked pretty lost."

"Anything else about them?"

"No." She shook her head. "I mean, I watched them leave. Watched them drive away. They just looked so tired and confused."

"Which way did they go?" Hank asked.

"They went north."

Hank thanked her and asked for the coffee to go.

"What about the apple pie?"

"It's all right," he said. "I only need the coffee now."

He walked outside and looked north down the highway. Then he lit a cigarette and got back into his car and kept moving in that same direction.

57

LYLE SAT AT THE COUNTER OF THE MARSHALL INN, A small diner right off the town's main strip. A feeling of total determination had swept into him, gripping him with an intensity he hadn't felt in years, since he first started as a deputy.

He was not going to be denied the truth.

He was not going to roll over for Curtis Alderson.

Not this time.

Not again.

No, never again.

His waitress, Nancy, poured him coffee and asked, "When you gonna ask me out, Lyle?"

"Soon as I have some time to take you out, sweetheart."

"You work too hard, darling."

"Lots of work to be done. This whole Alderson deal is a mess. Now those two kids are missing."

"Any luck finding them?"

"Just a couple leads here and there. But nothing concrete. Hopefully something pans out or someone comes forward."

Nancy leaned on the counter. "I got a question for you, darling."

"What's that?"

"How come there ain't been no big news about them being on the run? Or even much news about Beau Alderson? Town could use some attention."

Lyle shook his head. "Not attention like this. And besides, Curtis Alderson didn't want it."

"How you gonna find them if no one's out there looking?"

"I ran a secret wire to other agencies and departments. The word on them is out with the law."

Nancy stood back up and shook her head. "What a horrible thing that happened. Especially to an Alderson. It's unbelievable almost. I mean, just so, so bizarre how life can flip in an instant, on and off, just like a light or something."

"What do you mean?"

"I saw Beau Alderson with his friend earlier that afternoon and they looked like they were having a lot of fun. They were really drunk. But they were in great moods."

Lyle's body tensed immediately and he turned his full attention to Nancy. "What friend?" he asked.

"That Corey Rogers boy. I saw the two of them at the Alderson Market buying beer and cigarettes."

A huge break.

Lyle shot to his feet. "Thanks for the coffee, Nancy."

"What about your food, darling?"

Lyle set some money on the counter. "That should cover it."

He hurried out of the diner.

THEY FINALLY CAME TO A STOP UNDER A TREE. SHE took off her undershirt while he lay with his back against the tree. She tore one of her shirts into strips with her hands and teeth.

She took the first strip and put it on his face to wipe the blood away. He winced and finally tears fell from his eyes. Everything was catching up to them. The exhaustion and the unknown and the doubt and the law.

She cleaned all the blood away, using her spit to help stop the flow, then she began to wipe the blood from his chest and arms.

While she did it, all she could say over and over was, "This wasn't the way things were supposed to turn out."

And he said nothing. He just quivered and winced and hoped they could get back to moving north soon.

AS LYLE SPED AWAY FROM THE DINER, ADRENALINE
rushed through his veins. Things were clearing up. He felt
like a sheriff for the first time in a long time. A call from the
highway patrolman who discovered the pickup truck came
in. The patrolman told Lyle about two kids spotted at a diner
in Blairstown, South Dakota, who matched Gina's and Dru's
descriptions.

"This is fucking huge, Officer. Great work."

"We seized some blankets and a bag of clothes out of the
truck they were driving. We got the truck back at the station
and people combing it for clues."

"Excellent. Anyone see which way those kids ran off?"

"Nope. A couple folks at the diner who did notice them
said it was like they were a couple of ghosts. Left without
even being noticed."

"All right," Lyle said. "Thanks for the call. And great
work again."

"Thanks."

Lyle hung up. All the ducks were lining up. He hurriedly
called Marty.

"Marty, I just got a call that Dru and Gina were spotted
in Blairstown, South Dakota."

"That's a good break."

"I know. So I'm thinking now, why would they be near Blairstown?"

"They're heading north. Maybe to Canada."

"I'm betting there's a running route that cuts through Blairstown."

"Like drug running?"

"There's all sorts of 'em up that way and I bet Blairstown is a safe spot. That's what I'm thinking."

"Okay . . ."

"So if Dru knew about that being a running route, who told him?"

"No idea."

"Who was Jaime Weiben's best friend and partner in crime?"

"Carl Sheer was."

"Exactly. So what I'm thinking is that after they left the Alderson house, panic started setting in and he went to get help from the one person he knew had knowledge of the land and could help him."

"You think Carl still has contacts? Kid's been off the radar since Jaime went to jail."

"I think it's quite possible. So I need you to go out to Carl Sheer's place and question him," he said.

"You ain't gonna come with me, Lyle?"

"No, I've gotta see about something else."

"Should I take Brian?"

"No, no, no. You go by yourself and report everything you get only to me. Not a word to Brian about this."

"Yes, sir."

Lyle grinned and hit the gas pedal hard. Those two kids were gonna be safe. He was almost there. They were going to be picked up and protected by him personally, and finally, the truth was going to come out.

Finally, he was going to be able to sleep just a little bit easier at night.

He was so close.

Those two terrified kids were gonna be home soon.

60

THEY LIMPED AND LIMPED FOR WHAT SEEMED LIKE miles before they saw a farmhouse up ahead. There was nothing else around.

The house was yellow with chipped paint. One story high with a gravel driveway and a place in the front for a garden in the spring and summer.

They were careful and snuck up to it from the side. Both of them were sweating and trembling from nerves. After five minutes of just watching, they slid around the corner and looked through a large window.

Inside, sitting in a living room, were a very old man and woman. They could hear a radio playing. The old man sat on the couch in a flannel shirt and jeans and the old woman sat in a rocking chair knitting in a gray nightgown.

"We can't go in there, Gina," he said.

"We have to, baby. We have to clean up those cuts."

"They're listening to the radio. There's gotta be something about us on it by now. We'll get caught."

"We don't have a choice, Dru. Once those cuts get infected, we won't be able to go north no more. We'll die out here."

"We'll find another place to do it where we won't be seen."

"No we won't," she said, then ran to the door and knocked on it.

Whatever color was left in Dru's face disappeared. He swallowed the gulp of anxiety in his throat as he watched Gina standing at the door rubbing her hands together.

The old man answered and he looked at Gina before poking his head out of the door and seeing Dru standing a few feet back.

He wasn't fazed at all by the image of a bloody kid in his yard.

Then the old lady came to the door.

"Hi, dear," she said to Gina.

"We're so sorry to bother you but we need your help," Gina said. She pointed to Dru. "He had an accident."

"Oh, you poor things," the old lady said. "Come inside right now and we'll get you both cleaned up."

61

THE CHURCH WHERE BEAU ALDERSON'S MEMORIAL service was being held was the place Tina and Curtis had been married. Tina saw that as fitting. Curtis didn't like churches.

People filed in. It was set to start in twenty minutes. Lyle sat in his parked car across the street from the church until he saw Corey Rogers walk out in front of the old building and light a cigarette.

Lyle crossed the street. When Corey saw Lyle coming toward him, his shoulders trembled and his hand began to twitch.

"Corey Rogers," Lyle said.

Corey nodded. "Hey, Sherriff."

Corey's voice was shaky, a sure sign to Lyle of fear and nerves.

"I've got some questions for you, son."

Corey looked at the ground and started scratching the back of his head. "About what, sir?"

"How come you didn't come forward and tell anyone you were drinking with Beau Alderson the day he was killed?"

"'Cause I wasn't with him," Corey answered.

"Is that so?"

"It is. I promise." His voice was even more shaky, his hand moving quicker against his head.

"Well, I can place you buying beer with him earlier that same day."

"It wasn't me."

"Come on, son. Don't make this hard on yourself."

Pause.

"Now, you wanna go ahead and look at me while I talk to you?" Lyle asked.

Corey did. His eyes were white and the pupils were dilated. "What are you getting at?" he asked.

"Listen to me, Corey. If you're hiding something, you need to come clean now. I'm giving you this chance. Come clean before it gets worse."

Pause.

"What happened that night, Corey?" Lyle pressed.

"I said I wasn't with him."

The door to the church opened and Curtis Alderson emerged from it wearing a dark brown suit and a brown hat. "Corey," he snapped.

Corey turned around, shaking still.

"It's time to come inside now, son," Curtis said.

"Yes, sir." Corey dropped his cigarette and walked to Curtis.

"I didn't say nothing to him," Cory whispered so Lyle couldn't hear him.

Curtis grinned and patted Corey on the shoulder. "Of course you didn't. You did well for your daddy, son. Now go back inside."

Curtis waited for Corey to walk back in and then walked up to Lyle.

They stood at almost the same height. Their eyes were even and glared at each other's.

Curtis sighed. "You're still poking your head where it don't belong, Lyle."

"Whatever it is you're hiding from me, I'm gonna find it, Curtis."

"For the last time, Lyle. I'm not hiding anything. Now I gotta get inside. The service is about to start."

Curtis began to walk away.

And Lyle went, "We got a hit on them kids at a diner in Blairstown. We got the truck they were driving."

Curtis turned around. "That's good. I want them brought back here."

"We're getting close. So whatever it is you're trying to cover up, it comes to an end when we get those kids."

"Like I've said and will say for the last time, I ain't got nothing to hide."

"I guess we'll see about that, Curtis."

"Guess we will."

Lyle turned from Curtis and walked back to his car. Curtis watched him.

Lyle put the car in drive and made a U-turn. As he did,

he looked over and saw Curtis staring at him. He tipped his hat and sped off.

Curtis grabbed his phone after Lyle was out of sight. He called Hank, who answered after one ring.

"I got something new for you," he told him.

"What is it?"

"Those kids are somewhere near Blairstown in South Dakota. They're on foot now."

"Already on my way."

"Excellent."

62

MARTY GOT TO CARL'S TRAILER. HE SENSED IMMEDIATELY that something was off. It was dark inside but Carl's vehicles were parked in front. An eerie silence was cast over the scene. Everything was still.

Marty stepped out of his car, his right hand pressed against the gun in his holster.

He stepped up to the door and knocked.

No answer.

He knocked again.

Nothing.

"Carl Sheer!" he hollered. "Carl Sheer, if you're in there, answer me and come out."

Nothing still.

The eeriness grew and he began to shake from how unsettling this place felt. It was like in a horror movie when someone goes into a dark basement or enters a big house in the middle of the woods. There was suspense in the air. His face was sweating. Marty was a good deputy by every account, but he didn't have guts like Lyle. Not even close. He didn't have the same callousness and steadiness and calculation as his peer Deputy Fehr. He was a nice guy with a big heart who believed in justice and truth and the law and hated evil. His few years on the job, he'd never had to really confront it. Not yet.

He yelled out one more time before trying the door.

It was unlocked.

He pushed it open.

The hinges creaked and it made him shudder.

He stepped inside, turned on the lights, and his face went snow white.

His soul broke and his jaw dropped.

His eyes landed on the couch and all of its massive horror.

Dried blood splattered everywhere.

He choked down a mouthful of his own vomit.

Tears filled his eyes.

He followed the blood with them and watched the trail lead into the room at the other end of the home. The door to the room was closed. He pulled out his gun and walked toward it, his eyes holding steady on everything in front of him.

When he got to the door, the sweat on his face was like a pool. He took a deep breath, sucked in his stomach, and opened it.

Evil shit all over.

He saw the three bodies stacked on top of one another.

Carl on the bottom.

Haley in the middle.

The young child on top.

All facedown.

The smell, the rotting smell of death and flesh, had begun to set in the room and consume everything.

More vomit shot up from the bottom of his guts, and this time he couldn't swallow it back down. He ran out of the trailer and threw up in front of the stairs. He threw up so hard it forced him to the ground, to his hands and knees, where he threw up for the next few minutes.

When he was done, he wiped his mouth and got back to his feet. He began to cry so hard that it shook his entire body.

63.

THE HEATER WAS BLASTING IN LYLE'S CAR. HIS fingers gripped the steering wheel so tight his knuckles were white. He was ripe with excitement. As he neared the station, the lab tech called him on his cell phone.

"What do you got?" Lyle asked.

"This is gonna sound real strange," the tech said.

"What is it?"

"The prints . . ."

"Yes."

"Gina King's are all over the murder weapon too."

Lyle thought his heart was gonna stop. "Come again?"

"The girl's prints are all over the weapon."

He was stunned. "You're certain about this?"

"One hundred percent, Sheriff."

"Shit."

Pause.

"We could have got this all wrong about who killed Beau Alderson."

"What are you gonna do?"

Lyle slowed his car down and pulled to the side of the road. "I need to think for a second. Thanks for the information. You did good."

He hung up. He felt dizzy. He put his head in the palm of his hand and began to go over everything again.

The scene. The holes in the case. Curtis's interference. Everything that seemed off but was taken as truth, as common sense. Every single assumption that was failing and falling flat on its face.

His phone rang again.

It was Marty.

"What do you got for me?" Lyle asked him.

"It's not good."

"What did you find, Deputy?"

"Three dead bodies in the bedroom of Carl's trailer."

"Whose bodies?"

"Carl Sheer's. Haley Anderson's. And a baby boy."

Lyle felt sick but vindicated. His instincts had been right all along.

Marty asked, "What do I do, Lyle?"

"You call the paramedics and get them out there immediately. And don't touch anything else."

"But." Marty quivered.

"But what, Deputy?"

"I think you need to come out here yourself, Lyle," Marty said. "This is horrible stuff. Evil stuff."

"This is your thing now, Marty. I need to find out where those two kids are going. It's their only chance."

He paused.

Then he said, "Forces have been unleashed like I have

never seen around these parts and I need get to those two kids. They have the answers. They have the truth."

"How are you going to get them?"

"I'm gonna go to County and talk to Jaime Weiben. I'm gonna get some goddamn answers."

64

THEY SAT ON THE EDGE OF THE BATHTUB IN THE farmhouse's only bathroom. Gina bandaged Dru up with peroxide and gauze.

He was in her hands completely at that moment. She was his caretaker. His first-aid kit. His beating heart.

Every time she cleaned a cut, he shook in pain, but she was steady and calm and determined.

The scene at the fence played on repeat in her brain.

"You're an angel," he'd told her.

"You're beautiful," she'd said back.

It was a revealing part of their story. How in the absolute most dire circumstances, with forces out there hunting them, with the torture they'd each had to endure, the sheer truth of their feelings about each other had only enhanced and grown. Tangled up in a barbwire fence, bleeding, flesh opened, hunted, and those were the words out of their mouths as she untangled him from the tiny blades sticking into his skin.

The old woman knocked on the door.

"Come in," Gina said.

"Just wanted to let you two know that dinner is ready."

"Thank you," they replied in unison.

The old woman closed the door and Gina finished.

As they were about to leave the room, Dru grabbed Gina and pulled her into him. He squeezed her as hard as he could. He turned her face so that it was looking at his. He wiped the hair out of her eyes and put his face against hers.

"Thank you," he said.

"You don't have to thank me."

"I do, too. So thank you for being so fucking amazing."

"Baby," she said.

They kissed. They put their tongues in each other's mouths and kissed hard. Teeth knocking against teeth. Bones crashing into each other. Slobber and bit lips.

It was their first real kiss since they'd been on the run. After the kiss, he said, "You're the love of my life."

"You're the love of my life."

"We're gonna get there."

"I think so too."

They walked into the kitchen to eat for the first time that day.

The four of them sat around the table. The kitchen was old; white wallpaper with red and blue birds covered the walls. There were cupcakes on a plate by the kitchen sink. The radio was off. The plates and silverware and glasses were ancient and breaking.

They ate chicken noodle soup and bread and drank milk.

It was dark out and no one said much about anything.

The couple asked no questions and the two kids gave no information.

For dessert, they ate pecan pie.

When they were through, the old lady said, "I made a bed for both of you. You can rest up here for the night and Bob will take you into town tomorrow morning."

Dru and Gina traded an intense glance across the table.

"Wow," Gina said with caution. "Thanks so much for that. I mean, we sure do appreciate everything."

"Oh, sweetie," the old lady said. "You two are broken and need to be fixed. You stay here the night and we'll get you all taken care of tomorrow in town."

"Thanks again," Gina said. "It really means a lot."

After dinner they all sat in the living room. The old man listened to the radio and the old lady resumed her knitting with Gina on the couch beside her.

Dru sat in the rocking chair.

The news hour was quickly approaching and Dru stood up and signaled with his eyes for Gina to follow him into the kitchen.

She did.

They stood there and Dru whispered, "I packed a bag of blankets I got from one of their closets. Let's leave now."

"How do we get out?"

Dru pointed down the hallway to a room with a window.

"Are you sure?" she asked.

"We have to. We can't go into town with them. We have to go."

"Okay."

"We'll find a place to sleep after we walk for a while."

"I know," she said.

They walked quietly down the hall and into the room and Dru carefully slid the window all the way up and they climbed out of the warm house.

They hurried away as fast as they could.

65

DEPUTY FEHR AND CURTIS WALKED AROUND THE
front of one of Curtis's ranches. Curtis had put the deputy
on his payroll more than a year ago without Lyle knowing
it. He'd never done any major lifting for Curtis but he'd
turned his head and made the proper busts and fudged a
few reports.

He'd even been off-duty muscle for Curtis one night six
months ago, showing up at the house of a man who owed
Curtis money.

"So the other night I really saw something great in you,
Deputy. I saw someone who wants to be the boss. Someone
with ambition. Someone with the attitude that anything
which needs to be done can and will get done."

"I've always had that attitude for you."

"You have. But not with some of the larger, more
intense, and complex problems."

"But I can do that too and step up. That's me, Curtis. It's
who I am in my blood."

"Good," he said, patting Brian's shoulder. "Let's put you
to the test, then."

"Sure."

"Need you to do this job for me."

"Whatever you want, Curtis."

Curtis stopped and looked out into the sky and said, "Lyle has gone nuts. He's been running around, throwing wild accusations out about my family and me. You know what he did at my boy's memorial service?"

"No, sir."

"He cornered Corey Rogers and threatened him with false evidence and lies to make Corey talk to him."

"At his memorial service?"

"Yes. The old man has gone mad, Brian."

"I think he has too. I've been seeing it myself. He's taking some weird stances on this case. He's been working more independently and leaving me out of the picture."

"We need a new sheriff, son. What do you think about that? Election's in six months."

"I think I agree with you."

"You wanna be that new sheriff, Brian? Because I can make you sheriff." He snapped his fingers. "Just like that."

"I'm ready to do whatever it takes."

"You do this job for me and it's as good as yours."

"What's the job?"

"Corey Rogers."

"What about him?"

"I need him out of the picture. He could ruin a lot of things."

Brian tensed up. He knew what "out of the picture" meant coming from Curtis. He'd never killed anyone before, but he'd never been offered something like what Curtis was offering him. More power. More prestige. More money. He knew about Lyle's nice trucks and his nice boats and his cabin. He wanted that. He wanted to be the top dog.

"Can you do that for me?" Curtis asked.

Pause.

"Because I need to know," Curtis said. "I need to know that I can count on you."

"You can. Anything you want, Mr. Alderson."

Curtis smiled and patted Brian on the shoulder again. "You have a big future around here, son. A very bright future."

66

LYLE SAT DOWN AT A TABLE ACROSS FROM JAIME Weiben, the kid he put away, the kid he now needed answers from.

The two hadn't seen each other since Jaime pleaded guilty and was sentenced by a judge whom Curtis Alderson also owned. Jaime could still feel the boots slamming into his rib cage while he was pinned on the ground the day of his arrest. He could feel the two batons smashing into his legs while he was in cuffs. He felt the spit still, the huge glob of a loogie that Lyle had shot right into his face.

He hated Lyle.

Lyle hadn't given any thought to him until the case of Dru and Gina had broke open.

Jaime was handsome, almost a clone of James Dean, even after being locked up for years. He had brown hair combed neatly to the right and tattoos on his neck and arms. He was in amazing shape. Toned to the bone. He had a scar under his left eye that ran to the top of his lip.

"Well, well, well," he said with a smirk as Lyle scooted the chair up to the table. "Look what the cat drug in. So you finally came to apologize for roughing me up, Lyle?"

"You know why I'm here, Jaime."

Jaime leaned back. "No. I don't. Why don't you tell me?"

"Oh, come on. One of the guards told me that you've already been informed about why I'm here. Your brother is in trouble."

"I don't know nothing about that, Lyle. Kid ain't been to see me in two years."

"I think you do."

"What could I have? I ain't seen him. I don't even know what the hell's going on. Just heard an hour ago that he's on the run with some gal and that Alderson kid is dead. Fuck the Aldersons, anyway."

"Well, you ain't changed one bit, have you? Still the same pile of crap you were before."

"You still on the take, Lyle? Working for Curtis."

Lyle sighed. "You don't get it."

"I get it perfectly. You roughed me up after I was already subdued and smiled as I was being sentenced. I saw you there grinning in court that day."

"You robbed a store."

"You beat me up while I was in cuffs and lied about it to a judge and now you want me to help you. What could I know? Ain't nobody been here to see me about Dru. Anyway, you want to put him away is what it sounds like. I would never give you info to hurt my brother."

"I'm pretty certain he went to see your old pal Carl to get help before he left town with the girl."

"So what? I ain't talked to Carl since he came to visit me my first day in jail."

"If Dru did talk to Carl, where would he have told him to run to?"

"No idea."

"Listen to me, Jaime. I know you're suspicious and I know you don't like me and I sure as hell don't like you."

"So why are we talking? You're trying to take down my brother."

"Nope."

Jaime rolled his eyes. "Yeah right. And I believe you. Someone who lied to a judge after I filed a complaint against you for brutality."

Lyle had lost his patience. He yelled, "Get over it!"

He went, "I think your brother is innocent and every second I sit here getting attitude from you instead of answers is a second that I lose tracking him down."

"So what?"

"Where do you think Carl told him to go?"

"Ask Carl, Lyle."

"I can't, Jaime."

"Why not?"

"Carl's dead."

Jaime's jaw dropped and he slunk down in his chair. "What? No. Not Carl."

"I'm afraid it's true, Jaime. He was murdered along with his girlfriend and their baby boy. Shot and stuffed in the bedroom of his trailer."

Jaime felt sick. Carl had been his best friend since they

were kids. He'd planned on Carl helping him get started with a real job when he got out. That was the plan. To straighten his life out like Carl had after Jaime's arrest.

Lyle cleared his throat and said, "You get my seriousness now, Jaime? I need your help. Your brother and that girl need your help. You are their only chance right now. Okay? So where would Carl have told Dru to run to?"

Jaime squirmed, then his shoulders loosened up. He rubbed his face and went, "The one time that Carl came to see me, I told him to go to my mom's house and give my brother a message."

"Go on."

"I told Carl to tell my brother that if he ever got into trouble or needed any help of any kind, that he could ask Carl for it and Carl would help him."

"I need more than that. They were last spotted at a diner in Blairstown, South Dakota. That's a stolen-goods and drug-running route from the border. I know that."

Jaime knew right then where Carl had told Dru to run.

He said, "There's this place on the border."

"What place?"

"It's a safe place that Carl and I used to run things through. We always went through Blairstown. No one really knows what all goes on there. There's a lot of myth about it. It's Native land. Outlaw land."

"What's the place, Jamie?"

"People call it Jameson's Crossing. That's where Carl

would've told them go because you can hide there. He has some connections there still, I'm sure. You can get lost. Vanish just like that and never come back again."

"I've heard things about it," Lyle said. "Rumors and such."

"It's just after Red Valley."

"And you're positive that's where Carl would've told them to go?"

"If they were seen in Blairstown, then that's where they're heading."

"The place you can disappear," Lyle said, almost in an enchanted tone.

"Yeah," Jaime said back. "Forever."

67

LYLE WALKED OUT OF COUNTY AND PUT IN THE CALL for the surrounding counties, South Dakota, Montana, and the border patrol to set up roadblocks, and gave a description of Dru and Gina. He was certain Jamie was right. Criminals were creatures of habit. If the only route through Blairstown went to Jameson's Crossing, then he knew that's where they were heading.

Lyle had heard rumors about Jameson's Crossing through the years but had never been near that territory. Some said it was nothing, just a place whose decor remained unchanged and obsessed with the romance of the Wild West. Some said it was a myth, just a story about a place that had been passed on and built upon, a front for something else, an illusion, a pipe dream. Lyle had never been interested in it or asked much about it because it wasn't his business to know or care. Until now. And he believed it was real. He trusted Jaime's word on this. He watched Jaime's whole demeanor change when he'd told him that Carl and his family had been killed and that Dru had talked to Carl right before his death. Criminals, like Jaime, who'd been doing what they'd been doing for years—running drugs, holding up gas stations, selling drugs, moving stolen merchandise—aren't dumb. Sure, they get caught sometimes but it's usually not for a while and they know in their gut what a hit is and what it means. Jaime knew his little brother's situation and he knew, in his gut, that his brother was in big trouble. It showed in his reaction.

Lyle felt it in his gut too.

These were the moments when you believe the things that come out of the worst people's mouths.

And with that moment, decisive action had to begin.

The roadblocks were just the first step.

68

COREY POUNDED HIS EIGHTH SHOT OF WHISKEY AND
finished off his bottle of beer. He'd been at the bar for the
last four hours. His head was spinning and his stomach was
empty. His words were nothing but grunts and sounds mixed
with slobber that formed anything other than sentences.

He pushed the shot glass at the bartender and held
up his finger. The bartender walked over to him. He had
a beard and a gut and crossed his arms and leaned against
the bar.

"What?"

Corey pointed at the shot glass.

"I think you've had enough."

"One more," Corey slurred.

The bartender stood up straight. "Like I said, I think
you've had enough."

Corey tried to get to his feet but slipped and cracked his
chin open on the counter.

The guy beside him pulled Corey to his feet and the
bartender yelled, "Get the hell out of here, kid."

"Fuck off, fat man," Corey said back.

"Leave or that chin ain't gonna be the only thing
bleeding," the bartender snapped.

The man who helped Corey up walked him out the front door.

"Get your fucking hands off of me," Corey said.

Blood spilled from the cut on his chin.

"Hey, I just helped you," the man snorted back. "You need a cab."

"Fuck you. I'm walking."

"All right then, asshole. Walk."

He stumbled from the bar and stayed on the side of the road. He felt nothing but sick coming on. He'd been drunk since he and Curtis had talked. He'd even been buzzed at Beau's memorial service. During the actual service, he didn't feel anything but anger and guilt. He watched Curtis speak of his son as some totally innocent kid whose life was tragically taken for no reason and he wanted to puke.

The more he thought about Beau, the more he began to disown him. He began to dislike himself, but he wasn't man enough to turn himself in. He didn't wanna go to jail. The damage had already been done. His friend was dead. He had a guilty conscience for as long as he was alive. His secrets would give him nightmares forever.

Parked in a green, unmarked car across from the bar was Deputy Fehr. He wore a black stocking cap, black leather gloves, and a black coat.

When he finally saw Corey stumble out of the bar, he started following him.

Corey stopped to light a cigarette. His lighter didn't work. He kept at it but he couldn't get it lit. That's when Deputy Fehr made his move.

"Hey, man," he called out. "You need a light?"

"Yeah, that would be fucking great," Corey slurred.

The deputy had both hands in his jacket pockets. The one in the right gripped a gun with a silencer screwed into it.

As the deputy stepped toward him, Corey said, "I know you. You're a cop."

"I'm a deputy sheriff."

He could see the drunken gloss that had turned Corey's eyes into marbles. He smiled. Easy fucking target. Just squeeze the trigger and you win the game.

"What are you doing walking all the way—"

But before Cory could finish, Deputy Fehr had the gun drawn and pointed at Corey's chest.

"This is from Curtis Alderson," the deputy said. "Tell his son he says hi."

"What the fuck?"

"Bye-bye."

He shot Corey twice.

BANG!

BANG!

Corey staggered back, both hands over the two holes in him, blood gushing from them, before he fell down.

On the cool gravel off the side of the road, he choked on blood that poured out of the sides of his mouth. Tears flowed down his face. Deputy Fehr stepped over him.

"Any last words?" he asked.

Corey tried to say something but the blood and pain muffled it like a rag that had been shoved down his throat.

The deputy pointed the gun at Corey's head.

Corey closed his eyes.

Brian's shortcut to the top was just about to begin.

His first kill.

All that crap talk about hard work and putting in the time and working your way up was just that, crap.

He squeezed the trigger once more and blew half of Corey's face off.

Corey Rogers was dead.

He kicked Corey into a ditch and his body rolled to the bottom of it. After that, he walked back to his car and drove away. He drove down a series of dirt roads and grassy routes, through a short patch of trees, until he saw the shed, a bright light shining through the windows of it, with Curtis waiting for him.

The deputy got out and walked to Curtis, who stood like a giant in the cold night with the radiant light making a detailed outline of his body.

"It's done, Curtis," the deputy said. "Shot him three times and rolled him into the bottom of a ditch on East Monroe Road."

Curtis nodded. "Good job, Deputy. You did the right thing."

"I know I did."

Curtis stepped toward him and patted him on the shoulder. It sent shivers down Deputy Fehr's back.

"Now what?" the deputy asked.

"Now you give me the gun and I make it disappear forever."

"And about the job?"

"Anxious are we?"

Pause.

The deputy swallowed the lump of slobber in his throat.

"I kind of admire that in you," Curtis continued.

"Thank you."

Both men's breath blew like clouds from their mouths.

And Curtis said, "When Lyle finishes ruining his career, you will have my full endorsement and complete financial backing for your run at being the sheriff of Marshall County."

Deputy Fehr grinned and then began to laugh.

Curtis followed suit. "How does that sound? Sheriff Brian Fehr."

"That sounds like power, Curtis."

THEY COULDN'T SEE ANYTHING BUT THE BIG outlines of trees in the moonlight and the rest of the darkness that surrounded them. They were both freezing, shaking from the cold, and Dru's body was thrashed. He cried out anytime he had to move suddenly, reacting to the pain from his clothes rubbing against the cuts on his arms, his legs, and every time Gina heard him, another piece of her soul broke apart.

The sound of trickling water.

They followed the sound and found a small stream of water that had begun to thaw from its icy cover.

Dru dropped to his knees and felt around until he touched the water, parts of the stream still frozen, and he put his face into it and drank. The stream was deep, at least five feet, he thought, and when he was finished, he turned to Gina and wrapped his sore arms around her knees and said, "Tonight we sleep here."

Pause.

He looked up at her, his arms still hugging her knees. "That way, when we get up tomorrow, we have fresh water and I can keep the cuts clean."

"That's a good idea. I'm so exhausted anyway, love."

They took out the blankets they stole from the house and laid one on the ground. It was thick and soft. Then they pulled two more over them as snugly as they could.

They folded one of her sweaters and used it as a pillow, and then he turned to her and went, "Come here, baby."

"I'm right here," she said as she burrowed her face into his chest.

"There she is," he said, squeezing her tight.

She poked his nose with her finger and giggled. "You're silly."

"Silly, silly, silly." He laughed back.

They were cold but the body heat they were creating helped a lot. Even though both of them were brutally tired and still hungry and beaten, neither of them could close their eyes and sleep.

Dru looked up at the sky and Gina stared into the black nothing of night across Dru's chest.

"What do you think is happening back home?" she asked.

He lifted his head for a moment and answered, "I don't know. I don't even wanna think about it, baby. I'm sure it's, ya know, just lots of confusion and questions and pain. And I just hope my mom's still alive."

He laid his head back down on the sweater and she put hers against his chest and they sniffled and shuddered. The night quiet of the woods and fields of the Midwest in winter surrounded them.

A cool air.

The trickling water.

The night birds and the night animals stalked through their territory while the rest of the world slept.

"Do you miss home at all?" she asked.

"Just my mom. I mean, fuck that place. Do you miss it?" he asked her.

"I miss Katie so much. So much that it hurts. But no, I don't miss it. My stepmom doesn't mean much to me and my dad . . ."

She paused.

"What, Gina?"

"I mean he's been so busy getting ready to run for mayor and with his business and with Sammy and Katie, it's like I'm not even there to him anymore. It's like I left when my mom left."

They lay in silence again for a few more beautiful, peaceful minutes.

And then Dru said, "This is home now. Right here. What we have between us."

"Me and you," she said.

"Forever," he said back.

"And ever, baby."

It was a safe way to protect the pipe dream. The reassurance of hope amid the doomed reality that was closing in on them so brutally fast.

Dru

I'D FUCKED A FEW GIRLS BEFORE GINA. MOST OF THEM
were older than me or from other towns or both. They were
good girls from good families with college in their futures
and honor-roll accolades and proms on their minds. Or
girls whose biggest concern was where the keg was and what
kind of designer jeans so-and-so was wearing or staying up
late to talk on the phone and gossip. Basically, all of them
girls whose boyfriends didn't know how to fuck and whose
daddies would hate a guy like me.

I fit that bill so perfectly.

Gina knew that reputation. She was one of those girls, I'd
always thought, until we started hanging out and I saw the
most amazing and beautiful and careful and compassionate
side of someone I'd ever seen in my life.

She wanted me because of me.

Because I made her laugh.

Because I made her smile all the time and told her how
amazing and beautiful she was. I was always honest with her
and showed how much I appreciated her.

We were in love after the first week.

That was the easiest thing I'd ever accepted in my life.
How much I was in love with her from those very first days.

It was brilliant.

And then we fucked for the first time.

It was in a barn.

She wanted a "roll in the hay." She always talked about it, so that's what we did.

She drove over to my house. It was a Saturday and my mom was medicated and asleep, away again from all the pain for a few hours.

Gina showed up. She wore these tight blue jeans with huge holes in the knees, red cowgirl boots (although not the same ones she had when she was kid), a pink and blue plaid button-down shirt with the top button left open, and a white cowboy hat.

I watched from the kitchen window. It was sunny and warm for December, maybe in the midforties, and I had just finished making the last peanut butter and jelly sandwich. I set that sandwich in a wooden picnic basket along with a bag of Doritos and a six-pack of Old Milwaukee.

She came through the door and ran into my arms and we kissed. Her lips were glossy and sweet tasting and I remember snuggling my face against the side of her neck, the soft skin she had that smelled like vanilla and sandalwood and made the hairs on the back of my neck stand up.

"Ready for the picnic?" I asked.

"You know I am, baby."

We didn't use the barn on my land because there was no

hay in it. It hadn't been used for much since my dad became a drunk and let everything rot and go to fucking hell.

So we grabbed a red and black plaid blanket from the living room and drove two miles away to an old barn where there was a loft with hay in it.

We parked away from the gravel road so no one could see the truck. I broke open the chain lock with some wire cutters and took my beautiful baby's hand and led her to a small, wooden ladder.

"Right up there is your hay," I told her.

"Oh yeah?" She winked.

"Go ahead and climb, baby."

She climbed up and I could hear her giggle. A big explosion of hay went into the air. She started giggling harder, and when I got to the top of the ladder, my heart just melted as I watched her rolling in the hay, looking oh so immaculate and wonderful.

It was perfect.

We didn't fucking eat any of that food.

We drank the six-pack and we fucked again and again before taking a nap, naked, under the blanket, lying the same way we are now.

Gina

I WASN'T A VIRGIN WHEN DRU AND I FUCKED FOR THE
first time, but let me just say this: I hadn't been fucked until
Dru and I fucked for the first time!

Jeez Louise.

It was on a pile of hay inside a barn on a patch of
farmland right off a gravel road.

Just like in a movie or something.

And it was fucking amazing.

He undressed me and kissed me all over, my tits, my
neck, my stomach, then he ate me out until I pushed him
onto his back and took off his white T-shirt and unbuttoned
his jeans.

Before I sucked his dick, I took a big drink of beer and
he told me then that he would never let me go and that I was
his girl and that I was about to have the best sex of my life.

I believed him.

It gave me goose bumps.

And he was just dead-on fucking right.

I went down and he moaned and then he flipped me
on my back and held my legs against his shoulders and put
himself inside me. He fucked me so hard. I came right away
and then I came again and again.

And he went even harder.

He pinned my legs above my shoulders and fucked me for maybe twenty minutes, who the fuck knows or cares, actually, and then he pulled his amazing dick out and came all over my tits and stomach. I rubbed the come around and licked my fingers and then he chugged a whole beer and started fucking me again.

My first real fuck.

My first time with Dru.

On hay. In a barn. On a secluded plot of land, and then we fell asleep naked, my head resting on his chest, our bodies covered by a red and black plaid blanket.

It was so dreamy.

So fucking delicious.

70

IT WAS EARLY MORNING WHEN HANK WALKED INTO the last diner that Dru and Gina had been in, the one in Blairstown. He hadn't slept in two days but he wasn't tired. He didn't look tired. He was a driven man. He wasn't even driven by the money. He was driven by the job itself.

And Hank always got the job done.

When you're a fuck-up your whole life and do stupid things that get you in trouble and set you back, it labels you with a reputation that precedes everything from there on out:

That all's you are is a fuck-up.

What it does to some people is it gives them a chip on their shoulders. It gets them focused and dedicated and passionate. A guy like Hank, who did the dirty work to a degree of success unparalleled by any other of Curtis's henchmen, wasn't going to get notoriety or fame from it, but he was going to get respect. He was going to be the first one called. He was going to be the man people counted on. The pride that comes with that cannot be matched by any kind of money or pats on the back.

He was the best.

He was focused.

Undeterred.

Unrelenting.

And obsessively dedicated to that profession.

When you combine that all into the type of work he did, that made for one bleak outcome after another every time that Hank got the call.

He stood in the middle of the diner and looked around.

The bathroom.

He walked straight back and went inside. He noticed the window was still open. He didn't hesitate. He stepped onto the toilet and looked out at the same thing Dru and Gina had seen the morning before. At all the openness and brown on the edge of that town.

He stepped down.

He knew everything he needed to know. What direction they were going, where they could head, and most important, he knew they were on their feet and running.

He'd noticed a gravel road on his way into the town that went in that same direction. They couldn't be that far away.

He washed his hands in the sink and ran his wet fingers down the sides of his hair. After he dried his hands off, he exited the bathroom and went back outside and lit a cigarette and got into his car. Then he drove to the gravel road he'd seen on the way in and turned onto it, pressing the gas pedal just a little harder.

He was close to them.

Another job on the verge of being finished.

71

SHE SHOOK HIM UNTIL HE MOANED. HIS BODY FELT fractured, splintered, the cuts in his arms and legs were delicate and horrendous. He felt two warm lips touch him twice, first on the cheek and then on the lips.

He opened his eyes.

There was the face of an angel, smiling, pearly white teeth and chapped lips and those beautiful and dangerous eyes that could steal the heart of a man with one quick glance.

She was holding a strawberry cupcake with a lit candle in the middle of it.

"Hey," he said, groaning from the bruises and the fatigue. He sat up. "What's that for?"

"You don't know?"

He shook his head, a smile returning to his face, blood flowing a little quicker through his veins.

"It's for your birthday, silly. I didn't forget. Happy birthday, baby."

He'd forgotten. Through the whole journey and with a brain that had been feeling mushy from all the stress and anxiety of their situation, his birthday had totally slipped between the cracks.

"Damn, Gina," he said. "I can't believe I forgot my own birthday."

"You've had other things on your mind, love."

"But you remembered."

"Of course."

"That's amazing." Tears formed in his eyes. "That just . . . ya know . . . that means everything to me, love. Everything. No one's ever thought about me like that."

"I always will. I promise. Always."

"Baby."

"Seventeen," she said. "You're as old as me now, baby."

"That's right."

She laughed. "You better hurry up and make a wish and blow out the candle."

"Where did you get that?"

"There was a plate of them in the kitchen of that farmhouse. I stole one and found candles and matches in one of the drawers."

"Thank you so much." He closed his eyes.

"Wait, wait," she said.

"What?"

"Can't forget the song," she said, and sang him "Happy Birthday" in the most sweet and beautiful and calming voice ever.

He closed his eyes and blew out the candle.

"What did you wish for?" she asked.

"I'm not supposed to tell you that, silly. Otherwise it won't come true."

"Please," she said. "I've believed that for seventeen years and look at where we are right now."

They both started laughing and he leaned over and kissed the corner of her mouth.

"Okay," he said. "I'll tell you what I wished for."

"What?" She sat, excited, on her knees with her hands on them.

"For the sun to finally come out."

The best smile she'd had in days ripped across her face and she kissed him again and again. As he pulled back, she grabbed his hand and went, "No. No. I want you to make love to me."

His dick got rock solid. "Are you sure?"

"It's okay. It's you, baby. I need you to help me get rid of the sick feeling in my stomach. Be with me. I'll be all right."

He lunged back at her and put a hand on the side of her neck and the other one on the side of her face. They kissed with passion and purpose. It was gorgeous. She undid his jeans while he laid her gently on her back.

He unbuttoned her pants.

She jacked him off while he slid her jeans all the way off and then he slid himself inside of her and she said, "That's my boy."

He leaned down and kissed her neck.

72

LYLE WAS MAKING COFFEE IN THE CHEAP MOTEL room he'd rented the night before. He had driven most of the night and was in South Dakota, on his way to meet the sheriff of Lowell County, Montana, which Jameson's Crossing's jurisdiction fell under.

He poured himself a cup of the coffee and poured some water in it to cool it down. He took two sips and his cell rang. It was Marty.

"What've you got, Deputy?"

"We just got a call about a dead body in a ditch on East Monroe Road."

"Someone get hit walking home from the bar again?" Lyle asked.

"It was a homicide, Lyle."

"Come again?"

"Corey Rogers. He was shot three times."

Lyle's heart slid down the front of his chest. "Jesus Christ."

"Lyle," Marty said, his voice shaking. "Something very evil is happening."

"Where's Brian?"

"He's at the Rogerses' house talking to Corey's parents. Where are you?"

"I'm near where those officers found the truck those kids were driving."

"Evil is everywhere. I don't know how to stop it, Lyle."

Lyle cleared his throat and swallowed a glob of spit. "It stops when we get those two kids before anyone else can. That's where it all ends, Deputy. With those two kids."

73

JUST AS HE'D WISHED, THE SUN BROKE THROUGH the clouds.

It shone right on them, lighting up the whole area right as Gina was feeding Dru the last bite of the cupcake.

It was enchanting.

When it happened, both their faces filled with wild hope. His wish had come true. If that could come true, getting to Jameson's Crossing, something that seemed so far away, had to be able to come true.

He wiped his mouth and she reached down beyond him and scooped up a handful of water from the stream and he drank from her hand.

"We should go swimming," she said.

"In the creek?"

"Yeah, come on. Let's take a dip in the creek."

"We'll freeze," he said.

"We've been freezing, baby. It'll be fun."

Dru looked at the water and then back and Gina. She had an eager and happy look on her face.

How could he let that face down?

"All right," he said. "Let's do it."

They took off their clothes and jumped in. The water

was freezing but it didn't matter. They were like children all over again. They splashed and tackled each other. They laughed and they hugged.

At one point, she jumped on him and wrapped her legs tight around his body. She guided his dick inside of her and began to slide up and down on it. She moaned loudly and they kissed, and right before she was ready to come for the fourth time, she said, "Let's come at the same time, baby."

He nodded eagerly. "Okay."

A few seconds later, his hands tightened around her back, her thighs tensed, and they both came.

The day was off to a perfect start. Hope lived in the sun. It lived in the way their eyes sent secret messages to each other when they met in sudden glances or intense stares.

After he let go of her, they both waded in the water for a few more minutes and then crawled back onto the blankets and lay there, arms draped over each other's bare backs, and let the sun dry their bodies.

Gina

ONE OF MY FAVORITE TIMES EVER WITH DRU WAS on this freezing-cold night in January and this cute conversation we had that I think about all the time. It was after we watched *Breakfast at Tiffany's* at his house. It was Saturday. I love Audrey Hepburn so much. My mom and I used to watch *Roman Holiday* almost every single weekend.

Anyway, that night Dru and I were lying on the couch under, like, four blankets, our bodies pressed as snugly together as we could get them because it was so cold and cold air blew through the tiny cracks in the window frames. We'd been together for a little more than a month and had given each other these names. He called me his Cub and I called him my Pup. We would make noises instead of words sometimes.

Animal noises like, "Rrrrrrr!"

Or, "Roo, roo, roo." That was the one he liked to make. It was from *The Fox and the Hound*. When Copper tells Tod, "I'm a hound dog. Roo, roo, roo."

And that night we talked about how one day we wouldn't even be talking to each other in words, just noises. Just Pup and Cub talk, and he said, "That would be amazing. Our own secret language."

"No one would ever get us or understand us."

"No one has what we have. No one ever will either, baby."

"I love you, Pup," I told him.

"I love you, Cub," he said back.

"Rrrrrrrrr!" I went.

"Roo, roo, roo," he howled.

We laughed and he blew into my ear and told me I was beautiful. I kissed him. Then we made popcorn and watched *Vertigo*.

Of all the gorgeous nights I think about that the two of us of have shared, that sticks out as one of the best. It freezes the smile on my face. It makes me tear up with so much fucking happiness.

Dru

Me and Gina's family is gonna be beautiful. We'll have the most beautiful kids and we'll raise them right, with love. We won't fuck anything up with them. We won't abandon them or ignore them or pretend to listen to their problems. We'll give them everything we have to give, just like we're giving each other everything we got, and it'll be amazing. Our family and those pets and our future.

The life we're gonna have together.

Away from the madness and the pain and the nightmares.

The border is where everything starts all over.

Get there and the rest will be perfect.

"YOU KNOW WHAT I'M THINKING?" GINA ASKED Dru after they were dressed.

"What's that?" Dru asked back.

"We should carve our initials into each other," she said.

"Like give each other tattoos?"

"Yeah. Ya know, like when kids carve their initials into trees and stuff. Like that. We'll give each other tattoos."

"I'm into that," Dru said. "I have a pen that we can cut open for ink."

"Let's do it."

"Our initials on each other. Sounds like the perfect birthday idea."

"Yeah," she said with a huge smile. "It will signify us . . . forever. Me and you, Dru."

Dru picked up a piece of glass from near the creek with a nice jacked edge to cut skin with. Then he took the pen and snapped it in half with his teeth.

Gina sat down.

"Do me first," she said.

Dru nodded and knelt down beside her. She rolled up her left sleeve to her shoulder and took a deep breath.

"Whenever you're ready," she said.

With one hand holding the glass, he grabbed her arm above the elbow and put the glass to her skin.

"Go on," she said. "It can't hurt anywhere near as bad as you when you got into that fight with the fence yesterday."

Dru laughed. "Don't say funny shit. I'm about to cut you. I want it to look good."

"Okey dokey," she said. "No more jokes."

Dru grinned.

"Here we go, Gina."

He pressed the glass into her. Her body tensed and she sucked in a deep breath of air as he pressed harder. Blood began to run down her arm and she grabbed a handful of blanket and wiped the blood off with the corner of the blanket.

He slid the glass down to form the base of the *D*.

"How's that feeling?" he asked.

"It's fine, baby. I can take the pain easily."

So he kept going. It did hurt her but that girl was tough as nails. She was so resilient and so determined that a piece of broken glass slicing into her skin wasn't even gonna make her flinch.

Not that girl.

Not the future Gina Weiben.

He finished the *D* and then cut the *W* into her.

When he was done, he took the blanket from her and wiped the blood off her arm and began to pour the ink into the initials. He went over the cuts four times as she bit her lip, and when he was finished, he stood up and stepped back.

"Don't look that bad," he said. "Looks pretty good, actually."

She looked at it. "It is good, baby. You did it, so of course it's good."

"Thanks."

"Now," she said. "Sit down. It's your turn."

Dru sat down and Gina carved her initials into the part of his upper left arm that hadn't been mauled by the fence.

It was a beautiful moment. The two doomed lovers in the middle of the woods giving each other their permanent placement on the other one's body.

It was the best birthday of his life.

Sex.

Cupcakes.

Tattoos.

But just moments after she'd put the ink into his arm, something so tragic, so awful, happened.

Like that, the sun disappeared. It got sucked back into the clouds and everything went gray.

A few crows flew from a tree. The seriousness of their situation slammed back into them like thunder shakes the ground.

"Baby," Dru said. "We have to move now."

She nodded. "Yes, love. I know."

So they got their things together and started north, when Gina stopped.

"What is it?" Dru asked.

"Just this feeling I got," she said.

"What feeling, baby?"

"A feeling like I'll never swim in another creek again."

75

HANK DROVE UNTIL HE SAW THE FIRST HOUSE ON the road. He always trusted his gut reaction when he was on a job, and his instincts screamed at him that he needed to stop at this house and check it out.

Maybe he would derive something from it.

A nugget of information.

A clue.

He drove into the driveway and stopped the car and finished his cigarette. He sat there and stared at the house, thinking about what he was going to say to whomever he confronted.

He smoked another cigarette. The last one of the fourth pack he'd gone through since he'd left Curtis in the howling wind on top of that hill outside of Marshall.

He stepped out of the car and walked to the door and knocked on it.

The old man answered.

"Can I use your phone?" Hank asked.

"Is there something wrong?"

"I'm lost out here. I'm supposed to look at this guy's truck that's for sale and my cell's not working. I just need to call him and figure out how to get there."

"What's the man's name?"

"Johnson."

"Don't know any Johnsons around here."

"Well . . . maybe it wasn't Johnson. I have the guy's number so maybe I can use your phone and call him and figure it out."

The old man nodded. "Okay. Our house is open to anyone."

"Thank you."

Right after he let Hank in, the old man said, "Ain't had this much company in years."

Hank stopped dead in his tracks and turned back to him. "What's that mean?"

"Had some kids here just last night. Coupla runaways who had an accident."

"They look scared to you?"

"A bit. They were good kids, though. Snuck off last night without saying much."

Hank headed for the door.

"Didn't you need to use the phone?" the old man asked.

"Ya know," Hank said. He put a hand on his gun before restraining himself. The man obviously didn't know anything. "I just remembered where the place was."

The old man nodded. "Okay, then. I hope it works out for you."

"Me too," Hank said back.

Then he returned to his car, lit another cigarette, and drove until he found a road leading north.

He threw his cigarette out the window and turned on that road.

LYLE DROVE DOWN THAT ENDLESS HIGHWAY AS FAST as he could to a place that was maybe mythical, maybe real, or maybe just that fleeting dream people talk about at parties and happy hours and at bedtime.

Like Neverland. But for the crooked adults of this world.

He thought about those two kids on the run. How terrified they must be. And confused. And lost. And, hopefully, not dead.

He drove hard and steady but he couldn't drive away from his demons. All the jobs and the cover-ups and the trumped-up charges to keep Curtis Alderson's empire together. He'd long been tired of it. But he did it because he wanted the power and the prestige. Sheriff of Marshall County. All the off-the-book money Curtis paid him. And yet it wasn't enough anymore. He'd framed too many people. Busted too many stores and kids for stuff he should've looked away from. These two kids were his only chance at some form of redemption.

No, not redemption. That would never come. He'd thrown that away a long, long time before. But finding these kids was something. It was a chance to do the right thing for the first time in a while.

The first time in almost forever.

AS GINA AND DRU WALKED THROUGH THE WOODS, he held her hand loosely. There was nothing but dead trees and a vague, chilly wind. They were a long way away from Jameson's Crossing and they knew it. That's the thing with a harsh realm such as theirs. For moments it can disappear and things seem possible, actually anything does, but then the euphoria from those tiny moments dies and the reality settles back in. It sinks its teeth back into you, tears into your flesh, and poisons your blood, making you sick all over again. You're back to the hopelessness and the mess and the bleakness that the euphoria had watered down.

It was the same reality played on a newer landscape. A different day. With a different dead tree to walk by.

They were an hour away from the creek when Gina heard a rock fall from above and hit the ground. Dru hadn't noticed it. She squeezed his hand. There was something not right about the place they were in.

Another rock hit the ground.

Dru looked at her. "What was that?"

She shook her head before looking up to the tops of the trees.

"Oh my God," she snapped, ripping her hand out of Dru's, jumping back.

Dru turned to her and she pointed at the sky.

He looked up.

Sitting in a tree just up ahead of them on the ends of tree limbs, each one of them higher than the last, were three boys and a girl.

The boys all had shiny black hair, slicked neatly to the back or the sides. They were dressed in leather jackets with white T-shirts underneath them. They had on black jeans that were cuffed and wore black shoes with spikes. It was like a rural rockabilly thing, some throwback fifties gang. Extras from *Rebel Without a Cause.*

The girl also had black hair. She was wearing black tights under a black skirt. She also had a white shirt on under a black leather jacket. The girl was very pretty. Her lips were painted with bright red lipstick. Her eye shadow was black. Her skin was pale.

All their skin was pale.

Dru and Gina stopped on the spot.

When they did, one of the guys jumped down from the tree and approached them. He walked with confidence. His eyes radiated toughness and mystery. He had a cigarette behind his ear.

"And who the hell are you two?" he asked, putting the cigarette between his lips and lighting it with a silver Zippo.

"Nobody," said Dru, while Gina maneuvered behind him. He could feel her up against him. She was trembling.

The rest of the gang jumped down and stood behind the guy.

"Who are *you*?" Dru asked.

"I'm David," the guy said, his face chiseled like Dru's, but older and rougher. He turned to the other three. "And this is Denny, that's Garrett, and this pretty girl . . ."

"I'm Mattie," the girl said, with a side grin. "And I know who these two are, David."

"Oh yeah? Please indulge me, baby," David said.

"They're the two I saw on the front page of the paper when we were getting wine and cigarettes in town. They're missing from their town in Nebraska and the law is looking for them," Mattie answered.

Gina hooked her arms around Dru's right one and held it as tight as she could.

"Where you running to?" David asked.

"Don't tell them," Gina said.

All four of them laughed. "Awwww," David said. "Are you scared of us?"

"No," Dru answered.

"I think the girl might be," David said back.

"She's not. She's just tired. We're both tired and don't know where the fuck we are."

"You're in South Dakota," David said. "In the woods, near this house."

"What house?" Dru asked.

"This abandoned, beautiful two-story house that we took over and party at most of the days and nights."

Pause.

David looked over his shoulder at the rest of the gang, who inched closer to him.

He said something neither Dru or Gina could make out but the gang nodded in response.

He turned back to Dru and Gina.

"What's the place you're going to?"

"It's just this place," Dru answered. "I doubt you know what it is."

"Try me. Maybe we can help."

"Don't tell them," Gina whispered.

"It's okay, baby," he whispered back without moving his lips. "Maybe they can help."

"So," David pressed.

"It's called Jameson's Crossing."

The whole gang began to laugh in a sinister tone.

"You can't fucking walk to that place from here," Garrett chimed in.

Dru and Gina didn't say anything.

"He's right," David said. "We all know about that place. I've got a cousin that lives there and transports people into Canada. You two got any money?"

"Why?" asked Dru.

"'Cause I got a truck. Give you two a ride if you give me

some money. Gotta make a run up there soon anyway to bring some shit down here."

"Can you get us there by tomorrow?" Dru asked.

"Tomorrow night for sure," David said. "That's when I'm supposed to be there."

"What a coincidence," Gina snapped.

"Yeah," David said. "What a coincidence." He stared at Gina and licked his lips.

The whole gang laughed again.

A frigid and massive gust of wind cut through them all.

Gina pulled Dru even tighter. She whispered in his ear, "Don't trust them, love. You can't give them the rest of our money. You can't believe what they're saying."

But Dru saw an opening. A sliver of hope had returned with David and his gang. Forever began to blind his common sense.

He said, "No, they're right, Gina. We can't walk there. His truck is our only shot at making it."

He looked David in the eyes.

"We got money," he said. They still had a little more than three hundred dollars from Carl. "Where's the truck?"

"At the house," David answered.

"Where's the house?"

"It's not far from here," Mattie cut in. "Just a little deeper in the woods. There's a dirt path that leads to it."

"So come on," David said. "Just follow us."

Dru nodded but Gina hesitated. They looked at each

other. Gina's face was covered with worry. Dru's was smeared with desperation.

Gina shook her head no and Mattie said, "The house is really not that far. You wanna ride to that place, don't you?"

"Yeah," Dru said.

So they followed the gang deeper into the woods. David led the way, holding hands with Mattie, while the other two stayed back and trailed just a little behind Dru and Gina.

Gina felt sick and faint. Her head was fuzzy but she was with her boy and he'd promised nothing bad would ever happen to her again.

He promised, and if there was ever any time to put that faith in him to the test, it was then, with the end of their road quickly approaching. If he felt like this was the best way forward, then to her, it was the best way forward, even though the doubts were still there.

You can have doubts and keep your faith. It can make you stronger. Your faith in things grows more strong the more you bring doubt into the equation only to have that doubt be destroyed.

This was what she was banking on.

Twenty minutes later, they came upon a huge house with a blue truck parked in front of it.

The house was completely run-down. It had once been a beautiful white with bluejay blue trim, but the paint was chipped nearly all away. The roof was in shambles and falling apart completely. Boards with spray paint on them covered the windows. One of the boards read: *I hearby apologize for all the damage done.*

Gina shuddered and Dru pulled her closer to him and squeezed her hand even tighter.

"This is it," David said. "You guys have to check out the inside."

"I thought you were taking us to Jameson's Crossing."

"I am," David said. "I need to pack a bag. It's gonna be a few minutes. So just come inside and relax."

"I don't want to," Gina said.

"They seem all right," Dru said back. He looked in her eyes. "We're gonna make it. They'll get us to safety," he said.

She blinked and he poked her in the nose with his finger.

"Beep," she said.

"That's my girl," he said back.

"Come on now," David said. "Everything is fine. There's no law around here. You're safe. Its just gonna be a little bit before we take off. You two look tired, anyway. You can relax a little now."

"Sounds good," Dru said.

They followed the gang inside. The house was mostly bare. There were random pieces of furniture in the front room and the living room that it spilled into. There were tons of beer cans lying around, wine bottles, pizza boxes, and a record player.

Some posters of Joan Jett, the Misfits, James Dean, and Bettie Page were hanging around the living room.

The whole house creaked and shook with every gust of wind.

Gina's teeth chattered.

Garrett emerged from what appeared to be a kitchen carrying three full bottles of red wine.

"Let's have some drinks," he said.

"How about packing up and giving us that ride," Gina said back. "We need to go."

"Just relax," Mattie said. "You're safe here. No one knows about this place. We'll drink some wine and then get you on the road."

Pause.

"Sound good?" she asked.

David grabbed one of the bottles and took a drink and then he held the bottle out to Dru.

They stared at each other for a moment and then Dru took it out of his hand and looked at Gina.

"Just a few," he said. "It's my birthday."

"Well, happy fucking birthday, man," David said.

"Whoo hoo, it's a birthday party," said Mattie.

Dru took a couple of pulls and then tried to hand the bottle to Gina but she refused it.

"Suit yourself," he told her.

"Don't be mad at me," she said back.

"I'm not."

"Just be careful," she said.

That bottle got passed around and finished. The gang

seemed to ignore Dru and Gina. They spoke of a bank robbery a few towns over. A bar fight a couple of nights ago. They talked about some other friends of theirs in Bismarck and Helena. They talked about doing some business with a meth dealer in Blairstown.

Dru was buzzed. He'd never been much of a drinker. Just a few beers were all he needed. After four pulls of wine, with a stomach filled only with pieces of a cupcake, his head began to get fuzzy and his words became slow.

"Let's go to the living room and listen to records," Mattie said, noticing Dru's behavior.

All of them walked to the end of the front room, under an arched ceiling, and into a large room with the record player. David put on a Nick Cave record and Dru, Gina, and Mattie sat down next to one another on a green couch covered with cigarette burns and red wine stains, while the others sat on the floor. Another bottle was opened and the record spun on.

Mattie asked Dru, "So how old are you, man?"

"Seventeen."

She looked at Gina and slid a hand quickly down Gina's thigh while David watched. "How about you?"

"Same as him," Gina answered.

"Really nice," David said, as Dru took two huge drinks and passed the bottle back to Mattie.

That bottle got finished, another one opened, and a Velvet Underground record started spinning.

The exhaustion had already washed over Dru.

The alcohol did its job and his eyelids got really heavy. He tried to fight them but couldn't.

A few moments after the record had changed, his eyes shut all the way, and he passed out.

David looked at Mattie, who nodded, and then he looked at Denny and Garrett, who were smiling.

They all looked at Gina.

Dread seeped through her skin.

She turned her eyes on Dru.

It was no use.

There were more of them, anyway.

At least this way he wouldn't have to see it or hear it. At least this way he wouldn't have to know.

David stood up and said, "Your boy is sleeping."

"I know." She kissed her hand and touched his check. "He's so beautiful," she whispered.

David held a hand out to Gina.

"You a fighter?" he asked her.

"Used to be," she said.

"Used to be?" he responded.

"Yeah. But I'm too tired to fight right now," she said.

"So you're ready, then?"

Gina looked at Dru one more time. The black under his eyes. The fight in him that was gone. She got tears in her eyes.

She looked back at David. "Yeah, I'm ready."

Gina took David's hand and Mattie stood up and said, "This way, just follow him," pointing to a staircase going up.

David pulled Gina to her feet and took her up the stairs while Garrett and Denny followed behind them.

Once they were out of sight, Mattie sat down next to Dru and took all the money he had on him. She lit a cigarette as a bed upstairs squeaked and three guys moaned loudly.

Dru

IN MY DREAM, GINA AND I HAVE BUILT A TREEHOUSE in the forest. The forest is green and magical. There's a waterfall not far away that we can hear and there are deer and elk and bears and foxes. An owl's nest is in the next tree over and there are bluejays and cardinals that fly in the sky and sleep by us at night.

We've just come back from picking berries. It's daytime and we've been gone from Marshall for a while. I've got that beard she talked about me growing and I'm wearing a white shirt and jeans. Her skin is so dark now from the constant glare of the sun, it's almost like she's full Sioux. Her hair is near black and it shines, hanging down near the bottom of her back. She's wearing jean shorts that barely go down her thighs and a wife beater, and has on a headband with two red feathers sticking out of both sides of it.

We climb the rope ladder we made and when we get to the treehouse, we eat our berries and drink water out of a plastic milk jug we found near the waterfall.

It's a brilliant setup.

It was her idea to live in the forest. She wanted to live like a Native American. Combine the modern with the primitive. That's why we hunt food and gather berries and bathe in the waterfall. That's why we have a battery-run hot plate and a battery-run radio.

That's how cultures survive in modern times, she's always saying. Implementing the present with the past.

The house is nice.

We have bear-skin blankets and a window. We have a picture of us two dressed in Old Western outfits in an antique golden frame, but most important, she has a ring on her finger.

It's an antique we found in one of the towns a while ago. A gold band with a little diamond on it.

I traded some deer meat for it and proposed to her as we were sharing a root beer one afternoon, sipping it through a straw. We were listening to the radio when that song "Love Is Strange" by Mickey and Sylvia came on.

Gina hopped up and turned the volume louder and started dancing. I joined her. We danced to the whole song, smiling and laughing, and when it was over, I knew it was time.

I got down on my knee and just went for it.

"Marry me, Gina King."

And when I looked up, she was crying and nodding yes.

There was no formal ceremony.

We just walked to the top of this beautiful hill, covered with yellow tulips, and went through the vows we'd written together.

The whole thing was beautiful in my dream.

And then we were back eating the berries in the treehouse.

She pulls out a Ritchie Valens tape and rewinds it until she hears "We Belong Together."

We dance and we kiss, and then it begins to rain but the rain is warm so we climb back down to the ground. We're both barefoot. It gets muddy and nice. We're still kissing and still dancing and she tells me she's gotta be the luckiest girl in the world.

We kiss again and I pull back.

"And I gotta be the happiest guy in the world."

It's all so nice.

Every time I dream, she seems to be in it.

The girl of my dreams.

In all of my dreams.

Gina

I KNEW WHAT WAS COMING THE SECOND I REALIZED
Dru had passed out. I could've screamed, I could've yelled, I could've clawed and thrown some punches. But it wouldn't have mattered. Way out there, in that old house, miles away from any roads. Nah . . . it was better I didn't fight at all and not have my baby see that kind of evil and terror while he's completely helpless to do anything about it.

Never.

Never.

Never.

There wasn't even really a choice.

I let them take me upstairs and do whatever they wanted. This time my eyes were open. This time I watched what was happening to me but I still didn't feel it.

When it was over, they took all my clothes and left me lying there. I heard the front door shut and the truck start.

I sat up.

Gray light was coming through those tattered and broken windows.

I held my knees and laid my face against them.

A quick image of me and Dru dancing to Ritchie Valens in the rain once flashed through my head.

I smiled.

The image was lovely and it was the last one I wanted to see in my head.

I looked up finally and saw a knife lying on the floor.

It was time.

My heart and my head were both saying the same thing, and when that happens, you listen and do what they say because it doesn't happen very often.

I walked over to the knife and picked it up.

I gripped it hard.

It felt nice to hold it tight.

A sense of power engulfed me. A way out of this. It was my turn to take the reins. My turn to take a direction that didn't lead north anymore.

After I eased my grip, I turned around and left the room. My naked body was cold and there was a line of blood running down my legs. The wind moaned through the house. It sounded like a voice calling me home. It sounded like the end.

I saw the bathroom down the hallway.

The door was open.

I walked inside and turned on the water and I filled the bathtub to the top.

78

WHEN DRU WOKE UP, THE ROOM WAS EMPTY AND his throat was dry. He felt dizzy and lost. His wallet was gone. Gina was gone. The sky was getting dark again and the house was even darker.

A sick feeling began to settle in his stomach.

He stood up and yelled for Gina again and again.

Nothing.

He looked outside through a window and the truck was gone. A feeling of sick was growing stronger and he kept yelling for Gina but still heard nothing back from her.

Nothing.

Nothing.

Nothing.

He ran through all the downstairs rooms.

Nothing.

No sign of anyone.

His head started to ache.

He thought for a moment and then ran upstairs. He looked in every room until he found her. The life sank straight out of his body. He almost collapsed.

His soul floated away. He watched it. It had white wings and a huge heart in its mouth.

And there she was.

His beautiful baby.

The only thing he ever loved more than life.

She was lying in the bathtub full of red water. She was naked. Her wrists were slit, hanging over the sides of the tub, dripping blood, making huge puddles on the floor. Her eyes were closed.

He ran to her, grabbed his Gina, and tried to pull her out of the tub, but he was too weak. He clawed and pulled and cried and she fell out of his arms again and again. He stopped for a moment and knelt beside her. He kissed her forehead and begged her to say something.

Anything.

But she wasn't responding.

She was dead and he was begging her to come back and say something. He was apologizing for passing out and leaving her. He was screaming for her to just wake up.

"Please, baby!" he cried. "I'm sorry I fell asleep. Just wake up and say something. Come back to me!"

And he was still kissing her forehead.

He kissed it a million times at least and then he tried to pull her out of the bathtub again but he slipped on the water that had spilled over and she fell from his grasp one more time.

And so there he sat, tears streaming down his face, when he saw the knife out of the corner of his eye.

Wiping his face, he picked it up with one hand, grabbed

Gina's hand with the other, then put the knife to his neck.

He knew it was the right thing to do.

Forever wasn't going to happen in this cruel world. The illusion had been destroyed. His love had died. In life, people die with their illusions.

With the illusion gone and Gina in some other realm, the choice was pretty fucking clear.

So he looked back at her one more time. Looked at her naked body sunken in a huge puddle of red and destruction.

He didn't even question why she'd done it. He just wanted to hurry up and be back with her.

He said, "I love you forever, baby. Forever, somewhere else, somewhere nice for you, love."

He dug the knife deep into his neck, just enough to make it lethal.

The knife dropped from his hand and the blood gurgled and oozed from the cut and his mouth. He tried to lean forward to keep his hand with Gina's, but he fell the other way and crashed to the floor.

It wasn't long before he died in a bathroom next to his angel.

79

AFTER STOPPING BY THE NEXT TWO HOUSES AND getting nothing, Hank drove for eleven miles before he noticed this dirt path. He stopped at the beginning of it and stared. It led into a mass of dead trees.

His gut told him to turn on the path and drive. His gut told him that the two kids were somewhere in the darkness and dead of those woods.

He turned and drove slowly. Two miles later, the house appeared. He pulled up to it and got out.

He noticed the fresh marks of a vehicle that had recently left. He put his leather gloves on. He held his gun and surveyed the entire house before entering.

Darkness and death.

He sniffed.

Death.

He knew the scent of it so well.

It had been with him for years.

He went around to all the rooms on the first floor. There was a heaviness in that place. Everything sat in stillness, nothing moved or made a sound. It was intense. Sometimes the more quiet things get, the louder they really are.

When he was done on the first floor, he began to ascend the stairs.

He held the gun out in front of him and stepped slowly and carefully up each step. Every one of them creaked. After it did, he would stop and listen for anything. A shuffle. A whisper. A shhhhhh . . .

There was nothing.

Just a shaky house. A cool wind. Loud steps.

When he got to the top, he saw part of a shoe through an open door at the end of the hallway. He walked straight for the room and entered.

He didn't flinch.

There was no reaction. Just two more bodies.

He looked at the scene briefly.

The death.

The torture.

The end.

He knelt beside Dru and turned him on his back.

The blood made this sloshy sound. There was so much of it. He was impressed by how deep and hard Dru had been able to cut his throat. The floor around him was like a dark red wading pool. By tomorrow afternoon, he figured, the blood will have soaked through the hardwood floor.

Hank began to search Dru for the photo. He dug in his pockets and took off his red soaked shoes and socks but there was nothing.

The girl was naked so it wasn't on her. He was going to

have to search the house. He didn't like that idea. He never liked being in one place for too long on a job.

But he'd come too far not to do everything in his power to finish it.

There was too much carnage anyway.

And then it happened.

A whisper from above.

It startled him and he stood up. He looked down at Gina. Her eyes were open. She was staring straight up at him. It sent a coldness down his back like he'd never experienced.

He drew his gun on her.

She was barely breathing, trying to talk to him.

He shook off the chills and leaned down next to her and listened.

She was saying Dru's name.

Hank took a deep breath. It was the ugliest job he'd ever done. After he exhaled, he pulled her hair and asked, "Where's the picture?"

"Dru," she said again.

"The boy is dead," Hank said back. "Where's the picture?"

Nothing.

"Where is the picture that Curtis Alderson wants?" he pressed.

A grim smile sliced across her face and she shook her head from side to side very slowly.

"Why are you smiling?" Hank asked.

The thickness of the water made the tub look like it was filled with paint.

He asked again.

This time, the smile went away and her head stopped moving.

"Well," he pressed.

"No picture," she said. "That night it all happened. We burned it in the fireplace. No picture."

"Is that the truth?"

"Yes," she said.

Hank believed her. His gut told him she was telling him the truth. The picture was gone. It had never left the house. All this violence, this death, all this terror had been for nothing.

It was time to be done with it.

Tightening his grip on her hair, he applied a tiny bit of pressure just to let her know what was about to happen so she could prepare herself.

He watched her.

Even in her final moments, she displayed an angelic beauty. Hank thought she was beautiful too. He stared at her. She closed her lips, nodded at him, and shut her eyes.

She didn't struggle with him as he pushed her head all the way under the water.

He looked away as he did it.

He held her like that for four minutes. He counted the time in his head. When he let go, he couldn't even see the body in the water because it was so red. He stepped back. The rare emotional peak vanished just as quickly as it had come on.

He thought about the appropriate things to do with their bodies. As he ran over numerous scenarios in his head, he heard a creak in the hallway.

He turned to the doorway pointing his gun. Mattie was standing there, leaning against it, holding an unlit cigarette.

"Where did you come from?" he asked.

"The basement," she answered. "I heard someone come in."

"Is there anyone else here?"

She shook her head. "No. The boys went drinking somewhere."

Pause.

"Who are you?" she asked, lighting the cigarette.

"I'm the guy," Hank answered.

"The guy who does what?" She took a drag.

"I'm the guy who makes the secrets stay secret. Who are you?"

"I'm the girl," she answered.

"The girl who does what?"

"I'm the girl she told everything to after she cut her wrists. I couldn't watch her die anymore. So I went downstairs and hid."

"Did you know her before this?" he asked.

"No," she said.

"Why would you tell me all of that?"

She shrugged. "'Cause I don't care what happens to me anymore."

The last loose end.

Hank squeezed the trigger and shot Mattie in the throat. Blood sprayed and she slumped against the wall, gurgling for just a few seconds until her head fell sideways and the blood started running from her mouth.

It was all over.

Hank dragged all three bodies, one at a time, into the living room and laid them next to one another, a foot between each of them.

After that he went to his car and opened his trunk and took out three jugs of gasoline.

By the time they ID'd any of the bodies, he would be long gone and Curtis would be safe. Their story would fall on deaf ears because life would've moved on.

Another bigger, sexier story would come along and seize the attention of the populace.

The case would stay open but most likely never be looked at again.

That much was always a guarantee.

The way we move on so fast.

The way we don't like to face down the monsters.

He opened all three jugs of gasoline and doused the outside of the house with one. He poured the second jug on all three of the bodies and then started at the top of the stairs with the third one. He made a trail from the bodies all the way out to the gasoline he'd dumped outside. When he was done, he lit a cigarette with a match and then dropped the fire on the trail of gasoline.

The trail lit up big and bright.

It stormed into the house and the whole first floor went into flames.

He walked back to his car, took his phone out, and texted Curtis:

Picture is no more. Job is done. Everything is buried.

He watched the house burn until his cigarette was finished, then he lit another one and drove away.

80

CURTIS STOOD IN HIS OFFICE READING THE TEXT. HE smiled. A sense of relief washed over him as he texted Hank back:

6 p.m. tomorrow. Same spot as always.

Curtis sent it, put his phone away, then poured himself a bourbon. He walked to his desk and took the Polaroid out.

He stared at it. All this trouble for a picture. But anything to keep his name good and safe. It was worth it. The land deal could proceed with no issues.

He walked into the den and looked at it for the last time. He shook his head. His boy's body was going to be in the ground in two days. He'd lost something important to him, too.

He looked up and tossed the Polaroid into the fireplace, which was going. He watched it burn and disappear. The extinction of another trail that might have jeopardized all those years of hard work, all that money made. The extinction of another threat to his empire.

Tina walked in, holding her nose.

"What's that smell?" she asked.

He turned to her. "Just a rotten log."

"It smells horrible."

"Just another rotten log, but it's gone now. No more of that."

Pause.

"I love you, Tina."

"I love you too, Curtis."

Pause.

"We're gonna make it through this."

"We've always made it through everything," Curtis said. "Nothing can slow us down. Not Beau's death, not those kids who did it."

"I wonder if they'll ever find them."

Curtis shook his head and rubbed his hands together. "I promise you," he said. "I won't rest until those two kids have been found and brought back here."

"I feel so bad for Craig and Samantha."

"Me too," he said. "That horrible thing couldn't have happened to a better family."

Tina sighed. "Well, dinner's ready."

"What are we having?"

"Pasta and garlic bread. Your favorite."

"Great. I'm starving."

Curtis followed Tina out of the den while the smell of the burning picture went away for good.

81

AND JAMESON'S CROSSING DID IN FACT EXIST IN ALL
its mythical purity. It was hilly and brown with lots of trees
and valleys and dead meadows.

Lyle got there and met up with the sheriff of those parts.
He was introduced to the other officers who'd been notified
of Dru and Gina, and the two sheriffs then spent a day
driving around the enormous stretch of land.

"We got drug routes controlled by every group
imaginable. Any kind of criminal enterprise you can think
of you can find here."

They came to a stop sign on a paved road that turned
into dirt just up ahead.

"All of that," Lyle said. "Here?"

The other sheriff nodded. "Yeah. This is where people
come to disappear. In these hills and woods. If those kids
had enough money or a connect and they made it, they're
gone. Good-bye. They either got across the border or they're
somewhere deep in the woods and you'll never hear from
them again."

"What are you guys doing about it? You're the law and
you know about all of this."

"Nothing we can do. Most of the local law is on the

take. The FBI. and ATF agents up here, all on the take. Hell, most of my deputies are probably getting something to turn their heads the other way. Think you got problems on that damn border to the south? Nothing like we got around here."

"What about you?" Lyle asked. "You on the take?"

The other sheriff sighed and turned to Lyle.

"We all do what's best for us around here."

Lyle was satisfied with that answer. He nodded and stared straight ahead.

They drove around some more because Lyle wanted to feel this place. It was his last connection to those kids. The place was scary in lots of ways and he worried for them even more here than he would've back in Marshall or in jail. He had an almost nostalgic feeling toward them.

Those kids had changed a lot of people.

They drove on.

Lyle saw packs of wild horses and dogs. There was a small town with a saloon and a gambling hall that had been raided by a group of Indians on horseback the day before.

The place was a power struggle.

Change against the past.

And no one was winning.

And no one was giving an inch.

And so life just went on that way.

It wasn't an actual illusion, as in you couldn't touch it and see it. It existed. The illusion of it all was the idea of progress and moving forward. The illusion was that those kids, if they had made it there, would've been safe.

That would not have been the case in Lyle's mind.

They would've been eaten by their own. Robbed. Tortured. And buried in the hills.

This wasn't a safe zone or an easy way out for those kids. That was the illusion they were fed and what drove them.

But in reality, those kids were dead the moment Corey Rogers and Beau Alderson attacked that beautiful, sweet, and innocent little girl.

That was the truth of the matter.

The only way it all made sense.

At the end of the day, after Lyle was dropped off at his motel, he crossed the street and bought a bottle of Wild Turkey and went to his room. He sat on the edge of the bed, the bottle on the small desk next to it, the lamp lit low.

As he took a pull, he thought about everything, Carl Sheer and Haley and their little boy. Corey Rogers's dead body in a ditch. The land deal worth fifteen million dollars. Lyle came to his own conclusion that those kids were gone forever and that the real truth, the only real truth there was anymore, had died with them and their beautiful innocence.

His heart was broken. His spirit had drifted away.

He took another drink and his phone rang.

"What is it, Marty?"

"There was a break-in at the lab and the tire iron is gone and so are all of the reports pertaining to it."

Lyle rubbed his face. He'd never stood a chance. He felt foolish in a sense for having believed he did. But he also felt a tiny sense of worth for having tried his damnedest to track down Gina and Dru.

"Is that it?" Lyle asked.

"No. When are you coming back?"

"I'm leaving tomorrow morning."

"Lyle," Marty said.

"Yeah, Deputy."

"It doesn't feel the same here anymore."

"I don't know what to say to you about that."

Pause.

Lyle swallowed another pull. "The mask has been ripped off this whole thing forever, Deputy. But ya know what?"

"What?"

"It still doesn't matter. Because it's all there, right in the open, for everyone to see."

"What is, Lyle?"

"Exactly my point, Deputy. Because no one will ever see it."

"Huh?"

Lyle swallowed another drink and chuckled. "Never mind, Deputy. I'll see you tomorrow or the day after."

He hung up and drank another drink, then set the bottle down on the desk. He sighed. He took his hat off and stared at his badge. It meant nothing to him anymore. All those years and he'd forgotten the real meaning of the thing. Those kids had revived it for him but it was too late. He knew he could never put it on again.

He set the badge next to the Wild Turkey. Then Lyle closed his eyes and thought about his cabin in Canada.

Dru

I REALLY GOT IT AS I LAY ON THAT FLOOR BLEEDING
out of my throat. I got why she'd done what she'd done.
The illusion had died in her. She was tired of running. The
illusion will eventually die in all of us.

This wasn't some stupid, sappy teen suicide pact we'd
made. I was running after her. Chasing her. Because I
couldn't stand the thought of not being with her,
somewhere, I didn't give a fuck where, anywhere in this
gigantic universe. I mean, you ever fucking felt that before?
You ever had the gentle presence of another person slowly
become the meaning of your life? The pulse that makes
the blood flow. The reason to feel good when you wake up
and the reason you feel safe when you go to bed. The way
the world is just so goddamn beautiful and right because
she's in your life and the whole time she wasn't a part of it,
everything and every day was such a fucking struggle.

That's why I ran after her.

I followed her to a beach. It was raining and the waves
crashed all around us. Her face was like the moon at night,
leading me out of the darkness.

I followed her through a rain forest full of green plants
and exotic creatures. She was waiting for me by a river,

singing her favorite song, her voice like a perfect mixtape that makes every part of the day you listen to it fucking magical.

I followed her through a blizzard. There she was, smiling, pulling me along with her hand, her eyes like the stars, something I could stare into and be encompassed by the beauty of life.

And I followed her to a country house way outside of a town in Montana. And there she was again, sitting on a front porch swing in a yellow sundress, laughing, surrounded by those unruly dogs, her warm presence the whole reason my life was gorgeous and worth every second.

There was no going on without her. It devastated me to see her laying in that bathtub, but even in that state, she was still an angel, she was still my baby, she was still Gina King, the love of my life.

So I trailed on after her.

I never left the path.

Even in those last moments, as I felt the life leaving me, I can safely say I never lost my way.

TWO DAYS AFTER BEAU'S FUNERAL, LYLE WAS READY
to see Curtis. He turned onto the property where Tina had
told him Curtis was and drove his pickup to a fence that
Curtis was standing against, watching a couple of his new
colts being trained.

Curtis turned around when he heard Lyle's truck door
slam shut and nodded at him.

It was warm, in the fifties, and the sun had been out all
day.

Lyle walked right up to Curtis without nodding back
and handed his badge to him.

Curtis squeezed it. "What's this for, Sheriff?"

"I'm resigning, Curtis. Effective immediately."

Curtis shook his head and tried to hand the badge back
to Lyle, but Lyle wouldn't take it. "You resign to the mayor,
Lyle. You don't resign to me."

"I've already informed him. He put Deputy Fehr in
charge for the time being. But I thought it would be more
appropriate to hand in my badge to you because it's really
you I've been working for all these years."

Curtis grinned and said, "And you say this like it's been
bad for you, Lyle. Jesus Christ. You've made a lot of money

being my guy and never complained before this case. It's been so good for you."

"It's been bad for a lot of others."

"So what? Who cares about the others? So we cut some corners here and there and used our position to our advantage. That's why we're better than everyone else. That's why we have the power. Because neither of us came from anything but dirt, and now look at us." Curtis was poking his own chest as he said it. "Sheriff Lyle Cortland and millionaire thirty times over Curtis Alderson. That's what we wanted, and that's what we have."

"Had?" Lyle said.

"Well, maybe for you . . . but I still have it."

Lyle looked around at the horse barns and the acres of land.

"Yes, you do still have it," he told Curtis.

Curtis rubbed his chin and continued, "First rule of life, Sheriff, you help yourself before you give a shit about other people. No one helped us growing up. We made this ourselves. So screw your morality and your new fucking rules and your laws. There's only one rule that matters, Lyle."

"And what's that, Curtis?"

"If you can do it and get away with it, then do it and get away with it."

"You've done that to perfection, Curtis."

"And so have you."

"Not anymore."

"Good for you, Lyle. Good for fucking you."

Lyle looked at the ground and kicked some dirt up with his steel-toe boots. Then he looked back at Curtis and said, "I think I know what really happened, Curtis."

Curtis nodded. "I'm sure you've got some fine theories." Pause.

With a grin as big as the Cheshire cat's stretching across his face, Curtis said, "But can you prove any of it?"

Lyle shook his head. "No, I can't, Curtis. And you know that. The murder weapon with Gina's prints went missing from the lab five days ago. Corey Rogers is dead and so is Carl Sheer. And those kids, as much as I want them to be alive, I figure they're probably dead and buried somewhere too."

Curtis rubbed his chin. "You need to go home and get some sleep. Take a vacation. Get your good senses back, and who knows, maybe you come to me in a couple of months and I might have some work for you."

Lyle smirked. "You don't get it yet, Curtis. I'm done with it all. I am never going to talk to you again. It's over for me."

"Lyle, don't—"

"And the thing is," Lyle said, cutting Curtis off, "you did get away with this, plain and simple. And you'll get your precious land deal next and more millions and millions. You'll get your new sheriff in place who will do all your dirty deeds for you, and you'll get Craig King into office, and you'll still have your town and your county and your state, but the thing is, Curtis, one day . . . one day, you will have to answer. Maybe to the law or maybe to a higher power more powerful than even you."

"Like God, Lyle?"

"Maybe God. Maybe something else. But that will be your justice, Curtis. I can guarantee you that."

Erupting into a howling laughter, Curtis buckled over, then caught his breath after a few moments and said, "After all these years, Lyle, you still don't get it."

Lyle stared at him. "Get what?"

"I answer only to me. Always. Just me. And never to anyone else."

Lyle nodded and said, "Maybe you're right."

Curtis started laughing again, even harder this time, and Lyle turned from him and walked back to his truck.

He got in, the sound of Curtis's laugh still ringing in his ears, and then he started the truck and drove home.

Gina

I REALIZED I WASN'T DEAD WHEN I SLIPPED OUT OF
Dru's arms. I could've said something but I didn't want to. I
wanted this to end. He would've never let it end if he knew I
was alive. That's the kind warrior of he was. The kind of raw
passion he had in him to make the dream a possibility. But
we would've never made it anywhere. Not in my condition,
not on foot, and I would've eventually had to tell him about
what happened when he passed out at the house. I couldn't
let him think it was his fault and that he'd let me down and
that I would've been okay if he'd been awake.

No way.

Because I wouldn't have been.

It's better that this ended.

Otherwise we would've been caught and put in jail. We
would've been apart for a long time. Both of us would've
literally died of broken hearts behind bars.

This way was the only way.

This way we die together.

So I just listened to him fall to the floor. I felt him
grasping my hand. I wanted to grab back so badly but no, no
fucking way, we'd gone as far as we needed to go.

And so he died next to me.

It was truly romantic if you put it in the right light, the light that this story deserves.

I knew I wasn't that far off from death either.

It was comforting, actually.

Feeling my soul running after him. Seeing myself floating away from the horror, knowing my Dru was somewhere good and close, just waiting for me.

That's where my head was as I neared the final moments of breathing.

But then that man came in, interrupting those wonderful feelings, those lovely visions, and asked about the picture.

The fucking picture.

All the fury and the pain slammed into me again. If we'd just kept it. If I hadn't destroyed it. This life would've never happened.

I was ready to go.

Once he began to apply the pressure, pushing me under the water, I got happy. I knew I was going to be with Dru again.

When I had sunk as far as my broken body would let me, my mind totally cleared, everything went black, and I heard Dru calling my name. It felt so good to hear his voice. The sweet sound of him saying it over and over. I reached out blindly toward the sound when I felt a hand wrap around my mine.

It was his.

I would know his touch anywhere.

He was pulling me closer to him, pulling with gentle urgency.

Dru told me it was okay and that it was safe where he was as he led me through the darkness. We were so close, and then it got really warm.

There was a bright light.

And I saw his face.

He was smiling and beautiful.

We were one.

He wrapped me in his arms.

Dru had pulled me to safety.

And there we were, together again.

Forever.

THE CAR CREEPS TO THE END OF THE DRIVEWAY AND turns onto the gravel road, the tires kicking up a small cloud of dust that whips into a spiral in the dead air before disappearing just as quickly as it came. I roll my window down and swallow a heavy gulp of humidity and look at my mom and take a deep breath. She smiles real big, and it seems authentic, and this puts me at ease to a small degree. If she can feel good about my journey, then what is there for me to really, truly worry about?

My mom guides the car onto the boiling black asphalt in front of us, turns the radio up, and rolls her own window down halfway. Her long brown hair blows in the breeze coming in and shines in the sunlight. She looks so pretty. Way better than she ever has over the past six months.

She's wearing an olive green dress and white flats, and she slides her sunglasses over her eyes and says, "I'm so excited for you. You're going to do great out there, Kaden."

"I'm sure I will. It's gonna be fun. New, ya know."

"Something that you've never come close to living," she says.

I turn my eyes out the front of the window. It's so sunny today, and the sky is blue. White puffy clouds that look like zoo animals float everywhere above us. And a tiny bit of me still can't believe that I'm doing this. That I'm going to San Francisco to see Chuck Palahniuk read and stay with my cousin James Morgan, and most important, that I'm seeing the final wish of my brother through. My best friend in the world. I'm doing what he wanted us to do before he died in Iraq. I'm taking care of the rest of the business he couldn't be around to finish.

We glide past giant spaces of green country, horses, cows, hogs, and big houses that have stood in place for generations. My flight leaves the Cedar Rapids airport in two hours, and I am due in San Francisco at three twenty this afternoon.

That Patsy Cline song, "Walkin' After Midnight," comes on, and my mom looks at me and says, "Just remember one thing while you're running around out there with James."

"Sure."

"Don't put too much stock into everything he says. He goes off about a lot of things."

"Like what, Mom?"

She runs a hand through her hair and sighs. "Just things. He runs his mouth, and not everything is always worth listening to. He can get really carried away sometimes."

I have no idea what she's talking about. Not one stinking clue. So I shrug and I say, "Got it." And we barely speak the rest of the ride. The rest of the way spent with me thinking about my brother, Kenny, and how big of a kick he'd get out of knowing I was actually going through with this.

I miss him so much.

My mom pulls up in front of the United Airlines terminal. She gets out. I'm trying to show that I'm not nervous. For her sake, not mine. I step outside and walk to the back of the car and help her pull my suitcase from the trunk. Then she hands me three hundred dollars and says, "I know we already gave you three, but here's some more plus a prepaid phone card. I want to be sure you have everything you need out there."

"I'll be fine, Mom."

"I know you will, sweetie." She pats my head and hugs me and says, "Call me when you land. Okay?"

"Got it."

"I love you."

"Love you too, Mom."

She hugs me again, and I drag my suitcases into the airport and check in for my flight. I make it through security with no hassles and sit down next to these big windows that look out over the concourse and, beyond that, the endless miles of farmland and country that surround this place.

I have no idea of what to expect. I'm on my way to see my cousin, whom I've met once, in a city I've never been to, and the deep unknown of these two things combined is putting me on edge, so I slide my billfold out and pull a letter from it. The last communication I ever had with my older brother, Kenny. The words on the paper that changed my life forever when I first read them on that brutal winter day in December:

Kaden,

What's up, man? If you're getting this letter, you already know that I'm not making it back from this desert of murder and madness. I'm sorry I wasn't strong enough to. I'm so sorry, man. Sorry that I'll never be able to see you again and throw the football around with you again and talk about girls and go creek dipping and quarry jumping with you in the summer at Leland's property. I just wasn't ready and prepared, and maybe I just wasn't cut out for this day-to-day hell. That's what Iraq is, Kaden. It's hell. The brutal scent of death is around every corner and along every single road in this godforsaken place. This isn't just a bunch of American soldiers shooting at shit, this is having to bear over hundred-degree temperatures. Frozen night commands. This is trying to look at a hostile crowd of people of all ages and trying to figure out which one is trying to kill you that day. We know nothing about the people or the place we're going up against each day. The only thing we know is that it's becoming increasingly more difficult to figure out who the enemy really is. A group of insurgents who arrived here to fight the jihad from one of the neighboring countries? Or members of a family who seek revenge on the soldiers who've turned their relatives into collateral damage, destroyed their neighborhoods, driven their people out of the area, and turned their country into a lawless melting pot of religious ideology and horrific street justice more brutal than you are ever shown on the screen of the televisions back home. I've seen decapitated bodies slung from buildings while entering certain neighborhoods. Children missing hands and eyes. It's fucking sickening. Me and some of the other guys in our unit would get physically ill at times while we rampaged through houses and buildings, only to find a group of Sunni men lying face-first on the floor, hog-tied, bullet wounds in the back of their heads. Or a baby, man . . . I saw the body of this baby girl who couldn't have been more than three years old in a trash can in this house. Her throat had been slit and intestines pulled through her stomach. The rest of her family was found stacked together in a pile in the living room with all of their throats cut too, and there was a huge warning note written in Arabic about the consequences of working with the Iraqi Police and U.S. Commanders. I mean, what the fuck, man? What is this madness we've been committed to. Our presence, my presence, has brought brutal death to over one million Iraqis, and they're not all insurgents, Kaden. Hardly any of them really are. We shoot at everything that makes a sudden movement. We hog-tie men and women in the middle of the night in front of their children before whisking them away in black hoods under the rotten cloak of Bringing Democracy to these people, which is just a code phrase for American Imperialism. It's not right, and all of our soldiers should leave. I have already left, little bro. In a flag-draped coffin that I'm not sure I'm really worthy of being buried in. We need to leave now before more Iraqis are slaughtered on these killing fields, before more of our soldiers are bled to death in these blinding whirlwinds of sand.

I know what you must be thinking, Kaden. Who is this guy writing you this letter? Where did your older brother go? Where is the kid who was so eager to leave for this fight and win this war for this just country's noble cause?

Well, here I really am. This is who I was turned into. Telling you all of this is the responsible thing for me to do. Telling you how ashamed I was before my death by what I had taken part in: Blind homicide. Vast torture. The pointless destruction of homes. The massive roundup and incarceration of innocent Iraqis.

The list could go on, Kaden. And I'm certainly not the only one in my unit who grew despaired by how we all became complicit in the destroying of a country and its citizens' lives. Nobody is into it anymore. Most of us just want to go home. That was when I first started reading books again. One of the other soldiers on the base was really into this writer Chuck Palahniuk. He's the guy who wrote the book *Fight Club*. Anyway, this guy was always raving about Chuck's books and how they were really helping him cope with being in Iraq. He'd been fighting for two years, and the only moments of life he had enjoyed during those years were the moments of downtime when he was able to be swept away into another one of Chuck's stories and was almost able to completely forget for those few precious hours where he was and what he was facing. The true life-or-death scenarios he encountered in the neighborhoods and villages in and around Baghdad for fifteen hours a day.

The guy told me that anytime I wanted to get into one of his books, to just ask him. He had all of them there. I asked him what I should read first, and he told me to start with *Fight Club*. That I should read his books in the order they came out, because put together they reminded him of one giant text, each new novel a different chapter. So I asked him for *Fight Club*, and from the very first line of the first chapter I was hooked, Kaden. I read the entire book that same night. Those hours spent reading were some of the best I'd ever spent in my entire life. Something inside of me took a drastic turn. I felt awakened for the first time. Reading those books, it was like there was an author speaking directly to me and to the way I felt about my place in the world.

Most of the characters in his books were so easy to identify with. Characters who were lost and drifting amid a plastic culture. Characters who felt betrayed by the end results of doing what they were told would make them happy. It made me think hard about how natural the violence inside of us is. But how we should use it in ways other than killing people. The way we bottle things up and are scared of everything and scared of feeling life and living among each other. It was a revelation. A revelation that happened too late.

I mean, I always felt like that myself. How Dad always told us that you do this, you do that, you get through school, and you get a job, then get married and have some kids and then retire and then die. And that's Happiness. He raised us as if that's the only way of life there is and that anyone who strayed from that path was somehow not worthy in his eyes, and even though I think Mom didn't really agree with him, I don't think she knew how to ever go against his word and how he thought about shit.

It's strange to have all of these feelings about this right now. And it's so strange to write a letter to your best bud in the world in this fashion. Already dead. With no chance of ever being able to say this to you face-to-face, man. I can't say for certain or anything like that, but I really think that if I'd thought about what would've made ME truly happy in life beyond Dad's direct approval, then I don't think I would've joined the military.

And this is why I'm writing this letter to you, Kaden. Because I need to know that you heard all of this somehow. I want you to start getting into good shit right now and do something fucking rad with your life. I want you to be happy, man. Read Chuck Palahniuk. See if it's for you. My goal was to come back on leave and take you out to San Francisco this summer to catch him do a reading for his new book and meet him. Our cousin James, the author, he lives out there. I asked him about it in an e-mail, and he told me it would be rad to have us out there for that. But I'm not gonna make this one, buddy.

If you're reading this letter, you've already said good-bye to me. I thought about this for a couple of months. That's how important this is to me. I had to have the letter come from somebody in the States without sending it from here because of some of the vague information that's inside about operation details my unit was involved in. I couldn't have the military read it, so I had to pack it with Brady. It was also the only way to get it past Dad. I don't want you showing this letter to either him or Mom, Kaden. I'm gone. And they shouldn't have to have their final memories and thoughts about me rehashed and then smashed into rubble. Just let them have their peace about what they thought I still believed about this war and this military. You're the one who matters now. I love you. Be something. Be anything. Go see what the fuck is out there, man.

Your brother,
Kenny

About the Author

Jason Myers was born in Iowa and raised outside of the small town of Dysart. After high school he moved to San Francisco and studied film at the Academy of Art University. In 2007 his first book, *exit here.*, was released and has since gone on to become a cult classic. His second book, *The Mission*, was released in 2010. This is his third book. He currently lives and works in San Francisco.

Simon & Schuster's **Simon Teen**
e-newsletter delivers current updates on
the hottest titles, exciting sweepstakes, and
exclusive content from your favorite authors.

Visit **TEEN.SimonandSchuster.com** to
sign up, post your thoughts, and find out what
every avid reader is talking about!